# Solo Leveling

## III

### CHUGONG

YEN ON

NEW YORK

# Solo Leveling III

CHUGONG

Translation by Hye Young Im and J. Torres

This book is a work of fiction. Names, characters, places, and incidents are the product of the author's imagination or are used fictitiously. Any resemblance to actual events, locales, or persons, living or dead, is coincidental.

SOLO LEVELING Volume 3
© Chugong 2017 / D&C MEDIA
All rights reserved.
First published in Korea in 2017 by D&C MEDIA Co., Ltd.

English translation © 2021 by Yen Press, LLC

Yen On
150 West 30th Street, 19th Floor, New York, NY 10001

Visit us at yenpress.com ◊ facebook.com/yenpress ◊ twitter.com/yenpress
yenpress.tumblr.com ◊ instagram.com/yenpress

First Yen On Edition: October 2021

Yen On is an imprint of Yen Press, LLC.
The Yen On name and logo are trademarks of Yen Press, LLC.

The publisher is not responsible for websites (or their content) that are not owned by the publisher.

Library of Congress Cataloging-in-Publication Data
Names: Chugong, author. | Im, Hye Young, translator. | Torres, J., 1969– translator.
Title: Solo leveling / Chugong ; translation by Hye Young Im and J. Torres.
Other titles: Na honjaman rebereop. English
Description: First Yen On edition. | New York, NY : Yen On, 2021.
Identifiers: LCCN 2020047938 | ISBN 9781975319274 (v. 1 ; trade paperback) |
ISBN 9781975319298 (v. 2 ; trade paperback) | ISBN 9781975319311 (v. 3 ; trade paperback)
Subjects: GSAFD: Fantasy fiction.
Classification: LCC PL994.215.G66 N313 2021 | DDC 895.73/5—dc23
LC record available at https://lccn.loc.gov/2020047938

ISBNs: 978-1-9753-1931-1 (paperback)
978-1-9753-1932-8 (ebook)

1 3 5 7 9 10 8 6 4 2

LSC-C

Printed in the United States of America

# CONTENTS

# 1
## RANK EVALUATION

# 1

## RANK EVALUATION

The last time Jinwoo had stood at this particular crossroad, he'd chosen the blessed mystery box over the cursed one, which had given him the Demon's Castle key. That, in turn, had given him access to the Demon's Castle dungeon, where he'd gained plenty of things—he'd leveled up significantly, collected a ton of loot, and the gold... He'd saved up so much gold that he almost felt obligated to spend some.

*If I had to do it all over again, I'd make the same choice without a second thought.*

However...he was still curious about the road not taken. The blessed mystery box was supposed to give him something he wanted, and the cursed mystery box was supposed to give him something he needed, so what was inside the other box?

*The blessed mystery box definitely gave me what I wanted, after all.*

And now, Jinwoo had the perfect opportunity to satisfy his curiosity.

......

He nervously awaited the system's answer. For some reason, he felt as though it was being unusually slow.

*Ping!*

His worries were unnecessary, as the system soon responded.

\* \* \*

[You have selected Item: Cursed Mystery Box.]
[The chosen item will be supplied.]

*Hwoom.*
A small box appeared at Jinwoo's feet.
*Nice!*
He nervously picked it up. The weight of the box in his hands felt very familiar. *Could it be...?*
Jinwoo hastily tore into it, and his eyes widened as he saw the contents. "This is......"

\* \* \*

Jinwoo went straight home after exiting the Demon's Castle. The first thing he wanted to do was clean himself up, as he hadn't bathed once while inside the dungeon. He could've bought water from the shop, but there hadn't exactly been an optimal time or place to do so.
*Can't really wash up leisurely when you're surrounded by monsters......*
*Shaaaah.*
It wasn't until he was back in his apartment and relaxing his muscles under a hot shower that he actually felt like he was out of the dungeon.
*Home sweet home.*
Jinwoo got dressed in fresh clothes, draped a towel over his wet hair, and sat on the edge of his bed. It was time to sort things out. He first called up the stat window.
*Stats.*
*Ping!*
Dizzyingly long strings of letters materialized before his eyes. They landed on something in particular.

[Available ability points: 20]

\* \* \*

The points he'd received for completing the Demon Souls quest. Naturally, he invested all the points in intelligence.

*Ping!*

## 〖Stats〗

| Strength: | Stamina: | Agility: | Intelligence: | Perception: |
|-----------|----------|----------|---------------|-------------|
| 178 | 137 | 147 | 149 | 119 |

At long last, intelligence was barely higher than most of the other stats. Despite still being quite a bit behind the strength stat, it was a huge improvement, considering how he'd been ignoring it until recently.

Strength, stamina, agility, intelligence, and perception. They were balancing out nicely.

*Everything here is important.*

Jinwoo had been obsessed with every stat at different points, so he'd learned the unique qualities and advantages of each.

*Wait......*

Considering the state of things, what if he increased all his stats evenly instead of focusing on one? He'd be an all-rounded Player. Jinwoo's ambitious streak flared up. It was an idea he could happily ponder only because every single stat was at a satisfactory level.

*Once my intelligence surpasses strength, I should also increase the others bit by bit.*

With his mind made up, Jinwoo turned his attention toward the skill window.

And there was the third reward.

### [Reward 3. Mystery Reward]

If he was being honest, he had been much more preoccupied with the first and second rewards—any item of his choosing and twenty bonus points—and, besides slight curiosity, hadn't been very interested in the third.

But his jaw dropped once he saw what it was.

### [Reward 3 has been delivered.]

A scroll similar in size to the Demon's Castle entry permits simultaneously appeared in his hand.

*What's this?*

Caught off guard by the delivery method, Jinwoo opened the item in surprise.

### [RECIPE: ELIXIR OF LIFE]
### Learn how to craft the Elixir of Life.

Jinwoo stared down at the scroll.

*I can make it myself?*

Mage-type hunters were the only ones with the ability to craft weapons with mana...but Jinwoo supposed that he was also one of them.

*But to think I can craft something as long as I have the recipe......*

Jinwoo's heart started pounding as his mind raced. What would he be able to create?

*What's the elixir of life?*

Jinwoo read through the information for the Elixir of Life.

### [ITEM: ELIXIR OF LIFE]
### Acquisition Difficulty: S
### Category: Consumable
### A mystical potion that cures all diseases using powerful magic. An entire bottle must be consumed for the full effect of the potion.

*It can cure......all diseases?*

His bedridden mother immediately came to mind.

Thanks to Jinho, he had already confirmed multiple times that an item's effect worked on other people...which meant he could save his mother if he crafted this elixir. His hands trembled as he clutched the scroll excitedly.

The ingredients were straightforward as well.

*World Tree Fragments.*

He'd received those after defeating Vulcan on the fiftieth floor of the Demon's Castle.

*Spring Water from Echo Forest.*

He'd acquired that by defeating Metus the necromancer on the seventy-fifth floor.

And lastly...

*...Purified Blood of the Demon Monarch.*

This was an item he hadn't come across yet. However, based on the first two ingredients, it was easy to guess where he could find the blood of the Demon Monarch. He'd have to go higher.

*It's probably the ultimate boss on the highest floor of the Demon's Castle.*

That meant he'd be able to gather the ingredients for the elixir by clearing the entire dungeon.

That's when it occurred to Jinwoo.

"Oh."

A moan inadvertently slipped out of him at the revelation. The item in the cursed mystery box—the Elixir of Life—was supposedly the one thing he wanted most in the world.

*Mother......*

Tears welled up in Jinwoo's eyes at the thought of being able to see his mother healthy again.

Just then, a message arrived.

*Ping!*

[You may learn the Crafting skill using the Recipe: Elixir of Life.]

[Would you like to acquire the Crafting skill?]

* * *

The electronic sound snapped him back to reality. He would have to complete the raid of the Demon's Castle in order to make the Elixir of Life, so the faster he prepared, the sooner he could return home. There was no time to be sentimental.

"......Learn."

**[You can now craft Item: Elixir of Life.]**

*This isn't a dream, right?*

As if to answer his question, a new [Craft] space appeared in his skills window.

**[CRAFT]**
**Consumable: Elixir of Life (2/3)**

The numbers at the end probably indicated that he owned two out of the three necessary ingredients—the World Tree Fragments and Spring Water from Echo Forest.

*Hmm.*

Jinwoo opened up his inventory and took out the item next to the spring water. It was a necklace assembled by tying small animal skulls together.

**[ITEM: DEMON MONARCH'S NECKLACE]**
**Acquisition Difficulty: S**
**Category: Accessories**
**Agility +20, Intelligence +20**
**There is a set buff that will be revealed when worn with Demon Monarch's Earrings and Demon Monarch's Ring.**
**Set Buff 1. (Hidden)**
**Set Buff 2. (Hidden)**

* * *

Spring water wasn't the only item he'd gotten from Metus, Guide of Souls. He'd also been gifted this abhorrent necklace that screamed of poor taste.

*Why are all the neck accessories like this...?*

Jinwoo grimaced as he remembered the design of the dog collar he was currently equipped with, and he held up this new item to his neck.

*Ping!*

[Would you like to change Warden's Collar to Demon Monarch's Necklace?]

The advantages granted by the Warden's Collar and Demon Monarch's Necklace were similar: They both raised two stats by twenty points. However, the Demon Monarch's Necklace had an additional set buff.

*Change.*

*Hwoom.*

[You have put on Item: Demon Monarch's Necklace.]

The dog collar reappeared in Jinwoo's hand as the necklace made of skulls took its place. Jinwoo shoved it back into his inventory and checked the buffs for the set of Demon Monarch's accessories.

**[ITEM: DEMON MONARCH'S NECKLACE]**
Set Buff 1. All stats +5
Set Buff 2. (Hidden)

*Every stat increased by five.*

All his stats had gone up by five, and that was with just one of the set buffs revealed. There would be one more once he completed the entire set.

*The Demon Monarch's Ring......*

Taking into consideration that a set buff was usually more impressive when the actual set was complete, this was fantastic news. And yet, the S-rank accessories were only a small boon from the Demon's Castle. The real reward was his extreme jump in level.

Jinwoo smiled proudly when he saw that he now sat at level 77.

*I leveled up sixteen times in one week.*

He'd improved at a rate he could never have dreamed of in C-rank dungeons. It was his compensation for toiling in hell (?) for seven days. The Demon's Castle dungeon was unfinished, but there was no denying that this had been a successful raid.

There was just one thing Jinwoo couldn't wrap his mind around. He placed the item from the cursed mystery box directly under fluorescent light.

*What the heck is this thing?*

The pitch-black key appeared to be absorbing the light around it. An information screen didn't pop up, either.

*This is a first......*

Instance dungeon keys were ordinary enough items that they even appeared via regular mystery boxes from time to time, but he had never come across this kind before.

*Where am I supposed to use this?*

Maybe it was because it came from a cursed mystery box, but he also couldn't help feeling something ominous emanating from the key. It wasn't like he could get rid of it, either, given how much effort he'd put into obtaining it.

*I guess I'll need it someday.*

After all, the cursed mystery box was supposed to supply an item he needed.

Jinwoo rose to his feet after placing the key in inventory. He would need to acquire some artifacts if he wanted to complete the Demon's Castle raid.

*Got some stuff to sell, too.*

Unfortunately, the reality was that E-rank hunters had difficulty buying and selling high-level artifacts. Who wouldn't be suspicious of a low-rank hunter, especially one thought to be at rock bottom, trying to sell a valuable item that even a high-rank hunter would have difficulty acquiring? He'd have the same problem with buying anything.

As long as he was dragging along the label of E rank, he wouldn't be able to reveal where his money was coming from.

*And what would I say if someone asks where I'm planning to use the gear?* Talk about opening a can of worms.

"Then I guess it's time……"

It was time to stop pretending to be an E rank and receive a rank reevaluation. He was to be properly ranked based on his actual abilities.

A serious expression crossed his face.

*Since I've dragged myself up to this level, I won't be pushed around anymore, right?*

That had been his intention from the start. Despite the inconvenience, he'd stayed as an E rank to avoid being pulled in different directions by those higher than himself.

But now? Jinwoo hadn't been intimidated by Yoonho Baek, the guild master of White Tiger. No, he was confident he'd be able to hold his head high in front of anyone, not just Baek. There was no reason to hide his true abilities anymore.

*Ba-dump, ba-dump, ba-dump.*

The pounding of his heart seemed to increase in volume at the thought of shedding the E-rank label he'd been stuck with for so long.

He just had one thing to confirm before that.

Jinwoo turned on his hunter-exclusive phone. It had been a week since he'd last powered it up, so his missed calls and inbox were pretty full, but they were mostly from unknown numbers. Alas, he didn't have enough time to check each one.

*I guess they'll call back if it's urgent.*

Jinwoo mentally shrugged as he scrolled through his call history and found the number he was looking for.

*   *   *

*Tra-la-la...* ♪♪

The person on the other end swiftly answered before the second bar of the pleasant ringtone.

**"Boss!"**

Had he been in the dungeon too long? To think he was actually glad to hear that familiar voice. Jinwoo cracked a smile.

"Did the talk with your father go okay?"

**"Yes! It went better than okay, boss!"**

*Really?*

That was good to hear. Jinwoo couldn't get reevaluated before Jinho completed his deal with his father, but now that everything had been taken care of, there was nothing standing in his way. The result was obvious from the tone of Jinho's voice, but it was nice to hear him verbally confirm it.

**"Boss, I actually wanted to talk to you abou—"**

*Beep.*

*Huh?*

His phone had died and cut off the call.

*Thinking back, the battery was low even before I entered the Demon's Castle, so......*

Jinwoo was relieved he'd at least managed to check on the matter he'd called about. He started getting dressed. The Hunter's Association Headquarters wasn't far, so the reevaluation wasn't likely to take him long to complete.

"Oh, right." Jinwoo stopped at the front door and hurried back into the apartment.

He'd just recalled his sister. He left a short note for her on the dining table, in case disappearing again without saying a word after being away for a week would worry her.

Your brother was here.

* * *

Satisfied, Jinwoo headed out the door.

* * *

It had been a while since Jinwoo set foot inside the reception area of the rank evaluation office for awakened beings.

*Has it been four years already?*

Or was it five? Jinwoo was full of emotion as he stood in front of the receptionist, who addressed him without looking up. "ID and contact information, please."

Jinwoo vaguely remembered the procedure and had prepared all the necessary materials beforehand, so he swiftly handed over his ID and his phone number.

*Huh?*

The receptionist raised an eyebrow at Jinwoo's ID. "Sir, this is a hunter's license."

"Yes."

The receptionist clearly failed to understand him. "Sir, if you aren't satisfied with the evaluation result, that's not our department—"

"That's not it. I'd like to get reevaluated."

"Pardon?" The receptionist, who'd been glancing back and forth between Jinwoo's face and the picture on the license, raised a finger. "H-hold on, please."

The employee headed toward a high-strung middle-aged man seated behind him. "Assistant Manager, a hunter is here because he wants to get reevaluated."

"Reevaluated? What's his current rank?"

"E rank, sir."

The assistant manager craned his neck to check out Jinwoo. "This happens sometimes. There are hunters who can't accept reality and come back here hoping against hope after being stuck in a fantasy."

"Then him, too?"

The higher-up nodded. "Reawakened, my ass… He sees other hunters make tons of money and become famous, so he's in denial and thinks he's got a shot."

"Ah…"

"These guys are a pain to deal with, so just let him know that there's a fee for reevaluation and send him to get an assessment."

"Yessir." The receptionist went back to his post, his worries now assuaged.

The assistant manager watched his employee and Jinwoo from afar, tutting before turning back to his computer monitor. But…

His finger froze over the mouse. The name on the hunter's license… It sounded familiar.

*Where have I heard that name before?*

Once Jinwoo was on his merry way to the evaluation room, Kisoo quietly approached the receptionist. "The E-rank hunter just now— what was his name?"

"Mr. Jinwoo Sung. Do you know him?"

"No, that's not it……"

He definitely knew the name, but he couldn't remember from where—until it hit him.

*Oh!*

The favor! Someone had asked to be contacted if a Hunter Jinwoo Sung turned up. How could he have forgotten?

The assistant manager found a secluded area and hurriedly took out his phone.

*Riiing, riiing.*

**"This is Yoonho Baek."**

"President Baek, sir, I'm just calling about that hunter you mentioned before. You know, Hunter Jinwoo Sung? He's actually here. But how did you know he'd come…?"

**"Jinwoo Sung is there?"**

"Yes, he just came in for a reevaluation."

"......"

The conversation suddenly cut off with silence on the other end, but it didn't last long. This time, President Baek sounded urgent. **"Could you please delay the reevaluation even just a little bit? I'm on my way."**

The assistant manager cocked his head. Was he hearing things?

The guild master of the unparalleled White Tiger Guild sounded anxious.

*Who would've thunk it?*

In any case, the reevaluation process was out of his hands.

He scratched the side of his head as he replied, "He's already at the evaluation building, sir."

The bewildered assistant manager, Kisoo Jung, ended the phone call with President Baek.

*Wait, what the hell's going on?*

It was strange enough for an E-rank hunter to want to get reevaluated, but for the guild master of White Tiger to request he be notified of the results immediately on top of that?

*Is there really something here?*

There had to be for President Baek of all people to be so invested in the situation.

Kisoo shook his head.

*Nah, it can't be.*

Second awakenings were very rare. It was a few months ago by this point, but the whole association had been over the moon about a potential reawakened hunter who'd turned out to be a false alarm. That was the norm with reawakenings: True reawakenings were like finding a needle in a haystack, while misunderstandings were a dime a dozen.

*Many a hunter has come to be reevaluated and left with nothing but a lighter pocket......*

The White Tiger Guild must have made a huge mistake. Still, Kisoo couldn't refuse a favor for President Baek, considering his own relationship with the guild.

"I'll be right back."

"Huh? Where are you going, sir?"

"I just remembered that I have to do something in Building B."

Building B was where the mana evaluation room was located and was referred to as such by the employees of the association.

"Yessir."

"Call me right away if anything happens."

"Will do."

Kisoo brushed off the thought of a possible reawakening, but as he realized that President Baek was probably already on his way, he hurried over to Building B.

* * *

Jinwoo took a seat on the end of a bench in the waiting room. Currently, there were three others who'd arrived before him. Their apprehension was clear on their faces. Jinwoo completely understood how they felt.

*I mean, the result will dictate their entire lives going forward.*

He'd had the same thoughts when he first visited the association. *If I'm an A rank—or no, even a B rank would be fine. Or hell, maybe I'm an S rank?* He'd had those pipe dreams, so it had come as a shock when his evaluation revealed he was an E rank.

Jinwoo giggled to himself as he reminisced about four years ago.

*What is he laughing at?*

*Forget that—how can he laugh now?*

Jinwoo remained unconcerned despite the strange looks the others were sending him.

*Was he born with nerves of steel?*

*Guess he just doesn't get nervous.*

As Jinwoo betrayed no further emotion, the others blinked and awkwardly looked away.

*Nothing's really changed since then.*

He'd had a similar experience last time as well. Back then, he'd been on edge around the other hunters in the room but also curious about what ranks they'd gotten.

Grinning, he looked around the building's interior. For the most part, it was like the people inside it… Since the Hunter's Association itself had been formed less than ten years ago, the building was still clean, like new. It was almost exactly how he remembered it.

There was only one difference.

*Them.*

As Jinwoo scrutinized the sharply dressed men and women gathered across from him, the man sitting next to him spoke up.

"I heard they're all guild people."

"Guild people?"

"Yeah. Not many hunters join the small guilds, so they hang out here and try to sweet-talk awakened beings as soon as they get their results."

No wonder the air among them was frigid.

*The way they watch us is like hungry wolves, too.*

There was a reason for that.

"In case you weren't aware, it's best to avoid joining those guilds."

"Why's that?"

"Apparently, small guilds take on tons of dangerous raids, and their death rates for hunters are high."

Jinwoo nodded his understanding.

Obviously, small guilds were in a strange limbo. Unlike private strike squads, small guilds wouldn't be satisfied with tackling low-rank dungeons, but their hunters weren't good enough for high-rank missions. Because of this, unfortunate accidents were commonplace.

*That's why recruitment is important to them.*

They'd reached a point where they had to camp out in the association building to stalk and target newbies.

"Oh." The other man, who'd been dabbing the sweat off his bald head with a handkerchief, cautiously offered his hand to Jinwoo. "Shouldn't we introduce ourselves, since we were fated to meet like this? I'm Jung-hoon Yoon."

"I'm Jinwoo Sung."

Following that brief introduction, they went back to quietly waiting their turns.

"Next."

Because of the open concept of the waiting area, one could easily read the facial expressions of whoever had completed the test as well as those of the staff members. The awakened being who had just finished didn't look happy.

*I guess he's a D or E rank.*

The guild people seemed to have shared Jinwoo's assessment, as they didn't show any interest in the fellow as he passed by. It was quite an honest reaction.

It made one wonder if there wasn't another way to get the assessment.

"Next, please."

Another result, another disappointed hunter. This one headed to the exit with heavy footsteps, but it was to be expected.

*High-rank hunters wouldn't get paid the big bucks if they were that commonplace.*

For the average individual, even being a C-rank hunter would be like winning the lottery. They could make a lot of money by joining a private strike squad and, if they were lucky, could get into a large guild. Even the White Tiger Guild had four C ranks among their latest recruits. Entering a large guild would guarantee a salary comparable to that of doctors or lawyers.

Junghoon addressed him once more. "If you join a large guild, you get a big signing bonus, right?" The hand holding his handkerchief trembled slightly.

"I have some debt, you see. Can't live with my daughter because of it, too. That's why I'm quite nervous," Junghoon mumbled, then looked up hastily in shock and bowed his head apologetically at Jinwoo. "Oh boy, I can't believe I said that to someone I just met… I'm being a nuisance, aren't I? I tend to say too much when I'm nervous."

"It's fine." Jinwoo smiled and bowed back.

Junghoon clearly wasn't kidding about being anxious, as he took several deep breaths.

Yet another awakened being exited the evaluation room.

"Next, please."

It was Junghoon's turn. However, having broken into a cold sweat, Junghoon gently tugged on Jinwoo's sleeve. Perhaps he was ill?

"Are you feeling all right?" Jinwoo asked, concerned.

Junghoon shook his head. "No, I'm fine, but...would you like to go ahead of me? I'm feeling a little too worked up, so..." He looked desperate.

Was there any reason to reject the offer to go first? Jinwoo happily accepted. Who wouldn't be jittery if a few minutes could transform the rest of their life?

Jinwoo walked up to the no-nonsense staff member in Junghoon's place.

"Name?"

"Jinwoo Sung."

"Mr. Sung... Okay, please place your hand on that black panel and wait."

Jinwoo headed to the mana meter and did as instructed.

*Hmm? He's already been evaluated as an E rank.*

The employee looked over Jinwoo's paperwork. Most hunters who wanted to be reevaluated tended to be of E rank. After sending a pitiful look Jinwoo's way, they belatedly started up the mana meter.

*Blip.*

*Woom, woom, woom.*

The mana meter made a few noises for a brief moment, then suddenly stopped. The result appeared on the monitor.

*Huh? What's wrong with this thing?*

The tester looked perplexed and stopped Jinwoo as he drew back his hand. "Hold on, please."

"Pardon?"

"Let's try that one more time."

"Okay."

Jinwoo put his hand on the panel again.

*Blip.*

*Woom, woom, woom.*

*What?*

This had never happened before. The employee looked more and more frustrated. Why did the machine have to act up now of all times? They requested Jinwoo try it again.

"I'm very sorry, sir. Let's try it one last time."

"......"

Jinwoo decided to just keep his hand on the panel, due to all the retakes.

*Blip.*

*Woom, woom, woom.*

*Seriously, what the hell is going on?*

Beads of sweat appeared on the man's forehead.

*Murmur, murmur.*

By this point, others were beginning to notice that something odd was happening.

*Huh? What's going on?*

*How many times has this been?*

*Is there some kind of problem?*

The employee's brow grew sweatier the more attention he drew.

*Blip.*

*Woom, woom, woom.*

*For fuck's sake, what am I supposed to do?*

As panic began to set in...

"What's going on? Where's Changsik, and why are you doing every-thing alone?"

The employee spun around. Kisoo Jung, the assistant manager from reception, was here.

"Mr. Jung!" The tester was relieved at the unexpected backup. "Changsik went to the restroom."

"How dare he leave his post in the middle of—" Kisoo cut himself off.

*......Well, I did the same thing.*

*Cough, cough.*

Anyway, it appeared Kisoo had arrived just in time. Was the newbie having trouble in the absence of his superior? It was time for a veteran to show how it was done.

"So? What seems to be the problem?" Kisoo showed interest in the situation.

"The mana meter might be malfunctioning."

"It is?"

"Take a look, sir. It keeps showing an error message."

The employee stepped aside so Kisoo could check the monitor that displayed the results.

Kisoo froze. "......How long have you worked here?"

"About six months. Did I press something I shouldn't have?"

"That's not it. Just get Changsik over here immediately."

"What?"

"I don't care if he's in the restroom—get him here now!" Kisoo's voice rose.

The employee flinched. "Wh-what's wrong, sir?"

"This isn't an error. It's saying that it's off the charts! Don't you know what that means?"

"Um... So it's not an error message?"

*Why were all the newbies so slow?*

Kisoo's gaze turned from the rookie to the one being evaluated.

*To think this would happen......*

Jinwoo Sung, the man the guild master of the White Tiger Guild had asked Kisoo to report on.

Kisoo didn't take his eyes off Jinwoo as he explained. "It means we can't measure his mana levels with our mana meter, stupid."

"W-wait, then that means...?"

Did the newbie say they'd been here for only half a year? The last time this had happened was two years ago, so no wonder the kid hadn't realized what was going on.

Kisoo continued in a shaky voice. "Yeah... He's an S rank."

S for *special*. People often mistook it as a rank because the term was so widely used, but it actually stood for those whose mana levels were impossible to measure.

"Just hurry up and get Changsik."

"Right away, sir."

Changsik Kim was still pulling up his pants when he came running over after the employee's call.

"Huff, haah! Let me see." Changsik's face paled after checking the monitor. His gaze shook as it landed on Jinwoo.

*This is Korea's tenth......*

He approached Jinwoo.

Seeing him, Jinwoo finally took his hand off the black panel.

"Um... According to the mana meter, Mr. Sung..." Changsik abruptly remembered that Jinwoo was already a licensed hunter. "I mean, Hunter Jinwoo Sung. It's impossible to measure your mana levels with the current equipment. I'd have to receive permission from upper management to use a more sophisticated meter, so could we ask you to come back in three days?"

Changsik informed Jinwoo of the next step in the process. How long had it been since he'd last said these words? He could barely remember the previous time.

From his experience as a hunter, Jinwoo automatically knew what this meant.

*Perfect.*

His test was on hold. In other words, if the result was immeasurable on the more sophisticated machine in three days' time, he'd unequivocally be an S rank.

*It's all coming together.*

If he'd gotten an A-rank result today, he would've had to increase his abilities and come back to the association for yet another reevaluation.

But a reawakening was already rare enough, so would he tell people he'd had a re-reawakening? A second awakening was considered lucky, but people would be suspicious about a third. He wanted to avoid wasting any time in getting involved in something annoying.

*Whew.*

Jinwoo was relieved the results had come out in his favor. He then turned around.

"Huh?"

Everyone in the room was staring at him.

* * *

"Oh my, to think you'd come see me in person despite your busy schedule!"

"Please, you're Director Park of the association. A phone call just isn't good enough when talking to you."

The warm smile that accompanied President Jongin Choi's words had the older director chuckling.

The man in front of Director Park was the one who led the Hunters, Korea's top guild—the Ultimate Hunter, the individual who commanded the country's most powerful strike squad. How could Director Park not be delighted that such a person was humoring him?

Jongin held up a cigarette. "May I?"

"Oh, of course."

"Would you like one?"

"No, thank you."

Jongin lit the cigarette and brought it to his mouth, absolutely oozing with ease befitting someone who had achieved success at a very young age.

*Is this what you'd call charisma?*

As Director Park was gazing at Jongin as if entranced, the hunter suddenly said, "Seems like there's a commotion over in Building B."

"Building B?" The director looked in the direction of the evaluation room.

The director couldn't actually hear anything, but Jongin was an

S-rank hunter. His heightened senses couldn't be compared to the average person's, so if he could hear it, then it was most likely happening. How humiliating for this to be occurring in the presence of such a distinguished guest.

Director Park frowned. "I'll go and take a look."

"Wait." Jongin dropped the cigarette on the ground and stomped it out. "I'm intrigued as well." Jongin raised his head. His eyes shone, and he had an enigmatic smile. "I'll go with you."

\* \* \*

The entirety of Building B went dead silent in an instant.

*He said it was immeasurable......*

*Then does that mean he's an S rank?*

*I've only ever heard of immeasurable levels, but to think I'd witness it with my own eyes......*

*Gulp.*

The recruiters from various small guilds swallowed the lumps in their throats that formed as Jinwoo turned around. However, not a single one of them attempted to talk to him.

"......"

"......"

Had he been a C rank, it would've triggered mind games among them, and they would've been lining up to at least introduce themselves.

Had he been a B rank, they would've bombarded him with incredible proposals, guaranteeing things like managerial positions, shares of the guild, etc. It would've been a war zone. And no wonder, considering the value of having a B-rank hunter in one's guild, not to mention the incentives for anybody who could sign a B rank. It wasn't unheard of for B ranks to be sweet-talked into being a big fish in a little pond.

It was a different story when it came to A ranks and higher. A ranks received special treatment, whether they be from the smallest guilds or the largest. Becoming a member of an elite strike squad was a given, and since their main source of income was from high-rank dungeons, the rewards were incredible.

That wasn't all—if an A rank wasn't satisfied with any of the existing guilds, they also had the option of becoming a guild master. Since they could form a small- to medium-size guild themselves, was there any point in joining another? An A-rank hunter had that kind of power.

However…the man who had just been evaluated was said to be an S rank. Not even an A rank but an S rank—the highest level of awakened beings, of which there were only nine in all of South Korea.

*Does that mean there's now ten if you include him?*

*The tenth S-rank hunter……*

He was out of the recruiters' league.

*Gulp.*

The only thing they could do was stay quiet and let him pass by. He was just pie in the sky. Or so they thought at first, but…

*Wait a minute……*

*Isn't there an opportunity here?*

A few sly scouts were simultaneously struck with the same brilliant idea. What if they connected the S-rank awakened being with a large guild and received a commission? An S rank's signing bonus was tens of billions of won at least. Receiving even 1 percent of that amount would let them retire on the spot.

And if they were lucky enough to get in his good graces and be appointed as his personal assistant, they would be set for life. There was a rumor that one such PA had received a Porsche for their birthday.

*……Maybe I'll give it a go?*

*I'm no slouch when it comes to the art of persuasion……*

*Should I take the plunge?*

Countless thoughts ran through the recruiters' minds in a short period of time. The mortification of defeat would be fleeting, but the sweet thrill of victory would last a lifetime. They began inching toward Jinwoo while stealing furtive glances at one another.

Right then, someone pointed at the entrance of the building. "Huh? That's......!"

Perhaps it was because they were on edge, but the recruiters all turned simultaneously. Their eyes bulged at the sight.

"Whoa!"

The man entering Building B wore a fashionable suit. There wasn't a single person there who didn't know his name.

"Jong......Jongin Choi?"

"What's the president of the Hunters Guild doing here?"

Who else would it be? As if he was aware of the eyes on him, Jongin straightened out his suit jacket before striding over to Jinwoo.

*How did President Choi manage to get here so quickly?*

*Wait, is that guy already signed with the Hunters Guild?*

*They had intel on him? A top-tier guild really is built differently.*

They should have expected this. The recruiters readily accepted the inevitable. They were glad they hadn't spoken to Jinwoo. How pathetic would it have been if President Choi had walked in on them buttering Jinwoo up? It was clear to them where things were headed.

*President Choi completes the picture.*

*He's so cool...*

*The representative of the Hunters himself... S ranks really do get the VIP treatment.*

Their slight disappointment aside, the recruiters watched the meeting of an awakened being of the highest rank and the president of Korea's best guild with warmth in their eyes.

For his part, Jinwoo breathed a sigh at the sight of Jongin.

*That's a relief.*

He'd been in the middle of debating what to do about receiving so much attention, but President Choi had graciously diverted the spotlight, even if unknowingly. Jinwoo silently thanked him for the unexpected help as he walked straight past the guild president.

Jongin was caught off guard.

*What? Wait.*

Jongin hurriedly called out to Jinwoo. "Just a moment."

Jinwoo stopped in his tracks and looked back. "……?"

Jongin's eyes shone as he regarded Jinwoo's face.

*This man is number ten……*

Jongin had told Director Park some nonsense about finding out what was going on together, but to tell the truth, he was already completely filled in.

*It was impossible for me to miss all that chatter about immeasurable power and errors with the mana meter and whatnot.*

Thanks to that, he'd been presented with a huge opportunity. And an S rank to boot! If he could secure this man, the Hunters Guild would have three S-rank hunters in its ranks, and not only would it be the strongest guild in South Korea, but it would be able to hold its own with the top guilds of the world. How could Jongin not jump at the prospect?

*No need to borrow a mana meter.*

He could feel how strong Jinwoo was simply by making eye contact with him. Jinwoo was a top-class hunter without a doubt. There was no reason to wait three days.

"Ahem." Jongin cleared his throat and shot his signature winsome smile at Jinwoo. "I'm the president of the Hunters Guild, Jongin Choi."

Jinwoo knew that much. Jongin's face popped up on TV all the time. Although he was curious as to why this famous person had come all the way to the association to talk to him, he didn't have time for a leisurely chat.

He glanced at the clock on the wall.

*It's already 5:50.*

If he factored in transit time, it'd be a close call.

Upon seeing Jinwoo's impatience that clearly indicated he should get to the point, Jongin was slightly taken aback as he continued. "Oh, so…I hear you received your rank evaluation."

"Yes."

"Do you have a guild in mind?"

"No, not yet."

Jongin brightened upon hearing this.

*Nice, we're finished here.*

The Hunters was among the world's top three guilds—how sweet those words sounded. From this day on, it would no longer be a pipe dream.

*You're mine.*

Jongin clutched the welcome news close and spoke the words that might very well be recorded in history books. "I'd like to discuss that matter. Do you have a minute—?"

"I don't. Sorry." Jinwoo cut him off and promptly exited the association building.

"......" It had happened so fast, the thought of catching up to him didn't even cross Jongin's mind.

The association employee and recruiter onlookers were astonished as they belatedly realized what had happened.

"What the heck?"

"Was President Choi actually rejected?"

"It looked like he flat-out ignored President Choi."

*Murmur, murmur.*

It quickly turned clamorous in the building. Jongin did his best to keep his cool and turned to the man standing next to him.

"Director Park."

"Yes?" the director answered awkwardly.

"Did I forget to introduce myself just now?"

"I...I'm not quite sure myself..."

Of course, the director had been right next to Jongin for the whole encounter and had seen and heard everything. However, this wasn't the time for honesty, was it?

When the director clammed up, Jongin scratched his head in embarrassment.

*Did I come in too hot...?*

But there was no need for disappointment. He was still a step ahead of the other guilds.

*I'm the only one who knows about the new S rank.*

The reevaluation would be in three days. There was time before the official announcement.

*I want to arrange a meeting with him at least one more time before then......*

What would be the best approach? While Jongin pondered this, he caught sight of someone bolting toward the association building.

*......Is that?*

It was a face he knew well. As soon as the man pushed open the glass door, Jongin blurted out a question in surprise. "President Baek, why are you......?"

Baek's eyes widened when he recognized Jongin. "President Choi?"

Jongin scanned Yoonho's expression.

*He looks like he was caught doing something......*

Yoonho wasn't here because he'd heard something from his informant. He'd gotten here way too quickly for that.

*Considering the distance between the White Tiger Headquarters and the Hunter's Association......*

So that was it—President Baek must have been in on it from the start. He'd already known what was going to happen here.

*He's aware of that man's existence?*

No, Yoonho wouldn't have let him get evaluated if that were the case.

*If I were Yoonho, I would've signed the guy first before allowing the reevaluation.*

At that moment, all the puzzle pieces scattered in his mind started to come together.

*......Could it be?*

The White Tiger Guild, the training incident, the red gate, the nameless supporter, and the appearance of a new S-rank awakened being.

*"White Tiger got help from someone they don't want anyone else knowing about."*

*"Is it a new hunter who has yet to be diagnosed as an awakened being? Or a criminal whose identity needed to be concealed?"*

\* \* \*

Everything made sense now...... Jongin had found him.

*So it was him.*

Seeing as how President Baek had sprinted so hard that he was now huffing and puffing, it wasn't that he'd just let Jinwoo do whatever he wanted. No, it was that President Baek couldn't stop him.

President Choi smiled at President Baek.

*You let this slip through your fingers.*

But Jongin was different.

*I'll happily accept this golden opportunity.*

President Choi brushed past Yoonho without another word.

Yoonho looked around, but Jinwoo was nowhere to be seen.

*Am I too late?*

Yoonho let out a sigh, watching Jongin's back as he departed.

*Haah...*

To think the guild master of the Hunters Guild would also be here.

Yoonho scratched the back of his head and mumbled, "Things are getting complicated."

\* \* \*

Visiting hours at Seoul Ilshin Hospital were until eight PM.

"You're Kyunghye Park's guardian, correct?"

"Yes."

"You can go in. You're aware of when visiting hours end?"

"I am, yes."

Jinwoo headed toward his mother's hospital room. He'd been able to get to there in time by rushing.

*Click.*

Jinwoo opened the door, made his way over to the bedside, and quietly took a seat next to his mother, who remained motionless as if asleep.

*When I look at her, it's like she'll wake up as if nothing's wrong......*

But she was in a deep sleep from which she couldn't awaken. She was diagnosed with an illness that had first been discovered when gates began appearing.

*I think they said there were around ten or so patients with the same condition in this hospital alone.*

He gently took his mother's hand. "Mom......"

Fortunately, a life-support system that ran on essence stones kept his mother's hand from withering away, despite her having been in a coma for several years.

Unfortunately, essence stones were expensive. It cost more than 5 million won to keep the machine constantly operating for a month. If the association didn't cover medical bills for their hunters, it wouldn't have been something he as a young man in his twenties could have afforded. He was able to hold his mother's hand thanks to all his efforts to this point.

But things were different now. Instead of being satisfied with keeping her breathing, he had a chance to actually cure her. The Elixir of Life, the cure gifted to him by the system. Whether it would actually work or not was a matter for later. Getting it crafted was the current issue at hand.

"I'll save you."

In the absence of their father and despite her failing health, his mother had done her best to take care of her children. It wouldn't be long now before she was up and about again.

*Please hang on until then.*

How long had he been keeping watch over her? After a significant amount of time had passed, he stood. His visit having come to an end, Jinwoo soundlessly left the room and cautiously closed the door.

When he turned around, though, he was met with a familiar face.

"So you really were the one who took care of the magic beasts in the double dungeon...weren't you?" That low, deep voice and those sharp eyes—it was Jinchul Woo, the manager of the Hunter's Association's Surveillance Team.

Jinwoo didn't answer. He had no reason or desire to do so. Instead, he had a question of his own. "How did you know I was here?"

"I came up with a list of places I anticipated you'd be, and when I contacted the hospital, they told me you were here."

The association had paid for his mother's hospital bill until recently.

*Though not anymore.*

The hospital may very well have been the first place he checked. The Surveillance Team acted swiftly, as expected.

Jinwoo couldn't help snorting his laughter as he asked, "Did you go out of your way to find me to ask about what happened that day?"

Jinchul shook his head. "That's not it."

"Then what brings you here?"

"There is someone who would like to meet you. Will you please come with me?"

The Hunter's Association's Surveillance Team. Their main purpose was to keep track of and monitor hunters and to penalize those who broke the law. They were the last people with whom hunters wanted to cross paths.

Because of that, Jinwoo regarded Jinchul with distrust. "Is that an order?"

"No." Jinchul took off his sunglasses. He bowed at a near-perfect ninety-degree angle and asked courteously, "I would like to humbly ask that you do."

"……"

Jinwoo hadn't expected the intense man to go this far, and after deliberating for a bit, he made up his mind to at least find out who was behind all this.

"Who's asking for me?"

Jinchul finally straightened up. "President Gunhee Go of the Hunter's Association." He held up his hand and gestured to around the corner behind him.

"The president is right this way."

\* \* \*

At the president's office at the Hunter's Association, the doctor examining President Go looked grim. He lifted the stethoscope from President Go's chest.

"Mr. President."

"No, you don't need to say anything. I can tell from your expression." President Go chortled as he buttoned up his shirt.

The doctor stayed quiet.

*That he's even up and about...is nothing short of a miracle.*

Despite this, President Go was chugging along at full speed without slowing down. He'd even had his doctor examine him at his office because he didn't have time to go to the hospital.

"You know..." President Go slipped an arm through his suit jacket. "When healers and healing magic came into existence, I thought I could regain my youth, bid farewell to this old, haggard body." President Go chortled again. "But that wasn't the case."

"Have there been no advancements?"

"Apparently, there's nothing even a high-rank healer can do about old age."

Had healers been able to eliminate all diseases, hospitals throughout the country would have had to shut down, and doctors would have been out of work. Fortunately, or unfortunately, that wasn't the case.

Mana helped with regeneration. Healing magic was limited to mending physical wounds. It could miraculously regrow a severed arm, but it couldn't lower the fever of a child with a cold.

*Thanks to that, I'm still gainfully employed, but......*

The doctor watched over President Go, who was already prepping himself to head out for the next item on his agenda.

*I hope the president of all people can find a treatment, even if it's through magic.*

Currently, neither healing magic nor modern medicine was useful for President Go's condition. The only thing the doctor could offer was advice. "You require bed rest. You must rest, even for a little bit."

"I would like that, too." But what would happen to the Hunter's Association if he did? President Go's laugh implied that question.

*The association without me, Gunhee Go......*

Even at this moment, large guilds with deep pockets were expanding their influence by the minute. Their power was already comparable to a country's military might. The only reason the association had any leverage among the guilds wasn't because of the government behind them but because President Go led them. As soon as the association lost hold of the guilds' reins, they'd be running free like wild horses.

*Not...not yet...*

It wasn't quite time for President Go to retire. The association was the only thing keeping the large guilds in check. He couldn't leave before he could set up a viable plan B.

*I need to be here to show that the association is still going strong.*

He was an S rank above all S ranks. He was a vital part of the association. So until then, no matter what it took......

"Argh!" President Go cried out in pain. He grabbed his chest, wrinkling his immaculately pressed dress shirt.

"President Go, here......" The doctor held out a painkiller and a cup of water.

"Thank you."

The medicine gave him some measure of relief. Right then......

*Hmm?*

His phone rang, even though he'd ordered his secretary not to bother him while the doctor was here.

Frowning, he answered the call. "I'm in the middle of a physical."

The urgent voice of his male secretary came over the receiver.

**"I'm sorry, sir. Something pressing came up."**

"Did Japan call again?"

**"They did, but that's not it."**

President Go's eyebrows raised.

*A bigger problem than those damn Jeju ants?*

What could it possibly be?

"What is it?"

The secretary squeaked out a response just before President Go ran out of patience.

**"We've received word from the evaluation team."**

"Evaluation team?"

The job of the evaluation team consisted of rating gates and awakened beings. It wasn't a group that usually caused problems.

*Or maybe......*

Did they make another error measuring a gate? A scowl came over his face as he recalled the recent conflict with the White Tiger Guild.

His displeasure didn't last long. What the secretary told President Go was beyond anything he could have expected.

**"The evaluation team...... They said there was an awakened being with an immeasurable rank."**

\* \* \*

"President Go of the Hunter's Association?"

Had he heard that right? Jinwoo wasn't sure. The person referred to as the most powerful hunter in South Korea had come to the hospital at this time of night to meet him?

*That can't be......*

Although Jinwoo was half in disbelief, Jinchul gestured again and confirmed what Jinwoo thought he'd heard. "The president of the association is here."

Jinchul's eyes radiated anxiety as he awaited Jinwoo's response. It was clear he wasn't joking around.

*......This is seriously happening.*

Why was Gunhee Go looking for him? Jinwoo couldn't rein in his racing thoughts. It had to be because of the results of his reevaluation, right...?

*Is he trying to recruit me for the association?*

However, the association was a nonprofit organization. It wasn't necessary for the president to bring along a Surveillance Team member in order to scout a single hunter. Besides, he hadn't had his full evaluation yet. The more he thought about it, the curiouser it all was.

"Fine." Jinwoo agreed.

Jinchul's expression lit up so quickly that one could barely tell he'd ever been nervous.

"Thank you very much!" Sincerity rang in his voice.

*To think such an intimidating man could make those expressions.*

Jinwoo was fascinated as he followed Jinchul. When they turned the corner, Jinwoo caught sight of an old man seated on one of the hard chairs in the hospital waiting room.

*That's......*

Jinwoo gulped.

A god among gods—that's what S-rank hunter Gunhee Go was known as.

*Shp.*

President Go spotted him and rose from his seat. "Hunter Jinwoo Sung?"

Even though he was over eighty, Gunhee Go was an old man with a commanding presence. His physique reminded Jinwoo of a retired pro wrestler or a traditional *ssireum* wrestler but without the cocky attitude.

*He's different from what I expected.*

Jinwoo figured the man would come across as a formidable, but the secretary next to him wore a more menacing expression.

"Yes, I'm Jinwoo Sung," he answered.

President Go extended a hand with a pleased smile. "Nice to meet you. I'm Gunhee Go."

They shook hands, and President Go waved at a couple of chairs that had been arranged facing each other. "Have a seat."

"Thank you."

The president waited for Jinwoo to sit before doing the same.

A gold badge on President Go's jacket collar caught Jinwoo's eye. The man was both a congressman as well as the president of the Hunter's Association.

*And an S-rank awakened being to boot.*

President Go wasn't someone with whom people could easily get an audience. Countless individuals, from politicians to business tycoons from abroad, wanted to meet with him, which made this whole thing even stranger. Why was someone like Gunhee Go in a rush to meet little old Jinwoo?

*First Jongin Choi, now Gunhee Go?*

Jinwoo'd had the honor of meeting not one but two people regarded to be at the top. He hadn't even been officially confirmed to be an S rank yet—

President Go interrupted his musings. "Congratulations on becoming an S-rank hunter."

Jinwoo cocked his head. "My results haven't been confirmed yet."

The president shook his head. "To be honest, the reevaluation doesn't mean much."

"Pardon?"

He gently smiled at Jinwoo's confounded expression. "A sophisticated mana meter does give more precise measurements, but it's not designed to measure immeasurable quantities."

"Then why...?"

"You're asking why there is a reevaluation procedure at all?"

He was spot-on. If the results were the same, why drag out the process? President Go's answer was simple. "It's a grace period."

*Grace period...?*

Before Jinwoo could ask, President Go continued sheepishly. "That's how long we can get away with to reach out to hunters like you first."

*Ohhh.*

Jinwoo perfectly understood what he was implying.

"As you know, despite the size of the association, there aren't many excellent hunters like Manager Woo in our employ..."

*Because of the large guilds, right?*

"...because of the large guilds."

Jinwoo had hit the nail on the head.

"Who would come to the association when fame and money are guaranteed by large guilds?"

The income for hunters in the association wasn't meager, but it was petty cash compared to how much they could make in a large guild. Fame was the same.

"There are many who can list off the names of elite strike squad members, but very few know about Manager Woo."

At the mention of elite strike squads, Jinwoo recalled A-rank hunter Chul Kim. The perception stat allowed Jinwoo to appraise another person's ability. By his assessment, Jinchul was definitely in a class above Chul.

*Even though they're the same rank, their skills are on different levels.*

Jinwoo turned to look at Jinchul, who blushed and bowed his head at the president's compliments and Jinwoo's gaze.

*However......*

If Chul had managed to start working as a hunter, he would've had heaps more money and fame than Jinchul. That was the difference between a hunter from the association and a hunter from a guild.

"That's why we set up this little trick in case an extremely talented awakened being showed up at the association."

And that trick was the reevaluation?

*I mean, if you think about it......*

Once the results became public and word spread, it would be much harder for the association to approach such a person. It made sense for them to go about things this way.

"Let me get to the point." President Go's smile had vanished. "We're not a company, so we cannot promise to make you rich. However..."

President Go had been fiddling with something on his chest, and he now thrust out his fist, which was clenched tightly around something.

"...We can help you down a different path."

"What do you mean...?"

"I mean we can nurture you to have a different kind of power." He revealed the item in his hand. There, on his palm, lay his glittering gold badge.

*Does he mean...political power?*

Jinwoo just looked confused. "I don't understand."

"Pardon?"

"Why are you going so far for me?"

That was a valid question. President Go's eyes shone as he examined Jinwoo.

*Instead of being intimidated by me or tempted by the incredible opportunity right before his eyes, he's calmly voicing his doubts......*

Had he been too hasty? He'd heard that patience decreases with age, and that clearly wasn't wrong. President Go swallowed his laugh and continued.

"You know the top five guilds, don't you?"

How could Jinwoo not? He silently nodded.

"Currently, there is a delicate balance among the five monsters of Korea."

There were the Hunters, White Tiger, and the Reapers in Seoul, plus Fame and the Knights outside of Seoul.

"If you join one of the five guilds, no matter which, the balance will tip, and huge change will come."

The large guilds were already powerful enough to pierce the sky. But if one of them welcomed another S-rank hunter and claimed a spot above the rest? Would they deign to listen to the association then? The association's role was to maintain balance.

"You cannot control hunters with laws, regulations, or governmental authority."

Jinwoo'd had the same thought not too long ago. Magic beasts weren't the only monsters. Hunters could be just as monstrous—heck, based on power alone, hunters were arguably more dangerous.

"That is why we need the association." President Go's expression revealed the gravity of the situation. "And the association needs Hunter Jinwoo Sung."

They needed someone as powerful as Jinwoo. Gunhee's gaze was shrewd.

*I'd have to have him close by and keep an eye on him for a time, but......*
If Jinwoo accepted, Gunhee intended to give him all the support he needed. S ranks were worth that kind of treatment.

*That should be enough for him to understand.*
All that was left was...

For the first time in quite a while, President Go felt a mix of apprehension and excitement. He asked in a low voice, "What will you do, Hunter Sung?"

# 2
## PRESIDENT GO'S PROPOSAL

# 2
# PRESIDENT GO'S
# PROPOSAL

It wasn't a bad proposal. With the support of President Go, even a regular non-awakened person would be on the fast track to success. Congress, the government, the association, or even the media—it was hard to find a sector President Go's influence didn't reach. So for an S-rank hunter holding President Go's endorsement...

*The sky would be the limit.*

Jinwoo pictured himself in a sharp suit sitting next to Congressman Go. His heart fluttered.

*This is pretty much a once-in-a-lifetime opportunity.*

After all, this wasn't a path just anyone could take because they felt like it. However, there was a catch that hadn't been addressed.

*If I join the association, I can't level up anymore.*

High-rank hunters who worked for the association weren't expected to go out in the field. Their main job was dealing with other hunters, not magic beasts. Even if he received permission to attend an association raid...

*The association deals only with the D- or E-rank dungeons that guilds won't bother with.*

Would he be content with cleaning up low-rank monsters that no longer gave him experience points? No, he couldn't be.

*I want to become even stronger.*

He wanted to advance as much as he could, climb as high as possible. If it were unachievable, he might have surrendered, but to give up when he knew it was still attainable? No way in hell.

*As long as I keep leveling up, I can continue to develop my power.*

*Ba-dump. Ba-dump.*

He felt more excited now than when he was imagining a place for himself next to President Go.

Gunhee also noticed a change in Jinwoo.

*His breathing has sped up. Has he finally made a decision?*

He was hoping for good news.

*No, it absolutely has to be good news. I don't have much time left......*

President Go's heart pounded as fast as Jinwoo's while he awaited the young hunter's answer. Every second felt like a minute.

Jinwoo opened his mouth. "I'm sorry."

President Go froze.

*He looked so determined about something, though...... Was I seeing things?*

He couldn't hide his disappointment.

*In the end, Jinwoo Sung only amounted to this...*

President Go's offer hadn't been an empty promise. In fact, he'd intended to give much more than that.

*The first S rank in two years......*

He'd planned to keep Jinwoo close and to teach him everything he knew. And if Jinwoo demonstrated himself capable, President Go would have trained him to be his successor, as they needed someone very powerful to hold the association together when President Go was gone. In other words, he'd been ready to give Jinwoo everything he had.

And yet, this was the result.

*I've become a laughingstock.*

President Go grumbled as he lowered his arm with the gold badge.

"......Is it because of money?"

Jinwoo replied immediately. "No, sir."

President Go snorted in his mind.

*They all talk the talk, but...*

On the inside, they were the same. It always came down to money, and it was icing on the cake if fame followed. Of course, greed was a basic human instinct, so President Go didn't fault him for it. He'd simply grown weary of people who couldn't be honest.

"Then why did you reject my proposal?" Even though he knew the answer, President Go asked Jinwoo anyway, solely to observe the young man's reaction. But...

"I want to hunt," Jinwoo replied without hesitation.

It hit Gunhee like a freight train.

*What did he say?*

Gunhee felt like he'd had the wind knocked out of him. "You mean... You want to hunt magic beasts?"

"Yes." Jinwoo discarded any superfluous details in his explanation and spoke his truth. "I want to go through gates and kill magic beasts. That's where I belong."

*Unbelievable.*

President Go was shocked. A man occupying a position above so many could tell when someone was lying or telling the truth by looking them in the eyes, as the ability to do so was a crucial tool to achieve such a position in the first place. That was how President Go could tell.

*Those eyes... He's telling the truth.*

The way President Go was looking at Jinwoo completely changed.

*When was the last time I felt like this?*

Gunhee had already been past his prime when he was first awakened, so instead of fighting magic beasts, he'd contributed in another way. He'd established the association using the money gained from selling his business, gathered hunters, and used his popularity to enter Congress and pen laws for hunters. However, despite all his achievements, he held on to one fundamental regret he couldn't shed.

*If I were twenty or even ten years younger, I could've fought alongside young men like him......!*

*Ba-dump, ba-dump, ba-dump.*

President Go placed his hand on his chest. His heart, which was in danger of stopping at any moment, was now racing.

*To think my heart could still sound like this.*

The steady beat lifted his mood.

On the other hand, Jinwoo was nonplussed.

*Strange...*

When he'd refused the president's proposal, he'd been ready for the possibility of the association cutting ties with him, but instead, President Go actually seemed pleased.

*Well, I guess it doesn't matter either way......*

He'd said everything he wanted to say. Jinwoo stood. "I should get going. My sister is home alone."

"Thank you for your time." President Go stood up after him, then fished something out of his inner breast pocket and handed it to Jinwoo. "Take this."

It was his business card.

*......?*

"If you ever need my help, please feel free to contact me anytime." President Go beamed. Jinwoo's words were correct. Powerful hunters belonged in the dungeons, fighting. Even though he'd failed to recruit Jinwoo, as the president of the Hunter's Association and a fellow hunter, Gunhee wanted to do what he could to help Jinwoo. To put it more bluntly...

*I like this young man.*

He had some advice to impart as well. Though it could be seen as nagging, in his defense, nagging generally came from a place of concern. "It's impossible to raid high-rank dungeons on your own, so please be very prudent when choosing a guild."

Especially given that his choice would make huge waves.

An enigmatic smile flashed across Jinwoo's face for a brief moment at President Go's heartfelt advice. "Thank you."

Jinwoo put the business card in his wallet and left after exchanging quick good-byes with President Go and Jinchul.

"Whew..." President Go flopped back down in the chair as he let out a sigh.

"Are you okay, sir?" Appearing beside the elder man, Jinchul assumed President Go wasn't happy.

But President Go waved him off with a grin. "Yes, I'm fine."

Of course he was. He couldn't remember the last time he'd enjoyed meeting someone like this. President Go basked in the feeling for a bit before turning to his secretary and giving an order. "Clear my entire schedule for the day, will you?"

"But you have that meeting with the cabinet members..."

"Cancel everything, no exceptions." A grin spread across his face at his own words. "I don't wish to waste this feeling on those fossils today."

He wanted to ride this high for at least the day. Suddenly, President Go's eyes snapped to Jinchul. Jinchul was thrilled seeing the president's smile, which was a rare sight. "Did you have something you wanted to say to me, sir?"

"Nothing important, just......" Gunhee hesitated a second and tapped his chin. "Would you like to have a drink with me?"

Jinchul offered an awkward grin at the unexpected invitation. "I'm not very good at holding my alcohol... Is that okay with you, sir?"

"Huh, I didn't peg you as a lightweight." Gunhee playfully tutted. "Haven't you heard the saying, 'The size of the glass a man can drink determines the size of his world'?"

"Apologies, sir." Jinchul sheepishly rubbed the back of his neck and blushed.

"I'm kidding. I'm in such high spirits that I'm in the mood to joke." Truth be told, Gunhee actually had someone else he wanted to drink with. He turned his gaze toward the hallway through which Jinwoo had left.

*Hunter Jinwoo Sung......*

How much could he drink? Gunhee smiled wistfully as he hoped to share a drink with Jinwoo someday.

* * *

*Skrrrt.*

*Fshhh.*

Jinwoo stepped off the bus. He'd used Jinah as an excuse to leave, but when he checked his watch, he realized it wasn't quite time for her to come home. He leisurely made his way to their apartment.

*Zzzt, zzzt.*

He turned at the unfamiliar sound and noticed a streetlight blinking like it was about to go out. Upon a second glance, the surrounding area seemed too dark. Because they were quite a ways from the city center, dark and secluded places were a stone's throw from the main road.

A memory of a recent headline flashed in his mind. There were all those mysterious murder cases.

*Weren't all the victims women?*

His sister often walked down this street, usually late at night.

*We can't move, either, because Jinah's school is close by.*

He wound up worried for her sake. Capturing the criminal would be easy for Jinwoo, but he couldn't exactly wait for Jinah out here every night just because he was concerned for her. Was there anything else he could do?

Jinwoo folded his arms, then grinned as a thought crossed his mind.

*I can have others keep watch in my stead.*

They were perfect for this situation. "Come out." Shadow soldiers materialized at his call.

*Five should be enough.*

These soldiers had been well trained during the Demon's Castle raids. Just by looking at them, Jinwoo knew they could be relied upon.

"From now on, you guys are the neighborhood's vigilantes. Commence your patrol." As soon as he gave the order, the soldiers morphed back into shadows and moved out, gliding among the shadows cast by buildings and other structures.

*That's it. Make your way around cautiously so no one notices you.*

Awww, they were adorable.

There was no way someone on a murder spree could defeat the shadow soldiers unless they were a high-rank hunter themselves. Even then, Jinwoo would immediately sense if something happened to his troops.

And he was an S-rank hunter.

*Or maybe I should call myself an S-rank awakened being, since I haven't received the official license yet?*

That was beside the point. This neighborhood was now under the protection of an S-rank hunter or awakened being. The real estate prices would explode if people found out about this free twenty-four-hour security service, wouldn't they?

A smile blossomed on Jinwoo's face.

*Excellent.*

He felt like he could relax. Jinwoo surveyed his surroundings with a look of satisfaction on his face, then turned to leave.

\* \* \*

"I hustled my ass over here because you asked me to have dinner, and we're having Korean barbecue?"

"Huh? You looking down on thinly sliced pork belly?"

"……"

"I've got precious memories of eating here with the boss!" Jinho's face was flushed as he put down his drink and huffed.

"Fine, then why'd you bring me to this precious place?" Suhyun looked unamused. She'd been on the verge of sleep when she'd received Jinho's phone call.

**"Sis, comfort me, won't you?"**

**"Since when do you call me Sis?"**

**"Siiiis."**

* * *

She'd come to join him out of pity, yet he had the nerve to choose a restaurant like this. Suhyun had been born with a silver spoon in her mouth and currently worked as a model, so this place was obviously ill-suited to her. Despite having thrown on only the minimum amount of makeup and a hat before rushing out the door, a bunch of guys were still ogling her.

"So what's wrong? You gotta use words." Suhyun prodded Jinho as she poured soju into his empty shot glass.

"Look, look at this. Boss is avoiding my calls, right?" Jinho's voice was thick with tears as he handed her his phone. There was a long list of recent calls with one connected and four that failed. Jinho explained that the first had even been cut off mid-conversation.

"Did you ask me here just because you couldn't get in touch with some rando?"

Jinho's head bobbed up and down.

"Haaah..." Shaking her head in disbelief, Suhyun snatched the phone from him. "Give me that."

She hastily pressed the Call button.

*Riiing.*

The ringing promptly stopped. As it did, Suhyun's eyes flashed. "Hey, you."

"Yeah?" Jinho looked up at her.

"The ringing stops exactly after fifteen seconds. He's not avoiding your calls—his phone is off. And if your conversation got disconnected, it was probably because his phone ran out of battery."

"...Really?"

"If you don't believe me, try calling him again."

*Riiing.*

The ringing stopped exactly fifteen seconds later, just as she'd said.

"It's true." Jinho's face lit up.

"Happy now? I'm leaving."

Jinho grabbed Suhyun's sleeve as she abruptly stood to leave. "Siiis, let's finish this open bottle first!"

"You only call me Sis in times like this, huh?"

He usually addressed her as *you, dude,* or *hey.*

Eventually, Suhyun sat back down.

"Oh? You're gonna drink, too, Sis?"

"You said you're gonna finish your bottle first, right? Who knows how long that'll take if you're the only one drinking."

"You're the best, Sis."

"Yeah, whatever."

Bickering aside, they were having a good time together.

"By the way, who's this boss of yours?"

"You'll find out soon enough..."

*...as long as he joins the Yoojin Guild,* or so Jinho was about to say when something on the restaurant's wall-mounted TV caught his eye.

"Hey, isn't that...?"

Suhyun turned to look. A news report about the A-list actor Minsung Lee was being broadcast. Minsung spoke shyly to the many reporters swarming him.

**"I haven't finished filming yet, so... I'm still waiting for the evaluation report, but......"**

The caption on the bottom screen reported that Minsung was planning to visit the association for an evaluation soon.

"Wow, as expected of *hallyu* star Minsung Lee! Look how many reporters there are. There are some from China, too." Jinho couldn't help but be amazed.

However, Suhyun's eyebrows twitched. "How can he lie that casually in front of so many people?"

"Huh?"

"Those who know, know. That's entirely for show. He already got an A rank, but he's milking it for the publicity."

"Really? But he's Minsung Lee, the symbol of humility."

Suhyun clicked her tongue.

*Tsk.*

*How is everyone falling for that act?*

She resisted saying anything else, as she didn't want to talk behind someone's back, but Minsung's reputation was the worst among those who knew him. There was an incredibly huge discrepancy between his public persona and his actual character. He was exactly the type of person Suhyun despised.

She could've let him slide if he was merely two-faced, but he also would not leave her alone. Just recently, he'd called her out of the blue, trying to impress her now that he was a fellow hunter. She'd had a hard time getting him off the phone.

*What a fucking creep......*

Minsung's narcissism had been second to none even before his awakening, so how much more unbearable would he be now that he was an A-rank hunter? On top of that, his evaluation result looked primed to be broadcast all over the country.

*He's a mastermind when it comes to manipulating the media.*

Suhyun shook her head and downed the rest of her shot glass.

* * *

"Are you going to take responsibility if I get fired?"

"Excuse me? What does that mean?"

"The president of the association ordered us to keep our lips sealed about what happened yesterday. He said he'd find and punish whoever leaked the awakened being's information, no matter what it took."

"President Go said that? But he's never said that before, right?"

"How should I know what President Go is thinking?"

"......"

"If there's nothing else, I'll hang up."

"......I'll call you later."

*Click.*

The call ended just like that. The guild master of the Reapers Guild, Taegyu Lim, looked uneasy as he put down the phone.

*What is happening…?*

When he'd heard the news that a super rookie had appeared, the guild master himself immediately called their contact at the association. But this was the last thing he'd expected to hear.

Would he take responsibility if the employee got fired? No guild would dare hire someone who had fallen out of favor with President Go and gotten fired. Moreover, even if the awakened being was identified, there was no guarantee the Reapers Guild would be able to recruit them.

*"Find and punish the person no matter what it took," eh…?*

President Go could definitely do that.

*But has that old man gone senile? Why is he going out of his way when he's never done anything like this before?*

Just what sort of wind was blowing these days? To think information leaks would be banned outright. That was unprecedented. For that reason, the Reapers Guild had no choice but to twiddle their thumbs until the official announcement.

That wasn't the only thing Taegyu found unfair.

*Then how did Jongin Choi and Yoonho Baek find out and get to the association?*

Was it a difference in the depth of their intel? Had the Reapers' influence fallen so far in this industry? If the super rookie joined either the Hunters or White Tiger, the gap between them and the Reapers would widen to the point where catching up would be impossible. Things already looked bad for the Reapers, and now a gag order, of all things, stood in their way.

*Is the old man my archnemesis from a previous life?*

He had helped Yoonho form the White Tiger Guild after he left the Reapers. That resulted in the Reapers getting knocked out of the top guild spot. The Hunters and White Tiger had continued steadily advancing, but the Reapers had stagnated.

*Isn't it time Gunhee helped out the Reapers?!*

Taegyu felt a hot flash of resentment toward President Go. He was out of options. Despite being upset, all he could do at this point was anxiously pace back and forth.

\* \* \*

*And with that, the daily quest is complete.*

Jinwoo could surf the Internet without a care. There were two days left until the reevaluation. He'd turned on the computer to look up information about buying and selling artifacts.

*Whoa!*

Jinwoo's eyes widened as he looked over the auction site.

*Bids start in the hundreds of millions!*

And it wasn't just that. Decent artifacts went for several billion won.

*Although......*

Artifacts were lifelines for hunters. It went without saying that the better the gear, the safer it was. Hunters earned a hefty amount, so why scrimp on tools that helped them hunt faster and safer? It was understandable, but that didn't change the fact that he found it shocking. Jinwoo felt uneasy looking at the prices.

*It doesn't seem like I have enough money, do I?*

He couldn't find any fireproof equipment up for auction, but he didn't have close to enough money to buy any high-rank protective gear anyway.

*I thought I saved up enough, but......*

It certainly was a lot from an ordinary person's point of view, but from a hunter's perspective, his bank account was very much lacking. He had about 1,700,000,000 won saved up. Jinwoo would have no choice but to sell the Sphere of Avarice to purchase the equipment he wanted.

His expression changed when he started considering things from a seller's stance.

*Having to buy at a high price means I can also sell at a high price.*

*Click.*

He tapped his mouse to search for magic tools currently up for sale.
. . . . . .

No matter how hard he tried, he couldn't find anything that doubled damage dealt by magic. Adding 20 to 30 percent to one's original power was the best he could find, and even those items were unbelievably expensive.

*The prices for tools are absolutely insane.*

If he thought about it, a 20 percent increase wasn't that bad. Only high-rank—or no, only the highest-rank hunters could afford these prices, so if an item increased their power by 20 percent, that would actually make a huge difference. High-rank hunters paid these exorbitant prices because they understood this. Items that had just been put up for sale in real time were already gone. If an item that gave a 20 percent boost sold for that price and rate...

*How much should I put the sphere up for?*

Jinwoo swallowed nervously. It hadn't been long since Jinwoo couldn't even begin to dream of artifacts, so it was hard for him to grasp how much money he could earn for the sphere.

*I guess that's why auctions exist.*

Hopefully, when he put the Sphere of Avarice up for auction, it would go for big bucks. Jinwoo closed the browser window with a satisfied grin on his face.

According to his research, there were basically two ways to sell an item: the official route and the black market. However, there didn't seem to be an easy way to access the latter. Information online was quite limited.

*If people could access it with just a few clicks of their mouse, I guess it wouldn't be called the black market.*

Luckily, there was no need to sell the Sphere of Avarice that way, since there was nothing sketchy about it. The best method to sell it would be to let the authorities running the Item Exchange put it up for auction. Despite the taxes and commission fees, that would be the quickest route with no extra work on his end.

*The problem is, I'd have to explain how I acquired this......*

If an E-rank hunter came in offering an incredible item that shouldn't even exist, would they take it with no questions asked? The Korean Hunter's Auction House was the most established company for dealings between hunters. If there were any potential red flags, they wouldn't let it slide.

*And that's why I need the license.*

A new S-rank license, that is. He'd gotten reevaluated for that very reason, and the result had been a success. If what President Go had said was to be believed, he would receive the new license in two days without any problems.

Jinwoo had initially been a bit concerned that things would become problematic when he declined President Go's proposal, but......

*I'm glad the president doesn't seem the type to hold grudges.*

President Go had continued to beam at him even as they exchanged good-byes. Individuals who had a long history of sensing the atmosphere in the room were experts when it came to reading people, and Jinwoo was such a person. As an E-rank hunter, he'd lived his life constantly trying not to step on any toes for four years, so he was able to assess others via their facial expressions. President Go's didn't seem fake in any way from what Jinwoo could tell. Therefore, he had nothing to worry about and simply had to wait for the reevaluation in two days.

*So...what to do until then?*

Jinwoo leaned back in his chair. Two days. It wasn't enough time to start something but too much to do nothing.

*I'll take a peek.*

Jinwoo moved the cursor to the link for the job board on the official hunters' portal out of curiosity.

*Click.*

At the press of a button, tons of postings flooded the screen, especially from private strike squads looking to hire new members in his area.

......

The reason was obvious. Strike squads in these parts had been temporarily out of work due to Jinho and Jinwoo dominating the C-rank dungeons until recently. Those same strike squads were now rebounding and actively doing raids.

Jinwoo smiled wryly and clicked on to the next page.

*I can't level up in a C-rank dungeon anymore, though.*

The last time he'd been in a C-rank dungeon, it had taken him not one but two whole days' worth of constant raids just to level up once. And he was now fifteen levels higher than then. Had there been a visible experience gauge, these jobs would've barely made a dent.

*C-rank gates are pointless for me......*

Unfortunately, there were no postings for hunters to do any high-rank dungeon raids. It was considered suicidal for a private strike squad to attempt a high-rank dungeon, and guilds wouldn't post calls for replacement members on a site like this. Still...

*Should I try changing the terms of my search?*

Jinwoo filtered the results by high-rank dungeons only.

*Click.*

It wasn't like he expected to find anything, but he figured he'd try just in case. But then...

*......Oh?*

There was, in fact, a single listing.

* * *

"You said you're an E rank?"

"Yes."

"Have you done this kind of job before?"

"No, I haven't."

"So...what class are you?"

"I'm a brawler."

*That's good, at least.*

The foreman wearing a hard hat scanned Jinwoo from head to toe.

*His body looks toned for an E rank. His eyes are steady, too.*

Jinwoo calmly awaited the foreman's response. Eventually, the man laughed boisterously as he handed back Jinwoo's hunter license.

"Ha-ha-ha! There are lots of people like you here, Jinwoo. Welcome to the team. Relax, don't be nervous." The foreman was an energetic fellow even though he was well over forty and sported a mustache that fit him quite well. "Wait here until everyone else arrives. Don't forget your equipment before going in."

"Equipment...?"

"You can choose one from the pile over there."

"......Got it." Jinwoo nodded as he surveyed the heap of pickaxes.

At that moment, a middle-aged man with a towel around his neck rushed up to them. "Yoonsuk! Our team is seriously understaffed, too, so how could you just take the temp?"

"Nah, the collection team is fine as is. You gonna take responsibility if we don't finish our work before the gate closes?"

"Well, no, but—!"

The mustachioed man grinned at Jinwoo as he spun around the man with the towel. "Jinwoo, you wait here. I'll be right back."

"We can talk here! Where're you taking me?"

"Who knows? C'mon—follow me."

The two men continued their bickering as they headed off.

*Guess the other guy is from the collection team...?*

High-rank dungeons were humongous in scale, and since strike squads couldn't do everything by themselves, jobs were delegated to different teams. A strike squad attacked, an excavation team dug out precious stones, and a collection team gathered the remains of magic beasts. The excavation and collection teams entered the dungeon once every magic beast except the boss was slain.

Jinwoo had applied to work for an excavation team.

*......Is this the only equipment available?*

He reluctantly grabbed one. It was weak, but he could feel magic flowing through.

*They imbued it with mana.*

Modern electrical appliances didn't work in dungeons. For that reason, they had to resort to old-fashioned tools enhanced with magic.

......

As he gripped the pickax, he realized why those on the excavation team were often referred to as miners.

Jinwoo turned to take in the gate. There was a huge hole, incomparable in size to C-rank ones, suspended in midair right before his eyes.

*So this is an A-rank gate......*

This thing was why he was here in the first place.

*I want to see a high-rank dungeon with my own eyes.*

Even though all the magic beasts except the boss had been taken care of, he still wanted to see the inside of the dungeon for himself.

*I, too, have to raid these dungeons someday.*

Knowledge was power, and there were limits to what one could learn and experience indirectly through books and the Internet. The White Tiger Guild trainees had overlooked that fact and ended up paying for it dearly. The truth was, if it wasn't for Jinwoo, no one would've come out of that incident alive. To know something was very different from experiencing it.

That was why Jinwoo had applied for the excavation team: to gain firsthand knowledge of an A-rank dungeon while he had the chance. He'd doubted his decision for a second when he saw those shabby pickaxes, but those doubts cleared as soon as he laid eyes on the terrifying gate.

*I'm glad I came here.*

This was a great opportunity, since he had time to kill until the reevaluation.

The mustachioed foreman, Yoonsuk Bae, jogged up to Jinwoo with a smile, possibly because the talk had gone well. "Let's get inside. Everyone's ready to roll."

Jinwoo tightened his grip on the pickax with a grin and nodded.

\* \* \*

*Knock, knock.*

"I have the file you asked for, sir."

"Come in."

Jinchul entered the office of the association president, who welcomed Jinchul with a warm smile, as he'd been expecting him. As President Go opened the file, he was met with a familiar face—Jinwoo. Jinwoo was much younger in the ID photo but didn't look so different that President Go couldn't tell who it was.

"Hmm." The president grew serious as he perused Jinwoo's history as a hunter.

*He's been working as a hunter for four years even though he's among the weakest E-ranks?*

It was practically a death wish. Although the levels of the gates run by the association were lower than the ones managed by guilds or private strike squads, they were still too much for an E-rank hunter to handle. As Gunhee suspected, Jinwoo had spent much of his time as a hunter hospitalized.

"He endured well despite having so many injuries."

"Apparently, he couldn't quit the association due to his mother's medical bills."

"...It's difficult to find a young man like him these days." Gunhee's perception of Jinwoo shifted.

*I couldn't have imagined he was taking care of his sick mother and providing for his younger sister in his father's absence......*

Gunhee had been intrigued by Jinwoo because of his second awakening, but he hadn't expected to find this when delving deeper into his files. He was an even better man than the president had initially thought.

*Jinwoo's too good to let him go to a guild.*

The more he looked, the bigger his disappointment at his failure to recruit Jinwoo to the association.

He smacked his lips as he continued reading to the last page. He closed the file with a satisfied look on his face. "Good work."

"Thank you, sir." Jinchul took back the file and turned to leave but then spoke with some difficulty. "Ummm... Sir..."

"Hmm?" President Go looked up.

It was clear something was troubling Jinchul.

*For a man rumored not to spill a drop of blood if stabbed, he certainly looks human......*

Was what he wanted to say that difficult? He had President Go's full attention. "Is something the matter?"

Jinchul answered after dawdling. "I thought you should know... I received a report just before I came here that Hunter Jinwoo Sung joined a raid team."

"Already? Interesting. Which team?"

"The Hunters' raid team."

"Hmm... Hunters, huh?"

Jinwoo had chosen the Hunters. Moreover, it had taken him only a day to decide. The president's face hardened.

*Was everything he said yesterday just talk he went back on because of the enormous signing bonus?*

If so, that was quite dispiriting after Gunhee had been thrilled to meet a hunter worthy of the title. Although, based on his file and how he'd acted yesterday, Jinwoo didn't seem to be the type to go against his word that easily. There must have been another reason. Perhaps...

"The Hunters are certainly the best choice if he wants the opportunity to do battle with powerful magic beasts." President Go tried to work out Jinwoo's reasoning.

However, Jinchul quickly put an end to that. "I don't think that's it, sir."

"Is there something else you've heard?"

"According to what's been confirmed...Hunter Sung joined an excavation team, not a strike squad."

The president shot up from his chair. "What? An S-rank hunter applied as a miner?"

He sounded incredulous—and Jinchul'd had a similar reaction. No matter how many times he'd double-checked his intel, the facts remained the same.

*That's why I wasn't sure whether I should report this......*

What was Jinwoo thinking?

Jinchul broke out into a cold sweat. "That appears to be the case, sir."

President Go fell back onto his chair and guffawed. "What an unpredictable lad!"

\* \* \*

Jinwoo put on the hard hat and uniform provided and followed behind Yoonsuk the foreman. About twenty other hunters in identical hard hats were gathered near the gate.

Everyone turned to the foreman, who introduced Jinwoo. "This is Jinwoo Sung, who'll be working with us today."

"Hello." Jinwoo gave a quick bow and assessed the team's mood.

"......"

They all seemed pretty indifferent, which was understandable.

*All things considered...*

Jinwoo was a temp worker who they might or might not run into after today, but the other hunters were official employees contracted by the guild. There was no need to be particularly friendly to the newcomer.

"Come on, people... He's still our coworker." Yoonsuk gave an awkward laugh and then pointed at a menacing man standing toward the back of the group. "Sung, stick with Mok over there and ask him if there's anything you don't get. He's a man of few words, but he's been doing this the longest."

"...Yes, sir." Jinwoo headed to the one named Mok without any complaints.

Once they made eye contact, the man introduced himself quietly. "Jinsu Mok."

"I'm Jinwoo Sung."

And so ended the introductions. Jinsu's gaze shifted in the direction of the foreman.

*What nice people.*

Jinwoo followed Jinsu's gaze. In the distance, the foreman was having an intense conversation with someone who appeared to be another employee of the guild. With a bit of focus, Jinwoo was able to eavesdrop.

"......The raid party still isn't over? I was told they were almost done a while ago, but how long has it been?"

"They really don't have much left to do. This is for the safety of you and your team members, so please wait a little longer until they clear all the magic beasts."

"This is the third time I've heard that today."

"Oh, c'mon, sir. You know very well how much of a pain it'll be if everything isn't cleared properly and a hidden beast pops out while you're hard at work, right?"

The male employee, who could've been Yoonsuk's son, shot him an adorably cheeky grin, and Yoonsuk couldn't help but laugh at his antics.

"All right, fine."

"Oh? So are we set here?"

"Yeah, yeah. Now, shoo."

"Yessir. Once the attack team comes out, I'll fly back here to let you know. Oh, and don't forget—we're all going out for a drink after work. Okay?"

"All right already. Go, shoo, away with you."

Thankfully, it seemed the conversation had ended without conflict. The other employee had dealt with Yoonsuk well.

*People always assume that if you work for a large guild, you can go around yelling at everyone, but......*

Ordinary civilians worked in the guild offices while the hunters who worked on location were awakened beings. The workload that required awakened beings dwarfed their actual number, which meant it was impossible to hire or fire them willy-nilly—they weren't easily replaceable factory equipment. Consequently, regular employees had no choice but to walk on eggshells around them. Though jobs at top guilds were highly coveted positions, they had plenty of internal issues people weren't aware of.

At that moment…

……*Hmm?*

Jinwoo, who had been listening in on Yoonsuk's conversation, suddenly picked up on what the other hunters were whispering about.

"Did you hear? Today's newbie is an E rank."

*People are talking about me again?*

At times, Jinwoo resented his excellent hearing.

*But it's not like I can stand here blocking my ears……*

Jinwoo gave a bitter smile while the others cautiously continued gossiping.

"What? An E rank?"

"The foreman hired an E rank?"

"That's what I'm telling you."

Jinwoo could feel their gazes like he'd been smacked on the back of his head.

"Seriously, what was he thinking choosing an E?"

"Is he gonna get things done properly?"

"Right?"

"I wonder if we'll be able to finish the work in time today."

Uneasy voices came from every direction. Even though they spoke in hushed tones out of consideration of Jinwoo's feelings, their efforts were pointless.

Jinwoo swallowed a sudden urge to burst out laughing.

*I see there was a second reason for the chilly reception.*

As per usual, E ranks were given the cold shoulder. It was nothing new to Jinwoo, and he'd grown used to it.

*It's not like I'll be spending much time with them anyway.*

Just then…

There was a commotion in front of the gate.

"The raid party is out."

"I guess they're finally done."

The hunters on the excavation team brightened, as they were tired of waiting.

Yoonsuk, who'd been keeping an eye on the situation, gestured at his team. "Okay, everyone, let's move."

They grabbed their tools and trudged in the direction of the gate. Jinwoo moved with them, situating himself in the middle of the group.

"Good job, all."

"Nice work."

"Well done, everyone!"

Guild employees were welcoming the strike squad members returning from the raid. It seemed like strike squads were also referred to as the raid party.

*This is...the best strike squad in South Korea.*

With keen eyes, Jinwoo scanned the faces of the hunters considered to be of the highest rank. There was a familiar one among them.

*......Jongin Choi.*

The man was an S-rank mage hunter and the guild master of the Hunters Guild.

Jinwoo sensed that things would get complicated if Jongin recognized him, so he pulled his hard hat down as far as it would go. Luckily, those in the excavation team were dressed similarly to Jinwoo, so he was able to easily blend in.

As Jinwoo quietly watched the best strike squad march out of the dungeon, he had one thought.

*......Are they really the elite of the Hunters Guild?*

He couldn't help but be surprised. It was harder than he'd expected to find a hunter with a strong presence. Jongin Choi, who bore the title of the Ultimate Hunter, exuded a powerful magical signature, but aside from him, there was nobody else of note. ·

*Maybe they're weak?*

But that didn't make any sense. Jinwoo firmly shook his head. They were the select few hunters assigned to the elite strike squad of the number one guild in all of Korea.

*The guild master himself led the raid, so there's no way they'd choose anyone less than the best of the best to accompany him.*

The word *weak* was the furthest thing from them. Therefore, there could be only one explanation.

*That's how strong I've gotten.*

A smile played on Jinwoo's lips.

Strength was relative. His efforts over the last several months had paid off. Jinwoo's abilities had increased exponentially to a degree where he perceived a strike squad exiting an A-rank dungeon as weak. He was able to gauge his own strength by comparing it to other people's.

*Ba-dump, ba-dump, ba-dump.*

His heart was pounding in excitement.

At that very moment…without anyone prompting him or a single noise to alert him, Jinwoo was compelled to look toward the gate. A gasp escaped him.

*Whoa……*

A short-haired woman was strolling out of it.

The first things his eyes were drawn to were her large, clear eyes. He couldn't help but also note her fair complexion and the sharp features of her bare face.

Ninety-nine out of one hundred men surveyed would readily agree that she was pretty. However, it wasn't her outward appearance that first grabbed Jinwoo's attention but rather what she held inside.

There was an incredible well of power within her. An extraordinary amount of mana emanated from the expressionless woman.

*She's the same level as Jongin at the very least.*

She might even have been stronger than Jongin. She had an aura that completely overwhelmed others.

Once Jinwoo managed to recover from his surprise and logic took the front seat, he recalled her name.

*She's none other than……*

Haein Cha, the only female S-rank hunter in South Korea. She was one of the highest-ranked hunters who, along with Jongin, was regarded as a pillar of the Hunters Guild.

*There's no one else she could be.*

How many women in the country had such a presence?

Despite her status, however, Haein's face wasn't that well-known. She was extremely reluctant to appear on TV, so Jinwoo had never actually seen her until now.

*The rumors that she's strange-looking don't appear to be true, so I wonder why she hates cameras so much?*

Most other women in their early twenties seemed to love being in front of a camera—their cell phone cameras, that is.

Perhaps he'd been staring a little too intensely, as Haein's gaze swept toward Jinwoo's general direction.

*Stealth…shouldn't be necessary, right?*

As Jinwoo concealed himself, Haein's gaze passed over him, and she cocked her head in confusion.

*What was that? I thought I felt a strong presence just now?*

Had she been mistaken? Her initial assumption had been that President Go had dropped by the site, but the presence had completely disappeared as if she'd been imagining things.

*The president of the association would be too busy to show up unannounced.*

The price for her apparent misunderstanding was severe. Because Haein had enhanced her perception to chase the location of the presence, the foul stench around her was amplified and pierced her senses.

*Ack.*

Haein covered her nose with a handkerchief as she usually did and staggered away from the other hunters.

*Her perception is better than I thought.*

Jinwoo breathed a sigh of relief when he saw her walking away. With that, the raid party had exited the dungeon.

Yoonsuk, who had been waiting for this precise moment, turned toward his team. He clapped his hands together loudly and addressed them all in an upbeat voice. "Okay, it's our turn now, so let's do a good job!"

The collection team entered the gate first, as per procedure, followed by the excavation team.

Jinwoo paused right outside it.

......

As Jinwoo quietly appreciated the majesty of his first look at an A-rank gate, Yoonsuk came up to him.

"What're you doing, Sung? We have to go in, too."

"Right." With that short answer, Jinwoo followed the others and stepped through the portal.

A familiar notification promptly appeared.

**[You have entered the dungeon.]**

# 3
## THE PARAGON OF
## THE EXCAVATION TEAM

# 3

# THE PARAGON OF
# THE EXCAVATION TEAM

*There's wind blowing inside a dungeon?*

Jinwoo lifted his head. He felt an ominous breeze coming from deep within the cave as soon as he set foot inside the gate. Chills ran down his spine, and at the same time, Jinwoo realized what the wind truly was.

*It's not just any old wind.*

It was a wave of magic power. The magic power emanating from the A-rank dungeon boss was materializing as waves that Jinwoo could physically feel. Considering how S-rank dungeons were rare on an international level, it was feasible the source of this magic power would be one of the highest-level beasts Jinwoo would ever encounter.

*An A-rank dungeon boss......*

Jinwoo wanted to see it with his own eyes. And if there was a chance...

Despite the chill in the air that made his hair stand on end, he couldn't hide his grin. One could call it a hunter's instinct, but wouldn't any hunter want to try their hand at taking down a large beast when faced with one?

Suddenly...

*Thmp.*

Someone passed Jinwoo from behind and bumped his shoulder. "Hey, get a move on." Seonggu Lee glared at Jinwoo and grumbled.

The interior of an A-rank dungeon was massive. There was plenty of space to avoid people, but Seonggu had been irked with how the temp was standing there with no apparent intention to move. He'd purposefully bumped into Jinwoo in an attempt to embarrass him, but...

*What the hell is up with this bastard? He's like a concrete pillar or something.*

When he did, he'd ended up bouncing off Jinwoo, which further annoyed him.

*How is a shitty E rank so sturdy?*

The temp was a mere E rank while Seonggu was a C. Although he'd been relegated to the excavation team because his skills were lacking compared to other C ranks, he wasn't about to lose face in front of some E rank. Yet the newbie hadn't even flinched.

Seonggu's eyes narrowed.

*The balls on this asshole.*

As his temper rose, Seonggu gritted his teeth and raised his voice. "Hey, you, shouldn't you apologize for bumping into me?"

*Shf.*

Jinwoo turned to face him. Seonggu stumbled back, startled.

*Eek!*

It felt like lasers were shooting out of Jinwoo's eyes. As Seonggu found himself suddenly having trouble breathing, Jinwoo opened his mouth. "My apologies."

"N-no......," Seonggu stammered in a barely audible voice, "it's no big deal......sir."

Seonggu turned beet red as he realized what he'd said and hastily made his way past Jinwoo with his head down.

"Phew!" Seonggu felt more at ease once he'd put some distance between himself and the newbie.

*What was with those eyes? And why was he smiling like that?*

He'd met Jinwoo's gaze for only a brief moment, but his body had stiffened, and his voice wouldn't come out properly. Only the last shred of his pride had kept him from dropping his own gaze.

......*Is he really an E rank?*

Between the man's immovable body and terrifying eyes, Seonggu wasn't sure what to make of things. Well, whatever. He vigorously shook his head as if trying to empty it and scurried away.

"Oh boy." Jinwoo rubbed the back of his neck as he watched Seonggu take off.

*My guard was up because of the boss, so......*

He'd unintentionally terrified Seonggu. Practice. Practice would make perfect.

As he self-reflected on being hypersensitive, Jinwoo chased after the rest of the excavation team. He caught up to them in no time and tried to stay with the members at the back of the group.

*No one would be able to keep up with me if I walked at my own pace.*

Because of that, he adjusted his speed to that of his colleagues.

As they went deeper into the dungeon, the waves of magic power from the dungeon boss grew stronger.

*My perception's definitely pretty high.*

Even though the boss's lair was in the heart of the dungeon, he could easily feel its presence from near the entryway. It was making his heart race.

*Will I be able to focus on the excavation work in this condition?*

As if in answer to his question, several loud voices rang out. "Heave! Heave!"

The collection team, which had gone inside ahead of the excavation team, was hard at work. They had bound the carcass of an enormous magic beast with rope and were dragging it along.

"One, two!"

"Heave!"

Since brawlers were physically strong, things were moving along smoothly even without the help of tools.

Jinwoo reminded himself of the procedure for tackling high-rank dungeons. First, the strike squad would defeat all the magic beasts except for the boss. Then, the collection team would drag out the carcasses of said magic beasts. Lastly, the excavation team would retrieve all stones found on the cave walls. In order to maximize profits, nothing was left behind. Essence stones and gems found in dungeons were a given, but the remains of high-rank magic beasts were also worth a ton of money.

*Bones, hide, flesh—they say there's a use for every part of a high-rank magic beast.*

That was the difference between a magic beast from a low-rank dungeon and one from a high-rank dungeon.

Once the entirety of the dungeon was plundered, one last job remained.

*Defeat the boss and close the gate.*

These four steps had to be completed in order to claim that a high-rank dungeon was cleared perfectly. At least, that was how guilds looked at it.

However...

*If we're talking about manual labor, wouldn't my soldiers be enough?*

The thought entered Jinwoo's mind as he walked past some sweaty members of the collection team. In truth, his leveled-up shadow soldiers would be far more efficient than a group of C-rank-and-below hunters. If he divided his soldiers into teams for hunting, collection, and excavating...

*I might actually be able to raid a high-rank dungeon on my own.*

Jinwoo smiled to himself, feeling pleased. He'd come here on a reconnaissance mission, and he was glad he'd taken the time to do so.

"And why do you look so happy, Sung?" the foreman asked as he approached his new crewman. He was probably curious as to why an E-rank hunter experiencing a high-rank dungeon for the first time was quietly smiling to himself.

"I was surprised that the magic beasts are way bigger than I'd imagined."

The foreman seemed satisfied with Jinwoo's vague answer, as he called up his own memories in response. "You think? Remembering it now, my jaw hit the floor my first time."

Since they were already on the topic, Jinwoo asked him a few questions. "Even if the other magic beasts have been killed, the boss is still alive, right?"

"That's right, since the gate will close once the boss is eliminated."

This meant they couldn't kill the boss until all the collecting and the excavating work was complete.

"What happens if the boss comes out of its lair?"

"That rarely happens, but… In that case, we'd all be dead."

That much was obvious. The strike squad took a break outside the dungeon before going after the boss, and nobody on the collection or excavation teams was strong enough to face an A-rank dungeon boss. Fortunately, the boss usually remained in its lair until the dungeon break began.

That was why Yoonsuk showed no concern over that possibility.

"Aren't you scared that such a terrible creature is in the same space as you?"

"Not at all." Yoonsuk was resolute. "In the three years I've worked for the Hunters, there's never been an incident. Don't you worry, Sung."

Yoonsuk patted Jinwoo on the shoulder, and for a brief moment, Jinwoo found himself envious.

*They do say ignorance is bliss.*

Jinwoo's body vibrated from the magic power emanating from the boss's lair even when he was standing still. It looked like he was the only one who could sense the creature's power.

"Ah, here we go!" the foreman exclaimed happily upon sighting a stash of gems embedded along the cave wall.

The skilled excavation team members positioned themselves in front of the wall without prompting.

*Thud, thud.*

They dropped their bags and took hold of their pickaxes. Jinwoo also claimed a spot at the patch of gems.

*Can I just swing my pickax?*

He was worried about breaking both the gems and the pickax if he used brute strength.

*What should I do?*

He couldn't bring himself to start and stood in place, hesitant. That was when Jinsu, the expert excavator, caught his eye.

*Fwsh! Krak! Fwsh! Krak!*

There was a rhythm to the way Jinsu dug out the gems. Every time he struck the wall, a bunch more clinked as they fell to the ground.

*Okay, let's see......*

Jinsu was undeniably a veteran at this—his skill was apparent, and he was twice as fast as his colleagues.

Jinwoo's eyes flashed as he activated his perception stat. As time slowed, he carefully studied Jinsu's posture, breathing, and movements. Jinwoo played them over and over in his mind.

*Got it.*

He had the hang of it. He grabbed his pickax. His stance looked like a carbon copy of Jinsu's.

*Fwsh! Krak! Fwsh! Krak!*

Although the posture was identical to Jinsu's, Jinwoo's strength was incomparable. Each time he struck the wall, magic gems fell to the ground in large chunks.

*Fwsh! Krak! Fwsh! Krak!*

A clear ringing echoed from the end of the line. The other members of the excavation team started to realize something odd was happening.

"H-hold up."

"What's wrong?"

"Look over there."

"Whoa!"

"How is he…?"

One by one, they stopped working to stare blankly at Jinwoo. Eventually, even the dedicated Jinsu's hands came to a halt.

*......*

They were all speechless. The newbie E-rank miner was making short work of the gems!

"Come on, people! You're here to work, not to stand around and stare off into space!"

Yoonsuk, who'd been busy taking inventory of the gems, rushed over in surprise when he noticed his workers had ceased.

"Sir, take a look at that."

"At what?" He craned his neck, and his eyes widened at the sight. "Whoa!" He was taken aback when he saw Jinwoo working at about three times the speed of everyone else.

"Sir, didn't you say this was his first time?"

"......I did."

Seonggu, puzzled about Jinwoo's true identity, had to interject. "Is he really an E rank?"

"Of course—I checked his license. Do you think I'd hire someone without verifying his identity first?"

"Then what's with that?"

"......" Yoonsuk, who had continued to silently watch Jinwoo, swallowed and exclaimed eagerly, "There's no doubt about it... Sung was born to be a miner!"

No wonder Jinwoo's impressive pectoral muscles had drawn his attention ever since the interview.

*I've got an eye for these things.*

The foreman grinned from ear to ear.

\* \* \*

*Beep, beep, beep.*

The alarm on Yoonsuk's watch sounded. He checked the time.

*Oh boy, time flies......*

It was already lunchtime.

"All right, everyone, let's go eat."

"Yessir!"

Everyone put down their tools and dusted off their hands. When Jinwoo showed no signs of leaving while the others wandered off in small groups, Yoonsuk sidled up next to him.

"Aren't you going, Sung?"

"I'm okay, sir."

"But how are you gonna work without eating?"

"I'm fine. I had a late breakfast anyway."

"Really? Well, okay, then."

Yoonsuk had wanted to have some serious and deep conversations with Jinwoo regarding things like each other's futures, but it wasn't like he could forcibly drag him out. He headed toward the gate feeling a bit disgruntled.

At that moment, the corners of Jinwoo's mouth began to rise. The farther away his team members went, the more his smile grew.

*I can't waste this golden opportunity.*

He was finally alone, as both the excavation and collection teams had exited the dungeon. He had about an hour to himself. This was his chance to check out the boss hidden deep within the bowels of the dungeon.

Jinwoo put down the pickax and turned his eyes in the direction of the boss's lair. He could feel the magic beast's energy pulsing steadily.

*I'll just sneak a peek at it.*

He wasn't planning on actually doing anything.

*Ba-dump, ba-dump, ba-dump.*

Jinwoo's heart started racing at the mere thought of glimpsing the boss. He willed his heart to slow as he started off. He headed farther inside the cave, following the magic beast's energy.

How far did he go? Eventually, he came upon a cavernous room: the boss's lair. The cave's passageways were already enormously wide, but this was somehow bigger. Jinwoo had to wonder if all high-rank dungeons were this spacious. That was when he came upon the boss, and it instantly clicked why the dungeon had no choice but to be built this way.

*If that ever got out......*

A massive, one-eyed humanoid magic beast stood in silence at the farthest end of the lair. Jinwoo's eyes twinkled like those of a child who had a toy he'd wished for in his grasp.

*A giant-type magic beast.*

He'd heard much about them, but this was the first time he'd seen one in the flesh. Due to their size, it was next to impossible to get a giant's carcass out of the dungeon in time. The average person would never be able to see one unless there was a dungeon break. Simply being in the presence of this boss excited Jinwoo.

*It'd be a tough opponent.*

It was powerful to the point where the hair on the back of Jinwoo's neck stood up. Yet the thought that it might be impossible for him to beat the giant never crossed his mind.

*The me right now......*

He could definitely take it on. At that realization, he swallowed hard.

*Gulp.*

How many experience points would he get if he brought it down? During his weeklong ordeal in the Demon's Castle, he'd leveled up fifteen times. But if he could level up two or three times by killing one boss......

*No, I shouldn't do that.*

Despite his best intentions, Barca's Dagger and Knight Killer materialized in his hands. The logic that said he shouldn't do this was sharply at odds with his instinctual desire to defeat this creature. Even though it would be the wrong thing to do, Jinwoo really wanted to test how strong he'd become. But right then...

A sharp voice came from behind Jinwoo. "What do you think you're doing there?"

Jinwoo's heart dropped immediately.

*When did she...?*

He'd been so focused on the boss that he hadn't noticed her approach.

*I'm busted.*

Jinwoo pursed his lips, feeling crestfallen.

Oh well. He couldn't keep drooling over the boss with a witness there. Since the Hunters had paid for the permit to this raid, the dungeon boss could be considered their property. Besides, if he killed it now, the gate would close, and the guild would suffer a huge loss.

*That would be a mess.*

He was so intent on leveling up that he'd almost laid hands on some-one else's possessions.

The owner of the voice drew closer, and Jinwoo gave a sigh of relief as he came to his senses. "I asked what you were doing."

Jinwoo rearranged his expression into a sheepish grin. "I got lost and somehow ended up all the way here."

"You got lost?" She didn't sound convinced.

Jinwoo finally got a good look at the other person.

*Huh? That's…?*

It was someone he'd spotted right before he'd entered the dungeon—Haein Cha, the female S-rank hunter.

Haein scanned Jinwoo's hands as she approached him.

*I thought I saw him holding weapons of some kind?*

But there was nothing there. Was she imagining things? She glanced up and down at him.

*A hard hat and uniform… Is he on the excavation team?*

It appeared as though he was telling the truth about being lost. Haein didn't quite understand how it had happened, but that wasn't important. The boss's lair was a dangerous place, so she decided that her priority was to send him on his way.

"This is where the boss is." She covered her nose with her handker-chief as usual as she stopped in front of him. "Please get out of here. If you trigger its aggro, everyone in the dungeon could get killed."

"Oh, I'm sorry." Luckily, his acting seemed convincing enough.

Pleased with himself, Jinwoo walked past Haein. As he did…

*Hmm?*

Haein whipped around to look at Jinwoo. But that was impossible… Haein's eyes widened, and before she could stop herself, she called out to Jinwoo.

"Um, excuse me."

"Yes?"

"Could you face this way for a second?"

What could she possibly want? Feeling uneasy, Jinwoo tried to maintain his distance, like a thief with a guilty conscience facing his accuser. But Haein was right in front of him in no time.

"What...seems to be the problem?" Jinwoo asked, nonplussed, but Haein lightly inhaled without a word of explanation. She had already removed the handkerchief covering her face.

*What's going on?*

Jinwoo had no idea.

*Why is she smelling me?*

Jinwoo may have been bewildered, but Haein was completely thunderstruck.

*There's...no stench.*

This was the first time she'd ever encountered a hunter without that foul odor. Haein stared at Jinwoo with startled eyes.

Jinwoo was clearly baffled. "Is there a problem?"

"You... Are you really a hunter?"

Did he need to say it? He retrieved his hunter's license from around his neck and handed it to her. Haein took it and checked Jinwoo's face against the picture on his license.

*E rank... Jinwoo Sung...*

Was it because his rank was too low? There was no odor coming from Jinwoo. Rather, a pleasant scent wafted from him.

Jinwoo gently plucked his license out of Haein's hand. "May I leave now?"

"I......" Even though Haein had stopped Jinwoo, she realized she didn't have anything else to say to him or any reason to hold him up. "......No, it's nothing. Please be careful as you head back. It's easy to get lost in here."

"Right, thank you." Jinwoo nodded and started to head back toward the excavation site.

He was soon out of sight, but Haein couldn't help but stare after him for a long while.

*He smelled nice.*

* * *

The members of the excavation team who had finished their lunch were slowly trickling back from their break. Yoonsuk, who had been picking at his teeth as he walked, was startled to see Jinwoo returning from the depths of the dungeon.

"Whoa, whoa, why're you coming from that direction, Sung?"

"Oh, I......" Jinwoo briefly glanced back toward where the boss was.

*I can't say it's because I wanted to see what an A-rank dungeon boss looked like, right?*

Jinwoo's eyes darted back to the foreman again. "I got lost looking for a restroom."

"Oh boy, you should be careful! Things all look the same inside here, so it's hard to find your way back if you get lost. But it looks like you managed it okay?"

"I met Hunter Haein Cha, so..."

"Ah, Hunter Cha? She's making sure the boss doesn't come out. She's the type to worry excessively, like you." Yoonsuk chortled. Jinwoo's concern about the boss emerging from its lair seemed to have made a strong impression on him.

Jinwoo forced a laugh.

*He can laugh because he has no idea how scary the boss actually is.*

That was the difference between hunters assigned to manual labor and those in the strike squads. Haein was preparing for something other people dismissed because she knew very well how dangerous magic beasts could be.

*Despite her cold exterior, she's got another side to her.*

If the boss escaped, the ones in immediate danger wouldn't have been the strike squad but rather those on the excavation and collection teams. She was giving up her precious break time to make sure everyone was safe.

*......She's pretty amazing.*

That was Jinwoo's honest impression of Haein. Her peculiar habit suddenly came to mind.

*Why does she cover her nose with a handkerchief?*

Come to think of it, during their recent encounter, aside from that last moment, she'd also been diligently covering her nose.

"Sir..."

"Yes?" He could've gotten annoyed with Jinwoo by this point, but Yoonsuk responded kindly to his new employee every time he talked to him.

*He seemed pleased with the work I did earlier.*

Hard work pays off, after all. Because of this, Jinwoo was able to interrogate him as much as he pleased. In fact, Yoonsuk seemed to encourage it.

"Why so silent after calling me over, Sung?"

Jinwoo let out a laugh. "I was just wondering... Do you know why Hunter Cha always carries around a handkerchief?"

"Oh, that? It's because Hunter Cha is unique."

"Unique?" What was that supposed to mean?

Yoonsuk continued with his explanation. "Hunter Cha can pick up a scent that only hunters have, but apparently, it reeks."

"A hunter's scent?"

"She seems to have a heightened sense of smell."

A heightened sense of smell. Jinwoo knew something about that—he had exceptionally good hearing. His hearing hadn't been bad before, but it had gotten even better after he became an awakened being.

*I guess Haein's sense of smell is a similar case.*

Jinwoo somewhat understood her situation.

"Isn't that peculiar?" Yoonsuk kept going on as if he enjoyed how intensely Jinwoo was listening to him. "I've heard she has trouble breathing when she's around other hunters because of that."

"......"

Was that why...?

*She asked me if I was a hunter.*

Perhaps he didn't have the same stench other hunters had? The boss of the Ice Slayers from the red gate had said something similar.

*　*　*

*"We hear a constant voice in our heads that tells us to kill humans. But standing before you, I don't hear that voice."*

Was this the same sort of thing? Unlike other hunters, he had no scent and didn't trigger a voice ordering his elimination.

*It's because I'm a Player......*

He was the one and only person who'd received the system's benefits. But what was a "Player" exactly? For a fleeting moment, Jinwoo pondered the question of his identity, but he then shook his head to clear it.

*It's not like I'll be able to come up with an answer anytime soon.*

He put the matter out of his mind. It wasn't something he could solve by poring over it, and letting it occupy his thoughts would only wear him out.

*Krak! Krak!*

The ringing of pickaxes signaled that his colleagues had resumed their work. Jinwoo also grabbed his pickax.

*An A-rank boss... I wanted to try my hand at taking it down, though.*

What would've happened if Haein hadn't shown up when she did? What could've been...

*　*　*

Thanks to Jinwoo's brilliant performance, the excavation team finished work before dinnertime. That was two hours earlier than the foreman had predicted. The rest of the mining team regarded Jinwoo in a different light now.

"Good job, Jinwoo!"

"You handled it pretty well."

"The way those gems fell, I thought you were using an excavator!"

The other hunters surrounded Jinwoo and showered him with praise. Gone were the cool attitudes on display outside the gate.

Jinwoo wasn't displeased, either. His experience as a miner had been fascinating, and he'd achieved his goal of checking out an A-rank dungeon.

"Let's head out."

"Yessir!"

"Let's go!"

The excavation team moved with precision at Bae's order.

"One, two."

"Heave!"

The collection team was still hard at work. The excavation team left them behind in the dungeon and, after changing out of their uniforms, gathered together. Unlike the full-time employees, Jinwoo was paid immediately in cash.

"This is for you, Sung."

"Thank you."

Yoonsuk handed him an envelope with the day's wages. "We're going out for a team dinner. Would you like to join us?" He sounded casual, but his eyes were serious.

*It looks like he wants to talk to me about something......*

Jinwoo could feel Yoonsuk's desperation, but he politely declined. "I'm sorry, sir, I can't."

"All right...I see." Yoonsuk scratched his chin.

*It's best to discuss such matters over a drink, but......*

Yoonsuk quickly changed tactics. "I've met a lot of people while working this job."

"Sure."

"But I've never met anyone like you. You're a natural-born miner." Yoonsuk seemed to really like Jinwoo.

*Ha-ha...... Oh boy.*

Jinwoo smiled awkwardly, unable to agree or disagree. The foreman took Jinwoo's smile as a good sign and went straight to the point.

"I don't usually ask this, but...would you like to work for me? I'll be sure to make it worth your while."

This young man named Jinwoo Sung had done three to four times the work of an experienced miner on his first day. What kind of foreman would Yoonsuk be if he wasn't able to hold on to this rare talent? He really wanted to hire Jinwoo, even if it meant persuading management to give Jinwoo extra benefits on top of a salary.

But Jinwoo was firm. "I really appreciate it, but…I'm preparing to do some other work."

Hearing Jinwoo's rejection, Yoonsuk slumped, looking like a man who'd lost everything. "O-oh……"

Jinwoo tried not to laugh.

*He's a funny man.*

Yoonsuk wore his heart on his sleeve. He was likely thinking he'd found a rare gem among the E ranks.

Yoonsuk had an internal debate before cautiously asking, "How about tomorrow, then? Can you come back tomorrow?"

"Tomorrow? Hmm……"

Actually, he was free, since the reevaluation wasn't until the following day. On the other hand, there was no need for him to work as a miner again. He'd learned all he needed to know about raid protocol, and he'd gotten to check out the A-rank boss.

*Oh, wait!*

A thought popped into Jinwoo's mind just as he was about to decline the offer. "Is there another raid tomorrow?"

"Of course. And it's another A-rank gate."

"But how? This raid was only completed today."

It was common for strike squads to take a week off between missions. This raid had begun yesterday afternoon, which meant the elite members of the Hunters Guild would have been raiding for two days in a row: yesterday and today. Once the collection team was done and they finished off the boss, it would already be the dawn of the next morning. Jinwoo didn't understand how they could handle another mission tomorrow.

Foreman Bae was excited to see Jinwoo showing interest. "Raid party B will be doing the work in place of the A team tomorrow."

Raid party B? Were they trying to clear an A-rank dungeon with a second-tier squad?

"This is the power of the Hunters Guild. We're probably the only guild in Korea with the power to attack two A-rank gates at the same time with two separate teams," Yoonsuk said proudly.

"Are the Hunters' raids usually like this?"

"No, no. There's generally no need to separate the teams, but the schedules seemed to have gotten mixed up this time."

With two A-rank gates appearing simultaneously in the Hunters' territory, it sounded like President Choi had done some serious hustling to get the permits for both A-rank gates.

*Oh, is that why President Choi was at the association yesterday......?*

A busy person like Jongin would only be at the association for a good reason.

Jinwoo nodded. "So tomorrow's raid will be the first one done exclusively by the second raiding party?"

"That's right. But it's hard to call the Hunters' second party second-rate. They're better than the best squads of most other large guilds."

"Still, it'll be more dangerous tomorrow, won't it?"

Yoonsuk didn't know how to respond. That much was obvious. Two S ranks had attended today's raid, but only A ranks and lower would be at the raid tomorrow. Although Yoonsuk had heard that tomorrow's gate would be smaller than today's, the absence of the two S ranks was a big deal. After all, Jinwoo had been worried enough about the boss even with the S-rank strike squad close by.

*Still, I can't lie to him.*

The foreman had been planning to use the next day to persuade Jinwoo, but he'd have to abandon his idea with a heavy heart. "Of course, it will be much more dangerous. If something goes wrong, the entire raid might fail."

With that, Jinwoo's attitude changed. He didn't have to think too long about it. "Okay, then."

"If that's what you feel, I guess there is nothing I can do."

"Where should I report tomorrow?"

"What?" The unexpected reply made Yoonsuk's eyes go wide.

*I didn't say the wrong thing, did I?*

He was sure he'd told Jinwoo tomorrow would be more dangerous than today. The foreman had been about to give up on Jinwoo because of the doubtful expression on his face, but then this had happened. It looked like he wouldn't have to find another temp thanks to Jinwoo.

*That's not all.*

Jinwoo had completed the work of four or five people on his first day. Having personally witnessed the speed with which Jinwoo accomplished his work, a speed that had astonished the ace of the excavation team, Jinsu Mok...Yoonsuk felt like he'd secured a whole army upon hearing Jinwoo say he would return.

"Sung, you made the right decision!" His mustache wiggled as his face lit up.

To ensure Jinwoo didn't change his mind overnight, he threw in a bonus incentive. "I'll talk to my superiors and make a special request to double your pay for tomorrow."

"Is that okay?"

"Of course. I can definitely make it happen for you!" The foreman thumped his chest. "Don't worry about a thing and just show up tomorrow."

It wasn't any trouble at all. How could Yoonsuk feel bad about paying Jinwoo double the daily rate when he did the work of four or five miners? If he were the president, he would've paid Jinwoo triple the rate or more to secure their future relationship.

*To think there would be a day when I'd wish I was the president of the Hunters.*

Yoonsuk swallowed his laugh.

Jinwoo then asked, "Oh right, I have plans tomorrow night. What time do you think we'll be done by?"

That morning, he'd received a phone call from Jinho.

\*   \*   \*

**"Boss, is it okay if I come over sometime?"**

He'd seemed depressed.

*Even though he sounded completely fine yesterday......*

Jinwoo had been caught off guard by this, but he'd had to push their meeting until tomorrow because of the mining gig.

The foreman laughed heartily. "I've heard that tomorrow's dungeon is smaller than today's, so we'll likely be done by six."

Today's workday had ended at five. If anything, they'd probably finish earlier than today. Jinwoo nodded. That worked perfectly for him.

"I'll see you tomorrow, sir."

"All right, take care." Yoonsuk wore a pleased smile as he watched Jinwoo walk away.

*If I were married, I'd have a son about his age.*

Even from behind, Jinwoo looked sturdy and reliable. How great would it be if all new hires were like him? Yoonsuk couldn't stop smiling.

And he wasn't the only one. As he headed toward the bus stop, Jinwoo wore a slight grin as well.

*It's not like I'm hoping for the strike squad to fail tomorrow, but......*

If a problem occurred, he could be a big help to either the strike squad or the excavation team. That's why he'd changed his mind. Ironically, the success rate of A-rank gates was higher than lower-ranked ones, due to the fact that the association didn't hand out permits to just any old guild. And the guilds who got the opportunity always gave it everything they had.

*The Hunters Guild isn't going all out on tomorrow's raid.*

They'd divided their strike squad members into two separate teams to attack two different A-rank gates. The confidence of the number one guild in the business was on full display. But it meant things were that much more dangerous as well.

*I have nothing to lose no matter how it plays out.*

A successful raid would be the best result for everyone involved. On the other hand, if there was a problem, he'd step in to help the Hunters and take the kill for himself.

*Excellent.*

His smile was still present as he got on the bus.

\* \* \*

Later that night, Haein found herself tossing and turning in bed.

*Why is he the only one who's different?*

She was having a hard time falling asleep while her thoughts were preoccupied with the man she'd met in the boss's lair. Ever since she awakened two years ago, there had been no other exception to her condition. The unpleasant smell of hunters—or, to be more precise, awakened beings—constantly assaulted her nose.

Initially, she'd assumed it was a disease and had consulted many different doctors, but none of them helped. And then, during a consultation, one had carefully provided the following suggestion.

*"Could it be that you're detecting people's mana through your sense of smell, Hunter Cha?"*

It was a reasonable theory. The higher the rank, the worse the stench, and the lower the rank, the less it affected her. Of course, there was no smell from ordinary civilians. But...

*...He's the first one who actually smelled nice.*

Her heart suddenly skipped a beat as she thought back to today's events. Haein had been curious about who he was, so she'd looked him up on the association's website as soon as the raid finished.

E rank. Jinwoo Sung. The site had the same information she'd seen on his license.

*There's no contact number......*

What would she do with his number anyway?

Once she realized she wouldn't get any more useful information from the association's website, she called Myungki Jo, the director of the Hunters recruitment team, before she could think twice about it.

**"Is something wrong? Why are you calling me at this hour?"**

It was one o'clock in the morning. If Haein hadn't been the only female S-rank hunter in Korea and the vice president of the Hunters Guild, Myungki wouldn't have bothered picking up.

Hearing his voice thick with sleep, Haein momentarily regretted making the call. After a brief second of hesitation, she blurted out, "Can you please find out more about Hunter Jinwoo Sung?"

**"Pardon? You mean the E-rank hunter who used to be in the association?"**

Haein wasn't expecting that response. Myungki was the director of the recruitment team for the best guild in Korea. How did a person like him know an E-rank hunter by name?

"Is he an acquaintance of yours?"

**"Well, the thing is...President Choi made a similar request yesterday. He asked me for more information about Jinwoo."**

"President Choi did?"

**"Yes."**

"Do you know why?"

**"No, I wasn't told......"**

"...So what happened?"

A sigh came over the receiver.

**"I tried my best to find information on him, but the association has it all sealed up. I've never seen them classify information on a hunter who's not high rank, so I'm not sure what's going on."**

"Oh......"

**"But why do you want to know more about him? Is there something I can help you with?"**

"No, it's fine. Sorry for calling so late."

*Click.*

That conversation had been three hours ago. She'd mustered up the courage to make the call out of curiosity and had ended up with more questions than answers. He was an E-rank hunter whose identity was of interest to the president of the Hunters Guild but whose information was being closely guarded by the association.

*There's something going on here.*

No, she hoped there was something here. She wished it desperately. He just might be the key to helping her solve the mystery of the unique ability that had been plaguing her for the past two years, ever since she'd become an awakened being at the age of twenty-one.

*Will I be able to see him again?*

What if she never did? Uneasiness came creeping in. Fortunately, she remembered Jinwoo's hard hat. She recalled the Hunters Guild's mark on his hat and uniform.

*Right, he's on the excavation team.*

Unlike raiding party A, which she'd been on, the excavation team had more work to do today. If he was still on the team, she might be able to see him again.

*Let's drop by.*

As the vice president of the guild, it wouldn't be strange for Haein to visit a raid site.

*I'll stop in as per usual and take a quick look to see if he's there.*

How strange… She automatically felt more relaxed knowing that she might be able to meet him again.

*I need to get some sleep.*

Haein forced her eyes shut for the sake of carrying out the plan.

\* \* \*

The next morning, Jinwoo left his house at the crack of dawn. Yesterday, he'd joined the team in the middle of the raid, so he hadn't bothered to rush, but today was different.

*Was I worried for nothing?*

Jinwoo had been concerned he might've been too early, but many hunters were already milling around in front of the gate when he arrived.

"Oh? Sung! Sung!" Foreman Bae was the first to greet Jinwoo.

"Sung is here."

"Hey, Sung!"

Unlike yesterday, the other hunters greeted Jinwoo with warm gazes and waves. The excavation team needed every hand they could get, so a skilled colleague was always welcome. The other miners looked happy to see Jinwoo again.

*This feels...strange.*

Since becoming an E rank, Jinwoo had grown accustomed to getting a cold reception, so being welcomed for the first time was bewildering to him. Still, their genuine reactions felt good.

"......" Jinwoo silently nodded in greeting.

"One, two, three." The foreman wrote the numbers down as he counted out the team members. "Eighteen, nineteen. Nearly everyone is here."

That was good enough. It was acceptable to have one or two people missing on a day like today.

*Especially when you have two aces up your sleeve.*

He grinned as he locked eyes with Jinsu and Jinwoo. Jinsu averted his gaze, and Jinwoo just cocked his head. At that moment...

"Um, sir."

"Oh man, you startled me."

The sudden voice coming from beside him caused Yoonsuk to flinch. The ability to approach someone undetected was a testament to one's skills. And no wonder—the voice belonged to none other than Kihoon Son, the leader of today's strike squad. Yoonsuk looked at him with consternation.

"Sheesh. You scared the daylights out of me, Hunter Son."

"Sorry about that. Approaching silently has become a habit after getting used to it in dungeons." Kihoon gave an embarrassed laugh.

The foreman of the collection team unexpectedly popped out from behind Kihoon. "Stop grousing, old man..."

"Huh? You too? What business does the collection team foreman have with me?"

"What do you mean, why am I here? I'm here because I've got something to take care of."

Yoonsuk looked at Kihoon, puzzled.

Kihoon scanned the excavation team members. "Our luggage carrier is a no-show, so I'll have to borrow someone from the excavation team to help us out."

"What?" The foreman was incredulous. "If you need someone strong to carry things, you've got the collection team, so why us......?"

As if he'd been waiting for that response, the foreman of the collection team flew into a rage. "My men worked three straight hours of overtime without dinner to finish the job yesterday. And now you expect one of them to be the luggage carrier?"

The only reason the collection team had been forced to do so was because the excavation team had wrapped up their work so quickly.

*Well, we were scheduled until seven last night, too, but we finished around five thanks to Jinwoo......*

Seeing the fire in the other foreman's eyes and the veins popping out of his neck, Yoonsuk was at a loss for words.

His explanation finished, Kihoon turned to the excavation team. "Is there anyone willing to accompany the strike squad? You'll receive hazard pay as soon as the raid is over."

"......"

Kihoon looked around desperately, but no one stepped forward. Everyone either looked down at the ground or up at the sky to avoid making eye contact with him.

It was obvious why.

*No need to risk my life for a little money.*

*I wouldn't do it even if my own life was at stake......*

The highest rank among the excavation team hunters was C rank.

Most of them were D rank, and quite a few of them were Es. Yet, Kihoon wanted to take one of them into an A-rank dungeon, which was bound to be extremely dangerous.

They'd be hard-pressed to volunteer for a B-rank dungeon, but an A-rank one? If a magic beast merely touched them, they'd be dead. Heck, it meant instant death if they so much as stepped foot in the wrong place. It wasn't the kind of dungeon a low-rank hunter could handle. Even though a luggage carrier's job was simply to haul the strike squad's gear, compared to excavation, it was too much of a risk.

"No…one…?" Kihoon's face slowly crumpled. He wasn't sure how long it was going to take to find a replacement luggage carrier. He might lose half a day, maybe even the whole day if he was unlucky.

*This isn't good.*

He then made eye contact with one hunter.

*Oh?*

Unlike the others, he was looking straight at Kihoon.

That hunter was Jinwoo.

*Hmm……*

As Kihoon took in Jinwoo, Jinwoo also carefully sized up Kihoon.

*He seems pretty shrewd for a tank.*

Common sense dictated that tanks be the squad leaders. Kihoon had a slenderer build compared to other tanks. He was also quite tall, so he looked more like a basketball player than a hunter at first glance.

*……*

Jinwoo's eyes eventually turned from Kihoon.

"Whew." Kihoon exhaled the breath he'd been holding in. *What was that?* Kihoon had tensed up to the point where he'd forgotten to breathe. He wasn't sure why.

*Maybe I'm just nervous because this is my first time as a raid leader?*

He usually attended raids as the supporting tank, so today was special for him. He couldn't screw this up. Kihoon bent over and took some deep breaths, then straightened.

There was a bit of a commotion within the excavation team. He thought people were making a fuss about his condition but soon realized it wasn't about him. As he looked up, Kihoon's eyes took in the arm raised toward the sky.

It was the volunteer luggage carrier he'd been waiting for. Kihoon's expression brightened. Everyone's eyes locked on Jinwoo as he took a step forward.

"I'll do it."

# 4
## THE S-RANK LUGGAGE CARRIER

# 4

## THE S-RANK
## LUGGAGE CARRIER

An E-rank hunter volunteering to go inside an A-rank dungeon?! The group erupted in pandemonium.

"You want to go when it's absolutely swarming with high-level beasts in there?"

"What the heck are you thinking, Sung?"

"You're still young with so much to live for! Don't go risking your life just for a little bit of extra cash!"

The excavation team swarmed around Jinwoo.

Yoonsuk tried to smooth things over with Kihoon. "My goodness! That young man only started working yesterday, so he raised his hand out of pure ignorance."

"What's his rank?"

"He's a…" Yoonsuk glanced briefly at Jinwoo and lowered his voice. "He's an E rank, which is way too low, so why don't you pick someone else? It's too dangerous for him."

Kihoon deliberated seriously.

*That man is an E rank……?*

Kihoon had made eye contact with him earlier. He definitely didn't sense any kind of incredible magic power from him, but he had a certain… He couldn't explain, but…he could feel a sharp and focused energy coming from Jinwoo.

*I don't think he's an E rank.*

Kihoon didn't think Jinwoo was a hunter of the lowest rank. Of course, there was no reason for Yoonsuk to lie to him, but Kihoon was certain of that.

*Besides, do ranks even matter for luggage carriers?*

Their only responsibility was to haul the gear. If the luggage carrier at the rear of the group was in serious danger, then that meant the strike squad had already failed. If an A-rank hunter couldn't survive the raid, then what did it matter if the luggage carrier was a C rank or an E rank? Death would be inevitable.

Once Kihoon reached that point in his thought process, he decided he didn't want to waste any more time debating. There had been enough delays, and they hadn't even started the raid.

Kihoon gazed at Jinwoo. "No, I'll take him."

* * *

"Is it too heavy?" Kihoon asked.

Jinwoo shook his head. "No, I'm good."

The large pack on Jinwoo's back was filled with extra clothes, weapons, protective gear, and more for the strike squad. It was quite big, but it wasn't particularly heavy thanks to Jinwoo's high strength stat.

*It doesn't look like it's too much for him.*

After examining Jinwoo's condition, Kihoon turned toward the gate. Jinwoo also swiveled his head to take it in. A huge gate as big as yesterday's floated in midair before his very eyes.

*No, is this one a little bigger?*

Yet they said the amount of magic emanating from today's gate was less than the one from yesterday. Since the difficulty level of the raid was decided by the level of mana and not by the size of a gate, the second-unit hunters had been put in charge of this raid.

*Yeah... The mana coming from this gate is considerably weaker than yesterday's.*

Jinwoo could confirm that as he stood at the threshold. The association's evaluation appeared to be correct.

*But then why...?* A weird, ominous sensation passed him by, similar to the one he'd had before entering the red gate.

*......I'm sure it's nothing.*

Kihoon gave the order. "Let's move out."

The strike squad that had been waiting outside the gate started to head in. One by one, the hunters entered the dungeon.

......

Jinwoo, who'd been warily eyeing the gate, followed them.

**[You have entered the dungeon.]**

The interior of the dungeon seemed normal. Having felt anxious about his strange premonition earlier, Jinwoo let out a relieved sigh after noticing that the passageways were much smaller than the dungeon from yesterday.

*Whew.*

They fortunately hadn't been teleported to a different world, either, though this squad was fully capable of clearing a red gate. There were eleven A ranks and six B ranks. In a guild other than the Hunters, the members of this squad would never have been relegated to the second unit.

Jinwoo chuckled.

*I'm not even a member of the strike squad, so let's not get too invested in the situation.*

Both today and yesterday were technically vacation days for Jinwoo. He'd simply have more things to stare at today. There was no need to get all sensitive about having joined a "second-tier" group. And with that, he allowed himself to take a chill pill.

"No need to be too nervous." A female healer walking at Jinwoo's side, who looked to be in her late twenties, struck up a conversation. She was probably trying to lighten his mood after seeing his tense expression.

"Kihoon—our leader—and all the other hunters here are outstanding at their jobs. Except me anyway." The healer offered a friendly smile.

Jinwoo hadn't been afraid, but whatever nervousness he was holding on to was expelled like air from a deflating balloon at her mellow expression.

Jinwoo fought back a sudden urge to laugh and smiled back. "Oh, okay."

The healer looked pleased with the result.

The front-liners, having confirmed that the entrance was clear of magic beasts, gave the signal to advance. "Let's move."

Jinwoo and the healer kept up with the strike squad. They moved slowly in order to keep an eye out for potential threats.

"If it's too heavy, I could help you." The healer kept glancing at Jinwoo's cargo. He wordlessly handed over the carton of water he was holding in his left hand.

"Eek!"

He quickly took back the carton as she struggled to keep a hold of it. The whole squad froze and stared at her.

"I'm sorry! I'm sorry!" She bowed apologetically to everyone.

From that point on, she never offered to help Jinwoo again and kept glaring at him. Jinwoo held in his snickers and kept walking nonchalantly.

It had been a while since he'd had a laugh inside a dungeon. In these situations, if someone dropped their guard, they could find themselves in danger in the blink of an eye. Especially the places Jinwoo found himself in these days... It gave him chills to this moment whenever he thought about the level of difficulty of the higher floors inside the Demon's Castle.

However, today was different. He was a third-party member on this raid, which wasn't a bad position to be in every so often.

That was when…

Jinwoo halted. It took another beat before the other hunters in the strike squad picked up the same disturbance.

"They're coming!"

Every hunter in the squad instantly shifted into battle mode even before Kihoon gave any orders. It all happened in the blink of an eye.

Jinwoo was highly impressed.

*This is how high-rank hunters roll……*

They were on a totally different level compared to the motley crews he'd always been a part of before. Even the clumsy healer was ready with a clear, transparent glow around her hands.

*I'm guessing I won't have anything to do here.*

Jinwoo was both disappointed and relieved.

At that moment, the magic beasts came into view. Were they animals? Maybe dogs?

Kihoon narrowed his eyes.

*Tmp-tmp-tmp-tmp-tmp.*

A pack of magic beasts resembling hyenas was racing toward them. Their sizes were that of midsize cars.

Kihoon blinked in confusion.

*Dungeon jackals?*

His suspicions were confirmed as they drew closer. The magic beasts were indeed dungeon jackals. Kihoon lowered his shield and relaxed his defensive posture, not bothering with a Provocation skill. When one of the jackals leaped for his neck, he easily struck it down with his shield.

"Hnnn!"

"What?"

"Dungeon jackals?"

The other squad members also loosened their tense shoulders with mystified looks. Soon, the dying cries of the whimpering jackals echoed throughout the cave.

"Hnn!"

"Hnnnn!"

"Hnn!"

They eliminated the creatures swiftly. More than ten jackals were turned into jackal carcasses on the ground in no time. The hunters dusted themselves off, clearly baffled.

"What was that?"

"It was over even before I could cast a single spell."

"Why did jackals spawn in an A-rank dungeon?"

"Right?"

"Did those association idiots mess it up again?"

Their voices grew louder. Speaking in low tones was an absolute in dungeons, but even the basics flew out the door given the surprising appearance of the dungeon jackals.

"Hmm…" Kihoon scratched the back of his head as he stared at the corpses.

*Why did C-rank magic beasts appear here?*

Kihoon looked around with a mien of disbelief. Everyone else had similar expressions. All except one.

Jinwoo was gravely examining the dead jackals.

*These aren't ordinary monsters.*

Jinwoo squinted. The fur around the jackals' necks had been flattened—evidence that they'd been tied up somewhere.

*That means something in here was raising them……*

They had to be intelligent magic beasts. Jinwoo recalled the Ice Slayers from the red-gate incident. It was a well-established fact that magic beasts with intelligence were tricky to deal with no matter what species they were.

*My premonition…might be correct.*

This wasn't a good sign.

"What're you staring at so intently?" The healer also squinted at the jackals.

"Shh!" Jinwoo lifted his index finger.

*Thmp, thmp.*

*Thmp, thmp.*

He could hear the sound of marching farther inside.

*The real trouble is coming.*

Jinwoo straightened up. The other hunters finally caught on to the fact that something was very wrong.

"Oh, fuck……"

"G-get ready!" Kihoon forced out the command.

Finally, the silhouettes of the enemies slowly came into view on the other side of the dark cave. The hunters' eyes grew huge.

"High orcs?"

"What are high orcs doing here?"

High orc warriors that appeared to be well trained stood in a row. There were twenty-two in all. That many high orcs would've been tough opponents already, but high orc warriors were worse.

"Something…something's wrong," someone muttered quietly.

For a group of low-rank beasts to ambush them right before a confrontation with a group of magic beasts considered extremely powerful even among other high-rank enemies was highly unusual.

*Shp! Shp!*

The high orcs pointed their spears at the hunters.

*These hunters and high orcs are evenly matched.*

Jinwoo positioned himself in a corner. He wanted to observe the situation and look for an opportune time to intercede.

The healer clearly thought differently. "Please go hide yourself so you won't get hurt!"

Her words rubbed Jinwoo the wrong way. He closed his eyes and took a deep breath to try to settle his ire.

The battle began shortly afterward.

"Graaahhh!" Kihoon activated his Aggro skill to lure the high orcs to him, but the provocation didn't have much effect.

It wasn't long before the beasts and brawler-class hunters were fully engaged in battle.

*Shhhhk!*

*Shiiing!*

*Krak!*

Blood splattered everywhere, and screams rang out.

"Gaaah!"

Finally, the mage hunters rained their spells down on the orcs.

*Boom! Kaboom!*

Those struck by the arrows of exploding light lost their heads. But nothing came after the initial volley. Spells worked well against the orcs, but the problem was that casting took far too long.

"Aaargh!"

The orcs were proving to be superior in hand-to-hand combat.

"Heal! Heal!"

"H-hurry!"

The increasing injuries kept the healers occupied.

"H-Healer!"

The female healer from before was also busy running around and treating fallen hunters. "I'm coming! On my way!"

She dropped to her knees next to a hunter writhing in pain after losing an arm and started chanting.

*Hwoooom...*

Accompanied by a blinding light, the limb slowly started growing back. The light was that of a regeneration spell, which only A-rank healers had the ability to cast.

A long shadow fell on her as she was focusing on the wound. She looked up. A high orc she'd thought to be dead was brandishing an ax, seemingly heavily winded.

"Oh......" The blood drained from her face at the sight. Unfortunately, there were no allies nearby.

As the orc raised its ax, she shielded her patient with her body instead of running away. "No!"

She waited for the pain, but nothing happened. Every second felt like a minute. She peeked up at the orc.

She couldn't believe what she was seeing.

"A-argh..." The orc was floating, trembling in midair.

"How......?"

What was going on? She couldn't help but stare at the sight.

At that moment...

*Kri-krsh.*

The high orc's head split off from its body along with part of its spine, like someone had ripped it off by force.

*Whud!*

*......?*

The healer gaped at the orc's fallen remains.

"Huh......?"

The magic beast's head remained afloat.

*......Damn, got some blood on me.*

Jinwoo frowned, then chucked the orc head he'd been grasping.

*Krak!*

The severed head struck a second orc, sending it tumbling to the ground. That orc's neck was bent at a strange angle, and the chances of it getting back up seemed slim.

*Two down.*

Jinwoo darted in a different direction. He'd activated Stealth mode. Neither the high orcs nor the hunters could detect Jinwoo's whereabouts. Because he was trying to avoid being accused of interfering with another's raid, Jinwoo had been eyeing the perfect opportunity to jump in. But then he remembered his Stealth skill. With it, he could run around as he pleased with no repercussions.

Jinwoo's lips curled up into a grin.

*Shall I get started, then?*

That was when...

"Gaaaah!"

Jinwoo spotted the leader of the strike squad, Kihoon, locked in a desperate struggle against three high orcs.

# 5
## ATTACK OF THE HIGH ORCS

# 5

# ATTACK OF THE HIGH ORCS

Jinwoo sped toward Kihoon. He wasn't that far from the tank, but he wasn't particularly close, either. It took only a bit of force to launch himself off the ground and land right in front of the high orcs' broad backs.

*Tmp.*

He was struck by a thought as soon as he stuck the landing.

*I could take care of these orcs if I wanted to.*

But that would defeat the purpose of hiding himself with the Stealth skill. Kihoon and the rest were the elite of the Hunters Guild, the number one guild in Korea. With the exception of that silly healer, the rest of the hunters would immediately suspect Stealth was involved if they saw high orcs being torn in two by an invisible force.

*Being discovered wouldn't be an issue, but......*

Jinwoo didn't want to cause any trouble the day before his reevaluation results were to come out. He'd considered waiting until the raid had failed completely before stepping in, but then the damage would've been too great on the healer's side. Just look at the female healer—she'd narrowly avoided death.

Jinwoo's eyes were sparkling.

*I'll do what I can without being noticed.*

That was the course of action he decided on. His deliberation had lasted but a couple of seconds. He'd reflexively called Barca's Dagger and Knight Killer into his hands before he could fully form the thought.

*When did I summon these?*

He couldn't stop grinning. His pounding heart found its calm at the familiar grips in his hands. Thank goodness no one could see his face while Stealth was triggered. He didn't want people to think he was crazy, laughing while humans and high orcs were locked in a murderous melee. Especially the leader of the strike squad—Jinwoo didn't think Kihoon would take it well if he spotted Jinwoo grinning while he was busting his ass trying to fend off three orcs at once.

*Let's take care of these guys first.*

Jinwoo got to work. He crouched down and severed the Achilles tendon of one of the orcs.

"Graaaahhh!" The high orc warrior roared at the intense pain.

Jinwoo was just getting started. He fluidly stabbed the side of the second orc with Barca's Dagger and slashed the third in the back of the knee.

"Guuuh!"

"Aaaagh!"

The adrenaline from the battle wasn't enough to dull their pain, and the high orcs' muscles seized up from the unexpected attacks to their vulnerable areas.

That was enough. Like a tidal wave crashing over a dam, Kihoon slammed into the orcs with his own counterattack.

*Shhhk!*

"Grrraaah… Aaagh."

"Huff, huff." Kihoon raised his head. The sword in his hand had pierced the orc's heart.

"Guuuh…" The high orc's lips quivered, and its glaring gaze rolled up to reveal the whites of its eyes as its body slumped to the ground.

*Whud!*

Kihoon pumped his fist.

*Yes! I've got this!*

As Kihoon patted himself on the back and took down the other two orcs surrounding him, Jinwoo continued to run amok.

"Graaahhh!"

"Gaaahhh!"

Jinwoo moved about freely even as he perceived time to have slowed down for everyone else, going completely unnoticed as he tipped the scales.

*Shhhk!*

Wherever Jinwoo passed by, he left wounds both great and small on the orcs in his wake.

"Graaah!"

"Guh?"

As soon as the high orcs froze in surprise at an injury that appeared out of the blue, their fates were sealed. The elite hunters seized the opportunity to attack.

*It's…somehow gotten easier.*

*What the heck?*

*Are we really going to defeat this many high orcs without sustaining any damage?*

The strike squad was both confused and thrilled. They'd been prepared to experience one or two casualties, but everyone was fighting much better than expected.

*Splat!*

A hunter wielding a mace shattered the head of a high orc. That was when Jinwoo received some welcome news.

**[You have leveled up!]**

*Whoa.*

It had been worth all that effort. His level had increased. It looked like he still received experience points even if he didn't directly kill or deliver fatal damage to the enemies.

*I only finished off two of them myself.*

But he'd assisted with the kills of thirteen orcs. He hadn't expected his experience gauge to rise at all, so to level up was exciting. Jinwoo's enthusiasm made him go even faster.

*Shiiing!*

*Shhhk!*

"Graaaahhh!"

The battle was coming to an end with Jinwoo's help.

*Phew......*

Jinwoo stopped some distance away, stored his daggers in his inventory, and surveyed his surroundings.

*That should do it......*

Everything was wrapping up, and he'd earned himself an extra level.

Jinwoo glanced down. Close to twenty high orc cadavers littered the area.

*I could've gone up at least another level if I'd killed all of them, but alas...*

Unfortunately, the Hunters had paid big bucks for the permit, so this was their hunting ground. This was about all he could take.

*That's fine.*

Satisfied, Jinwoo lodged himself in a corner fitting for a luggage carrier in hiding.

"Graaah!"

The last remaining high orc screeched as it realized the tables had turned and that it was surrounded by hunters. The cries of the beast echoed loudly in the cave.

Jinwoo deactivated Stealth while he watched the high orc drop to the ground.

*Vwoom.*

The hunters were breathing heavily. No matter where they looked, not one orc remained.

"D-did we win?"

"Is it over?"

"Wait." Before they could celebrate their victory, Kihoon checked to see if there were any injured. "Injuries! Did anyone get hurt?"

Wounded hunters were actually rare among strike squads with high-rank healers. As long as they were still breathing, they could be healed. So Kihoon wasn't asking if anyone was hurt—he was asking if there were any casualties.

The female healer shook her head as his eyes met hers. There had been injuries but no fatalities, and the treatment for wounded hunters had just finished.

"Then......"

The strike squad cheered.

"We won!"

"We did it!"

"Yeaaah!"

Hunters happily embraced one another. Jinwoo watched the celebration with his arms crossed against his chest and a pleased look on his face.

*Were the high orcs that powerful, though?*

From his perspective, he didn't think so... Having had no prior experience with high-rank dungeons, Jinwoo couldn't really relate to their elation. Jinwoo also wasn't aware of the fact that hunters who raided A- or B-rank dungeons also took the amount of mana present in the dungeon into consideration when choosing one.

High orcs were considered to be extremely powerful magic beasts even for A-rank dungeons. That they'd defeated not just regular high orcs but close to twenty high orc warriors was just short of a miracle. Jinwoo, the true miracle worker behind this feat, had no idea how astonishing this was as he silently congratulated the squad's victory.

*Hmm?*

Among the revelers, the female healer was approaching Kihoon with a concerned look on her face. Her eyes made it clear she had something to tell him.

Jinwoo strained his ears.

"Um, Kihoon?"

"Yeah?"

"During the battle with the high orcs just now......" She slowly and carefully explained what she had witnessed. Her story was that a high orc floating in midair had torn off its own head and then attacked and killed another orc.

Her expression was totally serious.

"......" Kihoon was speechless.

"It's true, I swear!"

Jinwoo tried not to laugh at how red the healer's face became as she insisted she was telling the truth.

The victory celebration didn't last long. One by one, hunters gathered around Kihoon.

"Captain, are we going to continue?"

"Isn't it too dangerous? For high orcs to spawn this close to the entrance..."

"Maybe we should retreat for now?"

Kihoon pursed his lips as he surveyed the other side of the cave.

*It's not an easy decision.*

Jinwoo understood Kihoon's dilemma. In a guild with two S-rank hunters, this might be both his first and last chance to lead his own strike squad. To retreat this early during a raid so monumental in his career...

*Plenty of people in this situation would be tempted to clear the dungeon.*

But a wise leader...

Kihoon made up his mind and opened his mouth. Jinwoo's eyes narrowed. Fortunately, Kihoon wasn't a foolish man.

"We'll retreat for now."

The leader's decision was absolute in a dungeon. It was an unwritten rule that, as a member of a strike squad, one would follow the leader's orders. Wasn't there a wartime policy stating that disobeying a direct order was punishable by death? In some ways, a dungeon was even more dangerous than a war zone.

The type of leader a squad had could mean the difference between life and death, and Kihoon was one who didn't disappoint his teammates. Every member in the squad was relieved.

"Whew."

"I was really worried you'd want to go all the way, Kihoon."

Kihoon patted the shoulder of the hunter and cracked a smile. "I'm not insane."

"I know, but still, look at my hands! They're shaking."

"All right, quit exaggerating. Let's go, everyone."

Jinwoo heaved the pack back on, and the strike squad began mobilizing as per Kihoon's order, but this time in the opposite direction.

Jinwoo's smile was bittersweet.

*I wanted to go farther inside, though.*

But he was just a guest anyway, and as a guest, he wasn't in a position to criticize the master of the house.

Regrettably, this was as far as they'd go for today.

"Hmph……" The female healer joined Jinwoo, seemingly put out that Kihoon hadn't believed a word she'd said. "It's true, though."

She pouted then and looked up at Jinwoo with hope shining in her eyes. "You know, earlier, the high orc—"

"I didn't see a thing."

"Ugh……" Her hopes were dashed.

Jinwoo suppressed his laugh.

But they didn't get very far when, suddenly, the front line halted abruptly.

Kihoon raised his right hand. "S-stop!" The panic in his voice was clear.

The weary hunters trudging along and Jinwoo, who had been closely monitoring things at the back of the group in case an orc tried to ambush them from behind, all froze in place.

The hunters' murmurs grew louder.

"What's going on here?"

"There's something else?"

"Why is this passage blocked? It was fine earlier!"

Jinwoo pushed through the commotion and, upon reaching the front of the group, extended his hand.

He blinked in surprise.

*It's...blocked?*

There was an invisible barrier barring the way. His first thought was of instance dungeons and the walls that separated them from the real world, but he quickly ruled that out.

*No, it's something else.*

He sensed something artificial about this wall. Upon an assessment of the barrier, the mana making up its composition seemed to be from an intelligent magic beast.

*But...why?*

Why block the way out instead of in?

Just then...Jinwoo's head whipped around.

*......?*

As if it had been waiting for its cue, an alarmingly powerful wave of mana came from the other side of the cave like a mighty tsunami.

*No way......*

Could that be the dungeon boss? The scale of this wave of magic power was completely different from the amount of mana he'd felt from outside the dungeon or when he'd first stepped foot inside.

Other hunters shivered as if they could also feel the waves of mana.

"Wh-what?"

"I suddenly have goose bumps."

A thought struck Jinwoo as he watched the others' faces grow pale.

*Could there be a boss that can hide its presence......?*

The wall hadn't been there on the way in, and the boss had started baring its fangs after putting up the barrier.

*Was... Was it a trap to lure in the hunters?*

The thought sent chills up his spine.

And as he expected...

*Thmp, thmp.*

*Thmp, thmp.*

From the dark depths of the cave came the sound of countless foot-steps, even more than before. As the noise grew louder, the hunters grew quieter. Jinwoo would have found the situation fascinating if it wasn't so dire.

"Kihoon......"

"......"

They all fell totally silent.

Jinwoo's ears twitched as he concentrated. He took advantage of the momentary silence in his immediate surroundings to count the number of enemies by the sound of the footsteps.

*Thmp, thmp.*

*Thmp, thmp.*

His heightened hearing and high perception stat allowed him to dis-cern the sound of each footstep.

*Forty-eight, forty-nine, fifty, fifty-one.*

There were fifty-one distinct footfalls in total—and they sounded similar to the ones made by the high orc warriors earlier.

Jinwoo looked around.

......

Apprehension was clear on everyone's faces. It looked as though they'd also managed to approximate the number of encroaching ene-mies. They'd barely defeated twenty-two high orc warriors. Now, fifty-one were coming. More than double.

*......We don't stand a chance.*

At least, the strike squad didn't. Jinwoo turned to look at his own shadow. It seemed to be wavering.

*Whoooo!*

He could almost hear his shadow soldiers screaming for blood. Jin-woo turned around.

*BA-DUMP, BA-DUMP, BA-DUMP.*

His heart was full-on racing by this point.

*Wait for it......*

It wasn't yet time. Jinwoo talked himself down as he silently stared straight ahead.

Finally, the orcs emerged.

*Tmp.*

The high orcs came to a stop, leaving quite some space between themselves and the humans.

"Graaaawr."

"Grrrr."

They growled as if they could attack at any second. The aggression from the fifty-plus high orc warriors felt indescribable. This could end only one way.

"This is insane…"

"How the hell is this happening……?"

"Ngh……"

The hunters lamented. The overwhelming pressure forced them back, but they were also blocked from behind. What could they do?

They'd already readied themselves to fight, but now that it was time, no one was willing to make a move. Instead, they awaited a cue from Kihoon. He bit his lip.

*Shit……*

*If only President Choi or Hunter Cha was here…* He frowned. An S-rank hunter would have the power to turn the tide in a disadvantaged situation. If those two were here, the high orcs would've been dead on arrival.

*Why did this have to happen now of all times……?*

Why was this going down when they weren't around? Kihoon was so used to fighting alongside them that, in this moment, he realized just how utterly powerless he was without them. It pained him that the group didn't have an S rank, but he couldn't continue the pity party. It was time to make a call.

*Fighting here would be suicidal.*

Yet they had no choice with their escape route blocked.

That day he'd first decided to become a hunter, that first time he'd stepped inside a dungeon, and that time he'd ended up severely wounded and lost consciousness, he'd always known this day would come.

*Yeah, that's right.*

Kihoon resolved to die here and raised his sword.

*Shiiing.*

When he looked over his shoulder, the hunters awaiting his orders nodded. He turned back, positioning his shield under his chin, and glared at the orcs, who showed no signs that they were going to make a move.

*Looks like he finally made a decision.*

Jinwoo also got ready. He hid his right hand behind his back and materialized Barca's Dagger. Then he closed his eyes. His pounding heart actually calmed as the battle drew near.

*Ba-dump, ba-dump, ba-dump.*

He relaxed his muscles and regulated his breathing.

*......Okay.*

Jinwoo opened his shining eyes.

*Gulp.*

The hunters were so tense that they were having difficulty swallowing. Sweat dotted their foreheads. On the other hand, Jinwoo was having to tamp down his excitement.

*How much experience will they give me?*

There was a little smile dancing along his face.

That was when one of the high orcs moved forward. It pushed aside the others and glowered at the hunters with the eyes of a wild animal.

"Grrrrr..." It was much bigger than the others and had long fangs.

*Is that the head of the pack?*

Jinwoo's eyes narrowed. Wouldn't the battle be easier if he took it out right now? What should he do?

As Jinwoo debated his options while fiddling with the handle of Barca's Dagger, the high orc opened its mouth.

"Krerak shina wigdu araknaka!" Its voice was forceful, and its eyes were fixed on Kihoon, who stood at the front of the strike squad. "Krerak shina wigdu araknaka!"

The hunters exchanged looks.

"What was that?"

"Is it trying to talk to us?"

"What's it saying?"

At that moment, the orc's facial muscles began to contort. When its face stopped moving, a totally different voice emerged from the beast's mouth.

"Humans..." It was like someone else was talking through the creature's mouth. "Listen up, humans..."

Looking closer, they could see the orc's clear eyes from earlier had clouded like those of a rotting dead fish.

*Gasp!*

The hunters were gobsmacked. An orc was speaking the language of humans!

*How can an orc speak our language?*

*Magic? Is this some kind of magic?*

They couldn't close their mouths from the shock of this unexpected development.

The high orc captain continued. "I am...Kargalgan. I...want to... meet...you...humans. Follow...this...one."

A magic beast wanted to have a conversation with humans? Nothing like this had ever been reported before. Kihoon and the rest of the strike squad were incredibly confused by this turn of events.

"Kihoon, you don't believe what a magic beast is saying, do you?"

"Ignore it."

"It's a trap! Whether we get smashed to a pulp or not, let's end things right here, right now."

"Still, if we can communicate with it, maybe—"

"Dude! You've been to how many dungeons? And you still don't know how magic beasts think?"

The hunters' opinions had already become divided in this short period of time.

Kihoon was quiet for a moment before addressing the orc. "Kargalgan, were you the one who blocked the way out?"

"That is right... I am...the head shaman...of the prideful...orcs... You...cannot...break...my magic...with...only...human power."

"Is there any being stronger than you in this dungeon?"

"Who...would dare...fight...against...me?!"

The loud voice reverberated inside the hunters' ears. Most of the other hunters either grimaced or covered their ears, but Kihoon coolly nodded.

His suspicions had been confirmed. Whoever was speaking through this high orc had to be the boss of the dungeon. The boss was luring the hunters to its location because it couldn't leave the boss's lair until the dungeon break.

*I don't know its reasoning, but......*

The leader of the orcs raised its ax over its head at Kihoon's lack of response.

"Choose... Either...you...die...by...my...soldiers'...hands...or...you follow...them."

"We'll go."

Kihoon's immediate response raised eyebrows.

"Hoon, are you serious?"

"Kihoon!"

Kihoon ignored the others' protests and studied the orc's reactions.

"Follow...human."

With that, the high orc's clouded eyes faded back to their original color. They were once again like those of a wild animal.

It grunted. "Ashi tu reka."

And with that, the hostile high orc warriors really began to withdraw. The leader stayed behind and eventually gestured for Kihoon to follow.

"Let's go." Kihoon was the first to take a step, and the hesitant hunters trailed after him.

*What is Kihoon thinking?*

Jinwoo was puzzled. There were sure to be more high orcs, including the boss, inside the lair. Their chances of winning this battle had diminished even more. Jinwoo couldn't figure out the reasoning behind Kihoon's decision.

*Is he thinking of negotiating with the boss? In order to get back alive?*

The odds of that happening seemed low, though…

No. This might be good for Jinwoo. He'd initially thought this raid would end with him killing a few low-rank magic beasts, but he now had a chance to meet the boss.

Jinwoo sent his dagger back to the inventory and slowly tailed the group.

How long had they been walking? Kihoon gradually slowed his pace until he ended up next to Jinwoo.

He addressed him in a low voice. "Hunter Sung."

"Yes," Jinwoo responded while keeping his eyes straight ahead.

Kihoon fixed his gaze on the high orc as he continued. "As soon as we meet the boss…we're going to launch a surprise attack. It won't be able to keep up the barrier blocking the exit with magic regardless of whether the attack is successful."

He had a point. With the exception of curses, spell casters had to focus on a spell in order to maintain it. The higher the level of magic, the higher the level of concentration required.

But then what? Even if they succeeded in killing the boss or disrupting the spell, they would still be surrounded by high orc warriors and trapped inside the boss's lair. It wouldn't change the fact that it'd be next to impossible for the strike squad to get out alive.

Kihoon answered his unspoken doubts with a resolute look. "While they're focusing on us, you get out. Please contact the main strike squad as soon as you escape the dungeon."

By the time the strike squad with the S-rank hunters arrived, it would all be over. Kihoon intended to lay down his life.

"Are you planning to go down with the boss?"

Jinwoo glanced at Kihoon. The squad leader's face was stoic, but his eyes never wavered.

"Our job is to close the gate, not to get out of the dungeon alive. That's why they pay us the big bucks." Kihoon spoke firmly. "This is what we're trained to do. But that's not the case for you. There's no need for you to die here. Please get out alive."

Jinwoo felt the conviction in Kihoon's voice. His words reflected his steely determination.

Nothing Jinwoo could say would assuage Kihoon in this moment, so he simply nodded in reply.

* * *

Haein arrived at the gate. She'd pulled her cap down low so barely anyone recognized her. She walked around in search of the excavation team.

A few hunters glanced her way as she passed by and, assuming she was one of the guild administrators, didn't pay her any further attention.

Haein spotted Yoonsuk in the distance. The excavation team was huddled around him.

*Ba-dump, ba-dump.*

Her heart began to race. Keeping her distance, she scanned their faces.

*Where is he......?*

She couldn't find Jinwoo, and disappointment crashed over her.

*Did he quit the team?*

She decided to give it another minute. He could have just left the area for a bit.

Three more minutes.

No, five.

Just like that, Haein ended up waiting for fifteen minutes, but there were no signs of Jinwoo.

"Haah..." She turned to go with a long sigh. After taking a couple of steps, though, she found herself walking back. She took off her cap and, with a deep breath, walked toward Yoonsuk.

The excavation team's eyes were on her. Luckily, the stench from them was tolerable because their ranks were on the lower end.

"Oh?" Yoonsuk recognized Haein and quickly ran up to her. "Hunter Cha, isn't it your day off?"

"Hello." Haein briefly greeted Yoonsuk and, checking to make sure she wouldn't be heard, carefully asked, "Um, is…Hunter Jinwoo Sung here?"

"Sung?" Yoonsuk blinked in surprise at the name. "Sung went inside the dungeon to stand in for an absent luggage carrier…"

"A luggage carrier?" Haein was taken aback. "Are you saying he went *inside* the gate?"

The foreman furiously nodded as if he couldn't believe it, either. "That's right."

An E-rank hunter had volunteered as a luggage carrier and gone inside an A-rank dungeon? It wasn't like he had multiple lives.

*What was he thinking?*

Haein then recalled him standing in the boss's lair yesterday with a weapon in hand. So it wasn't just her imagination. And that wasn't the only suspicious thing. She hadn't thought anything of it at the time, but when she considered it long and hard, it was definitely strange for someone who'd been a hunter for four years to lose his way in a dungeon.

*I need to get to the bottom of this.*

Haein needed to find out for herself what Jinwoo was doing in the Hunters Guild, and in order to do that, she had no choice but to go inside the dungeon herself. She was the guild's vice president and an active S-rank hunter. No one would stop her if she wanted to enter the dungeon in the middle of a raid.

Haein bit the nail on her thumb as she internally debated with herself before making a final decision. "I'll have to go inside the gate."

Yoonsuk's eyes widened. "Oh dear… Was there an accident? Should I call the guild for backup?"

"No, this is a personal matter. I have some business with him, so you don't need to worry about it."

"Oh…I see."

Haein turned to face the gate, but something felt like it was missing from her side.

*Oh... My weapon......*

Haein patted her hips and belatedly realized she'd left her sword at home. It was her day off, so who could've predicted that she would be entering a dungeon today?

She gave a slight frown.

*I believe Kihoon and the squad members are all skilled, but......*

It wouldn't be wise to set foot inside a dungeon without a weapon.

Haein turned to Yoonsuk.

"Is there anything else...?" Yoonsuk blinked innocently.

"Do you perhaps have a weapon I could borrow, sir?"

"Pardon?" Yoonsuk thought for a second before calling out to a passing hunter.

"Hey, Seok! Could you bring me one of our tools?"

"Yessir."

Seok speedily brought them one of the pickaxes used by the excavation team.

"......" Haein stared at it. "Do... Do you have anything else?"

"Anything else like...?"

"Like a sword or a spear."

"Sorry......"

"......" She gave a small sigh. "Understood."

Haein politely rejected the offered pickax and headed toward the gate.

Yoonsuk worriedly called out after her. "Hunter Cha, are you sure it's okay to go in without a weapon?"

Haein paused, thought about it for a moment, then hastily walked back to take the pickax.

He laughed heartily. "Good thinking. It's never a smart idea to go in there empty-handed."

"Well then......"

As Haein retreated, Yoonsuk didn't notice that her ears had turned bright red.

* * *

The members of the strike squad looked to be steadfast. As they walked quietly toward their fate in total silence, the female healer approached Jinwoo and started rummaging through the gear on his back.

Jinwoo turned his head to the side. "What're you doing?"

"Just a second." She pulled out a cute little purse. "I've always gotten strangely anxious when I'm separated from this for too long." She explained without anyone prompting her.

She then took out a notebook and pen from the purse and started to scribble something down. Her head bumped into Jinwoo's shoulder a few times because she wasn't looking where she was going.

*Scritch.*

She soon closed her notebook. She took her purse, which she'd slung over her shoulder while writing, and shoved it back in the gear pack, but she held on to the notebook. She thrust it at Jinwoo, who'd been eyeing her warily.

"......?"

The female healer choked back tears as Jinwoo stared at the notebook in his hand. "I've written a message for my family. Please give this to them when you get out."

If he laughed here, she would probably feel hurt, right?

"I'll hang on to this, but I doubt I'll get the chance to deliver it to your family."

"That's okay." She nodded sympathetically.

*With these orc warriors watching us so intensely, it'll be hard for him to escape.*

Plus, the luggage carrier was but an E rank.

She didn't yet understand what Jinwoo was getting at.

Soon, they arrived at the lair. The other hunters' trepidation was palpable, and Jinwoo could feel it on his skin. They were all in this together.

......

Jinwoo surveyed the area. It was a wide cavern, bigger than the giant's lair from yesterday, but it didn't feel bigger because of all the high orcs filling the room. There were over twice as many of them here as the force that had been sent to escort them.

*There's about a hundred… No, maybe a little more?*

No wonder there hadn't been magic beasts elsewhere in the dungeon—they were all here.

Kihoon looked at the rows of orcs, and the blood drained from his face.

*If this many high orcs ever escaped the gate……*

There were enough of them to destroy a small city before the strongest hunters could arrive.

Kihoon's back broke out in a cold sweat.

*We need to get rid of the boss at least.*

He swallowed hard and dug down on his resolve.

High orcs cleared the way so the hunters could pass.

"Ah shak." The high orc leader waved them through. The squad followed their escort to an altar in a corner of the lair.

"Look!" One of the hunters pointed to the top of the altar.

There stood a high orc shaman decked out in all manner of accessories, including a mask, bone necklace, and bone earrings.

*That's the boss……*

Kihoon stiffened. He could tell that most of the massive amounts of mana filling the dungeon originated from this magic beast. The four lugs guarding it with shrew gazes also didn't seem to be the typical high orc.

*This isn't good.*

Would they be able get past those guards to take down the boss once and for all? Each of the hunters had similar concerns.

They stopped in front of the shaman. The tension between the high orcs and humans as they regarded each other from a distance was absolutely electrifying.

"Heh-heh." The shaman wasn't bothered at all. It opened its hideous maw and cackled from beneath its creepy mask. "Welcome, humans."

The strike squad members exchanged looks.

*Once Kihoon gives the signal......*

*We all charge at the same time......*

*Aim directly for the shaman......*

They were waiting for a good time to pounce.

But then...the air around them started growing colder. This squad consisted of the best of the best, so they all reacted immediately to the change in temperature.

The cause of this was the shaman. As it took off its mask, the sheer power of its magic burst out in full force.

*Hwoooosh!*

Terrifying waves of magic flared. The hunters all froze like a herd of deer that had come face-to-face with a tiger.

"Oh m-my God......"

"How could anyone have this much mana...?"

"Th-that's who we have to fight?"

Frustration, lamentation, resentment, and regret—the shaman sneered as it took in the varying emotions on the hunters' faces.

"Are you afraid of me, humans?"

Kihoon bit down hard on his lip and forced himself to take a step forward to ask, "Why did you bring us all the way here? You could've let your warriors kill us."

The shaman gave a creepy, bone-chilling leer. "For entertainment."

"What?" Kihoon didn't know what to say. That's why the beast had brought them here?

The shaman continued. "While we bide our time, I'm going to kill you people one by one for my minions' amusement!"

*Graaaaaah!*

The high orc warriors cheered. The hunters crumbled under the pressure from the orcs and had difficulty breathing.

One hunter began to cry.

"However..." The shaman paused. Its gaze stopped on Jinwoo. "...There is something odd among you humans."

At that, Kihoon's eyes lit up.

*It's distracted, so this is our chance!*

The veins in his neck strained. "Now!" Kihoon bellowed, pulling out his sword as he rushed forward.

But there was only silence behind him.

*Huh......?*

He looked back at his colleagues as he ran and saw them glued to their spots. They had lost the will to fight in the face of this overwhelming power.

His heart sank.

*No......*

But someone had to do this. He couldn't stop here. He faced forward again. The shaman continued jeering at them, and its guards were just standing there. This could be their one and only chance. Whether it be by luck or by providence, as long as his sword could reach...

*Tmp, tmp, tmp!*

Kihoon charged with all his strength and raised his blade high.

"Yaaaaah!"

But he bounced off something well before he could strike.

*Crash!*

It was a magical force field.

"Uggghhh!" Kihoon was knocked to the ground and tumbled a few times, but he didn't roll around for long.

"Here's the first volunteer."

With the shaman's ridicule, Kihoon's body shot into the air.

*Hwoooom!*

It was antigravity magic.

"......"

The shaman's lips continuously moved as it magically hoisted Kihoon as high as a two-story building, then cast a different spell.

"......"

Gravity acceleration.

*Wham!*

Kihoon instantly slammed into the ground.

"Guh!"

Even before his mind could fully process the pain, his body was rising into the air again.

"Antigravity."

*Heh-heh-heh!*

The shaman and other orcs were cackling so hard, their fangs were on full display.

*Wham!*

"Argh!"

*Hwoooom!*

*Wham!*

"Gah!"

The shaman toyed with Kihoon, raising and dropping him again and again. The fourth time the hunter hit the ground, blood splattered out of his mouth.

His comrades watched with their faces turning ashen. Yet none dared to help him.

"K-Kihoon……"

They could only stand there trembling as they watched him break.

*Thud.*

The female healer fell to the ground as she lost the strength in her legs.

The shaman eventually raised Kihoon's body into the air for a fifth time. "This one's lasting longer than I expected."

"Nghhh……" A moan escaped from Kihoon. He'd kept his grip on his sword this entire time, as if there was still hope.

*Hwoooom!*

*Wham!*

*Hwoooom!*

*Wham!*

*Hwoooom!*

Kihoon's blade finally dropped from his hand as he was driven into the ground multiple times.

*Klang!*

Just then…Kihoon's falling body vanished.

"Huh?" The shaman blinked. Where could that bag of broken bones have gone? The boss scanned the lair for Kihoon's presence.

*That's……?*

It located Kihoon lying in a corner nearby. Beside him was another man—Jinwoo.

Jinwoo had laid Kihoon on the ground and was now glowering at the shaman.

"May I ask you something, Captain?"

"……?" Kihoon still hadn't quite processed what had happened to him.

"Am I okay to kill all the magic beasts present?"

"What…are you talking about…?"

As the disgruntled shaman pointed with its chin, one of the guards dashed toward Jinwoo, swinging its machete.

With his eyes aglow, Jinwoo fixed his gaze on the approaching beast and extended his palm.

*Ruler's Hand.*

The guard flew into the air as if he'd been snatched up by a giant hand.

"G-gaaah?" The beast flailed in vain.

*How……?!*

The shaman's mouth dropped open.

When Jinwoo pointed his finger down…

*Wham!*

The guard hurtled to the ground. Cracks formed where it'd landed from the impact. But Jinwoo didn't stop there. He raised the guard's body back into the air again just as the shaman had done to Kihoon.

*Wham!*

*Wham!*

*Wham!*

The guard cried out as it ricocheted between the ceiling and the ground like a basketball being dribbled and eventually got its head stuck in the ceiling.

*Wham!*

*Crumble.*

Debris fell from above. High orcs and hunters alike were aghast at the sight of the guard's dangling body.

Kihoon was shaking as he asked Jinwoo, "Just who…are you…?"

"I'll ask again."

This was the Hunters' hunting ground, and there was only one person here who could speak for them.

"Am I okay…to kill all the magic beasts present?"

Kihoon had reached the point where the true identity of the luggage carrier didn't matter to him anymore. He was vexed. He was mortified for getting played with like a toy by a damn magic beast. Tears fell from his eyes.

"Please…please go ahead."

That was all Jinwoo needed.

As he got to his feet, the orcs started closing in. Behind them was the shaman, who smirked at Jinwoo.

"Interesting skills you have there, especially for a mere human." With a wave of the shaman's fingers, the orcs surrounded Jinwoo. "But I wonder how far your little party tricks will get you?"

Jinwoo's gaze turned frosty. He'd never liked magic beasts, but for the first time, he had an intense desire to slay one. "I'm saving you for last."

If the beast could be amused, it could also be frightened.

Jinwoo chanted, "My shadows…"

His daggers appeared in his grasp.

"Come forth."

\* \* \*

*Skrrrrch.*

A black car pulled over to the side of the road. Sunglasses and a black suit—the man who got out of the driver's seat was Jinchul from the Hunter's Association's Surveillance Team. Three other men, all members of the Surveillance Team, also got out of the car.

"Manager Woo, weren't we heading back to the association?"

"There's something I need to do." Jinchul turned his head toward the gate in the distance.

*A-rank gates will never not be frightening.*

He squinted. What if that gigantic gate opened and all the magic beasts burst out at once? Just thinking about it made his hair stand on end.

*But why did he apply to be a miner at a horrible place like this?*

And for not one but two whole days. Even if President Go hadn't asked him personally to check out the situation, Jinchul would've come to scope things out of his own accord.

*I can't exactly…dig up information on him.*

The other party was an S-rank awakened being. It'd be difficult for him, an A rank, to run an investigation on Jinwoo without getting caught. So he'd decided to boldly come greet him outright. His plan was to tell Jinwoo that he'd had some errands nearby and was dropping in to say hello, then ask him a few questions.

*He wouldn't think it was strange that I have a few questions, right?*

Anyone would be curious to know why a confirmed S-rank hunter was subjecting himself to manual labor. Besides, Jinwoo had caught the attention of the Hunter's Association. Even the president had taken a particular liking to him and was monitoring his every move.

*No, not strange at all.*

It was perfectly natural to be curious and completely normal to ask questions. Jinchul kept telling himself that as he searched for a staff member of the Hunters Guild.

"Excuse me, I'm looking for the excavation team."

"May I ask who…?"

"We're from the association."

The staff checked Jinchul's ID and pointed him toward the area where the mining team was waiting. "Right over there."

"Thank you."

Four members from the Surveillance Team were here to see the excavation team. The foreman seemed to have been told by someone as he rushed over to meet them. "Hello, hello, what brings the Association's Surveillance Team here?"

The excavation team had been relaxing, but now they looked anxious. The words *surveillance team* weighed heavily on hunters. They were the judge, jury, and sometimes even executioner of awakened beings who other hunters couldn't handle. Such was the authority of the Surveillance Team.

"What's going on?"

"Surveillance Team hunters are here."

"The Surveillance Team...?"

Something was going down. With their interests piqued, they slowly gathered around Yoonsuk.

Jinchul took off his sunglasses.

......

He looked around for Jinwoo to no avail, then finally asked the foreman, "Where can I find Hunter Jinwoo Sung?"

"I knew it!" One hunter suddenly leaped forward. It was Seonggu, who had purposely bumped into Jinwoo yesterday.

He spoke so animatedly that he was practically spitting everywhere. "That bastard turned and smiled at me with the eyes of a killer! Man, it scares the bejesus out of me just thinking about it."

Jinchul frowned slightly.

*The eyes of a killer?*

What had happened between them?

Everyone started talking at once.

Jinchul ignored the commotion and focused on Seonggu. "What exactly happened?"

"Oh, um......" Seonggu stopped himself from answering when he realized that it wasn't exactly a tale that painted him in the best light, so he waved away Jinchul's question. "It wasn't a big deal, but the point is, his eyes were scary!"

"......" Jinchul turned back to Yoonsuk. "Where is Hunter Jinwoo Sung now?"

"Sung is...inside the gate."

Jinwoo went inside an active A-rank dungeon? Jinchul's eyes widened. "Why?"

"Our luggage carrier was a no-show. No one else volunteered for the job, so Sung went in his place."

"......"

"There is one thing..."

"What is it?"

"I'm sure it's nothing, but...Hunter Cha, Hunter Haein Cha, was looking for Sung just now and followed him inside the dungeon. I thought that was quite odd..." The foreman's confusion was clear on his face.

Jinchul's thoughts were jumbled after hearing this news.

*Haein Cha, the vice president of the Hunters Guild, was looking for Jinwoo? Not only that, she followed him into the dungeon?*

What in the world? Jinchul had only come to check on Jinwoo, but he felt like he had stumbled onto something big.

*First, I should examine the gate.*

That seemed to be all he could do at this point.

"I'd like to take a look at the gate."

"Certainly."

The foreman chuckled and waved at him to go ahead.

Seonggu hurriedly stopped Jinchul as he was about to depart with his subordinates. "Oh, sir!" Seonggu had an expectant look on his face. "Did that jerk Jinwoo Sung cause some kind of trouble? Did he kill someone? He looked like he'd have no problem doing that."

Jinchul's eye twitched. Suddenly, he understood why Jinwoo had glared at Seonggu.

*Jinwoo could probably send him flying with a snap of his fingers......*

But there were too many eyes on him right now. As a hunter of the association, he couldn't lose his cool at civilians. It was one of the downsides of working for the government.

Jinchul sighed deeply and responded as politely as he could. "Everything will be explained on the news tomorrow night."

The answer satisfied Seonggu, and his reply was brash and assertive. "See! Didn't I tell you he was suspicious?"

"He didn't look it, though..."

"Yeah, he was a good worker, too."

Seonggu ignored his colleagues' lack of support and continued bragging about his ability to spot bad apples.

*Tsk.*

Jinchul was clearly unimpressed by Seonggu's antics as he turned to the gate instead. But...Jinchul instinctively halted a few steps away from the entrance.

"Manager Woo?" His subordinates curiously looked at the stunned expression on his face.

*That can't... This doesn't make sense.*

Jinchul took out his phone and pulled up the association website. He navigated to the A-rank gate the Hunters Guild was supposed to be raiding today.

His eyes widened.

*Why does it list such a low mana reading?*

He couldn't help but shake his head.

*The measurement is wrong.*

Not all A-rank hunters were built the same, and Jinchul was one of the elite among A ranks. His gut was telling him that the measurement of the gate's mana level was off.

He quickly gave an order to one of his subordinates. "Mana meter."

Seeing the grave look on Jinchul's face, the subordinate quickly ran to fetch the meter from the car. The small mana meter used by the

Surveillance Team was much more precise than those used by regular association employees. This particular mana meter rarely malfunctioned or gave false readings, as it utilized high-quality essence stones that cost over a billion won.

*Beep!*

The meter had finished its assessment.

*Just as I suspected......*

There was a major difference from the association's measurement. This meant potentially huge problems if the guild had organized a strike squad based on the previous assessment.

*They should be fine, since there are two S ranks, but......*

As Jinchul picked the mana meter off the ground...

*Hwoooom...*

The gate began to vibrate. Jinchul's body shook from the sudden burst of magic power, as did those of his three subordinates, despite their perception being not quite at his level.

"M-Manager Woo?"

"What just happened?"

Jinchul looked at the youngest of his subordinates, whose face had turned pale. "Are you okay?"

"I-I'm fine."

At his subordinate's answer, Jinchul carefully inspected the back of his own hands. They were covered in tiny goose bumps.

Jinchul straightened up. "We're going in."

"Pardon?"

"You mean inside the dungeon?"

Jinchul was firm. "If you're scared, you may stay behind."

At this point, he was the only one who knew the reading was wrong. It was his sworn duty to inform the hunters inside. After all, the responsibilities of those in the Hunter's Association included managing, monitoring, and aiding other hunters.

"N-no, sir."

"We're coming."

Jinchul nodded. "And, you—stay behind and report the new reading to the association."

"Wh-what?"

"Can you do that?"

When Jinchul squeezed the shoulder of the tense youngest subordinate, the man found it in himself to nod affirmatively.

"Yes, sir. I can."

Jinchul turned to look at the gate. The immense power coming from the dungeon aside, there was yet another incredible source of mana emanating its power in waves.

*What the hell is going on in there?*

With Jinchul in the lead, the Surveillance Team threw themselves into the dungeon.

\* \* \*

Meanwhile, Haein was tracking down the whereabouts of the strike squad within the dungeon.

*Strange. Why aren't there any traces of magic beasts?*

In a regular dungeon, there would be a path of carcasses littering the ground from the entrance all the way to the boss's lair. But no matter where she looked, Haein couldn't find any. Were all the magic beasts gathered in one place?

*Oh?*

As she was pondering the possibilities, she finally came across some cadavers.

*Tmp, tmp, tmp!*

Haein, the S-rank brawler that she was, made her way to the battleground lightning quick.

*How is that possible?!*

Her eyes were round as she surveyed the field. All the dead bodies were high orc warriors, easily distinguishable from ordinary orcs by their red skin and long lower canines.

*How did Kihoon's squad defeat this many high orcs?*

More surprisingly, she saw no signs of fallen hunters. Although, had there been any casualties, the strike squad likely would've retreated and saved her this trip.

*Have I been underestimating A- and B-rank hunters?*

It was possible. From what she could observe, the battle appeared to have been a decisive victory for the hunters. But...

*What is this...?*

Something caught Haein's eye, and she crouched to inspect one of the corpses. What she saw surprised her. She quickly checked the other remains.

*Here... And here, too...*

Her suspicions were slowly being confirmed.

*But how...?*

How could this be? Almost all the high orc carcasses had wounds inflicted by a short, sharp weapon.

*These attacks weren't fatal, but......*

They would be enough to immobilize the high orcs. It was as if the other hunters had merely contributed the finishing touches on a masterpiece for which someone else had done most of the work. It could be said that one hunter had massacred twenty high orcs.

Only two of the orcs had died differently. One had been forcefully decapitated while the other had received a fatal blow to the head.

*Then, with the exception of these two, a single person took down the rest?*

Was that even possible? Despite her confidence in her own speed, she doubted she could accomplish the same feat. Plus, as far as she knew, there weren't any assassin-class hunters assigned to Kihoon's squad who used a short sword or dagger.

*A dagger?*

That brought a certain image to mind. She was certain the man standing in front of the boss's lair yesterday, Jinwoo, had been holding some kind of short weapon in each hand.

*Is he responsible for all this?*

As she was arriving at a conclusion, Haein suddenly whipped around to face the depths of the dungeon. Her face was grim. She'd felt a wave of magic so powerful that it seemed more akin to a vibration, the likes of which she'd never experienced before. The air itself had reverberated.

*No!*

She bit her lip. If this was the boss's magic power, no one from Kihoon's squad would survive. She sprinted toward the lair as fast as she could.

\* \* \*

"Come forth."

It all began with those words.

*Fwiiiish...*

His magic energy cast vibrations stronger than the shaman's. But that wasn't the only change. As he revealed his power, the shadow beneath Jinwoo's feet began expanding as well. Like ink poured into water, the shadow spread out at a terrifying rate.

"Whoa!"

"Wh-what's that?"

The strike squad hunters were astonished as they watched the shadow passing beneath their feet. How to process this? Even the most experienced hunters had never seen or heard of such a phenomenon. Fear started creeping into their hearts.

Kihoon could witness everything from where he lay helpless, trembling.

*What...what is he trying to do?*

He got his answer once the shadow covered the entire floor of the lair.

*Shhhhhf...*

The black surface rippled as shadows in black armor rose from the ground.

**[Skill: Monarch's Domain has been activated.]**

[Abilities of all shadow soldiers fighting on the surface of your shadow will increase by 50 percent.]

Jinwoo smiled lightly.

*Excellent.*

Monarch's Domain was a job-exclusive skill he'd acquired after reaching level 70 in the Demon's Castle. As the soldiers' abilities increased even further, Jinwoo could sense their morale. Naturally, satisfaction was written all over his face.

The fifty summoned shadow soldiers surrounded Jinwoo like bodyguards.

"G-grrr!"

"Grahhh!"

The high orc warriors, despite being known for their bravery, retreated after becoming intimidated by Jinwoo and his soldiers.

"Th-the orcs are backing down!"

"What is happening......?"

Although the unbelievable circumstances had the hunters quaking in their boots, they began to have hope.

"Did you feel that, too?"

"Yeah."

"Does any of this...make sense?"

The mage hunters who were sensitive to mana couldn't stop their own hearts from racing in response. To think that the source of the unbelievably huge amount of magic was the E-rank hunter they'd brought as backup.

*To start, is this even magic?*

*It's more sinister than the shaman's...!*

The sheer force of the magic filling the boss's lair was making it hard to breathe. The hunters were relieved that the one wielding this much power was on their side.

Conversely, the high orcs were very nervous. With the shadow soldiers' appearance, the odds had gone from 1 hunter against 150 orcs to 50 soldiers against 150 orcs. Moreover, these weren't just any 50 soldiers. They were much stronger than their number indicated.

As if out to prove this point, Jinwoo charged first.

When he did, the shaman yelled, "Why're you all standing around?! Kill that human at once!"

Galvanized by the voice imbued with magic, the high orcs raised their weapons and roared. "Graaaaah!"

*Sh-shiiiing, shhhk!*

Monarch's Domain affected only the shadow soldiers, but despite the lack of buffs, Jinwoo was already on another level.

"Aaargh!"

"Graaah, gaaaaah!"

The orcs screamed.

Both bodies and blood flew everywhere as Jinwoo swung his two daggers. At the speed he was moving, Jinwoo's actions were a blur of afterimages, even in the eyes of the elite hunters.

"Hey......"

"Yeah, he's like the vice president."

Haein's nickname was "the Dancer." Even though she was usually so collected, when she was on the attack, her movements looked like she was dancing at a fast tempo, which was how she'd earned the nickname. It embarrassed Haein, so she'd forbidden people from using it, which meant the title wasn't widely known. Still, it came up now and then.

The luggage carrier's movements were at the same level as Haein's or maybe even superior. If she was a graceful dancer, then Jinwoo was a typhoon. He crushed magic beasts from the eye of a storm.

*Graaaaah!*

The shadow soldiers also held their own. His soldiers—led by Tank, the previous head of the ice bears—charged at their enemies.

Iron held the front line. As his prebattle ritual, he puffed out his chest and bellowed.

*Gwooooh!*

*    *    *

[Iron is using Skill: Epic Taunt.]
[The debuff has been canceled out by the opponent's high resistance level.]

Enraged that his skill didn't work, Iron shrieked loudly and began smashing the orcs with his mighty iron hammer.

*Whoosh!*

*Krak!*

*Crunch!*

"Argh!"

"Gaaah!"

Some of the hunters actually felt pity for the orcs in Iron's way.

In complete contrast to Iron, Igris efficiently but mercifully cut the enemies' throats. The orcs that died at Igris's hand didn't even have time to scream.

*Shhhk!*

Each time Igris swung his sword, another orc lost its head. It wasn't as easy for the regular shadow soldiers to deal with the high orcs, but they had endless strength and infinite regeneration on their side. While the infantry soldiers preoccupied the orcs, mage soldiers were able to rain down a torrent of fire.

*Kaboom!*

*Fwoom!*

The number of high orcs dwindled quickly. The shaman's puffy cheeks quivered.

*How dare this measly human…!*

Its eyes were fixed on Jinwoo as its first target. The soldiers in black armor had been summoned by that human! Once the human was dead, his troops would disappear, too.

The shaman started casting a spell on Jinwoo. "……" Its lips moved rapidly.

The Song of Impediment, the Song of Blindness, the Song of High
Fever, the Song of Extreme Pain, and the Song of Sleep—five powerful
curses were completed in no time and aimed at the enemy.

"Done!" The shaman leered.

Jinwoo sensed the traces of mana traveling toward him as soon as the
curses were completed.

*Magic?*

Jinwoo and the shaman made eye contact.

It sneered at him.

*It's too late, human.*

Unlike ordinary magic, curses were inescapable. Once cast, that was
the end. They'd turn him into a walking corpse primed to be slashed
into pieces by the high orc warriors' machetes. It would be the perfect
end for a human who didn't know his place.

But at that moment...

Jinwoo heard that familiar electric sound.

*Ping!*

[An irregular status condition has occurred.]
[The irregular status condition has been removed by Buff:
Immunity.]

*Ping, ping, ping!*
More alerts sounded in quick succession.

[Curse: Impediment has been removed.]
[Curse: Blindness has been removed.]
......
......

The five curses were eliminated before they could have any effect.
*Heh.*

Jinwoo was the one smiling now. This was the buff he'd received when he had first become a Player.

**[THE GREAT SPELL CASTER KANDIARU'S BLESSING]**
**Long-lasting Buff: Health and Longevity: You are immunized against all diseases, poisons, and any other debuffs. Your healing ability increases exponentially when you are asleep.**

Thanks to this blessing, Jinwoo didn't have to worry about magic that affected his physical condition, like curses.

"Wh-what?!" The shaman shuddered. As the boss of an A-rank dungeon, it immediately detected that its curses had been dispelled by some kind of force.

*How could he block curses set by me?*

It didn't make sense. In order to neutralize someone's curse, you needed purification magic or a blessing from a higher-level spell caster.

*Does that mean one of these humans is a higher-level spell caster than I am?*

Before it could ponder this any further, shooting pain from its foot caused it to screech in agony. "Aaaargh!" When it looked down, it saw that a dagger had pierced its foot. "Grrrr…"

It was Jinwoo's dagger, Knight Killer.

The shaman looked up in a murderous rage. "How dare you…!"

Jinwoo slashed at another incoming orc, then silently mouthed a message to the shaman.

*"Sit tight and wait your turn."*

In other words, don't do anything rash.

The shaman's glowering face was as red as a ripened tomato. "How dare a puny human…!" It still had the energy to get enraged.

Jinwoo's expression grew cold. In truth, he could've disposed of the shaman as soon as the battle began but hadn't because he'd wanted to instill some fear in the shaman just as it had to his fellow hunters. However, it looked like he hadn't done enough to shake the beast. Its eyes were still animated.

Well, then...

*All right. I'll give you a show.*

Time to put the power of a necromancer on full display. The Shadow Monarch regarded his surroundings as if a delicious feast had been spread out before him. Black eddies of smoke rose from the dead bodies of the high orcs like they'd been awaiting Jinwoo's call.

And call them he did.

"Arise."

**[Beginning Shadow Extraction attempt.]**

Along with the system's message came a horrible cry of death from out of nowhere.

*Gaaaaah!*

The shaman's eyes popped out. "What is this...?!" It couldn't even complete its sentence.

It was interrupted by the sight of black hands rising from the shadows of the high orc corpses.

**[Shadow Extraction successful.]**

Jinwoo smiled at the new recruits joining his shadow army.

*My warriors have become undead...!*

The shaman trembled. Fifty of its warriors had lost their lives. That was about the same number of new soldiers swathed in black armor.

*That means all his soldiers were...?*

The shaman realized that this mysterious human wasn't commanding any ordinary army. It also realized just how disadvantaged they now were.

The battle of 50 soldiers versus 150 high orcs was now an even 100 versus 100. High orc warriors who'd fought bravely against enemies more powerful than them in the past had lost the will to fight upon seeing their fallen comrades reborn as shadow soldiers.

"G-grrrr..."

"Grawr..."

"Grrr..."

The usually fearless high orc warriors were visibly falling back. This was their greatest nightmare—becoming an undead minion of the enemy instead of dying gloriously in battle and going to a warrior's heaven. Jinwoo's show of power was having its intended effect.

*It worked on the warriors, but what about the shaman?*

He examined the look on its face.

*Oh-ho.*

Jinwoo brightened.

Finally. The terror was clear in its eyes.

The shaman trembled as it recalled the one with the ability to turn the dead into shadows. There couldn't be two beings with the same power. That was him.

*That's him... Then how did we come to be here?*

As soon as the shaman became aware of "itself" and "themselves," its mind was wiped clean. The only emotion left was terror.

Jinwoo was satisfied.

*That's right. Stay just like that.*

He was saving the shaman for last. His plan to instill some fear into the shaman had been successful. He turned, smiling, then blinked as a familiar face at the cave entrance caught his attention.

*Who is that again?*

She was vaguely familiar, yet not to him. It took him a moment to remember her name. Haein Cha, one of the S-rank hunters in the Hunters Guild.

*But what is she doing here?*

Yet Jinwoo's surprise at seeing her didn't hold a candle to Haein's complete astonishment as she took in the sight of Jinwoo and his shadow soldiers.

# 6
## FANG

# 6

# FANG

*Minions?*

That was Haein's first guess upon seeing the shadow soldiers, but there were too many of them to be considered minions. Mage hunters with the ability to control minions were generally only able to command one at a time, and if a hunter could summon two, they were thought to be of the highest caliber. She wasn't aware of any summoner who could control three.

And yet how many minions were there?

*Unbelievable!*

One person had summoned over a hundred. It hadn't taken him long, either. He'd called up several dozen minions at once.

*I wouldn't have believed it if I hadn't seen it with my own eyes.*

She was Haein Cha, one of the top ten hunters in Korea, and she was blown away by his abilities. In any case…

*There's no time for this.*

She looked past the shadow soldiers to the strike squad. They appeared to be in trouble. A few of them sat on the ground as if their legs had given out. Regardless of who Jinwoo was or what he was capable of, helping him with the orcs was her top priority.

*Think quick and move fast.* Adjusting the grip on her weapon with both hands, Haein took a step forward. But then...

She made eye contact with Jinwoo. The message in his eyes was clear. He didn't need her help. *Don't get in the way and just observe.*

She couldn't understand.

*Why......?*

She knew that Jinwoo could control an entire battalion, but there were almost as many high orcs, not to mention their more powerful boss, to contend with. Plus, if Jinwoo had summoned and was orchestrating such a large force simultaneously, his mana had to be very low, if not completely depleted.

*How is he going to do this all alone?*

Haein was puzzled but willingly lowered her weapon. It wasn't just because all she had at her disposal was a pickax borrowed from the excavation team. She genuinely wanted to see what Hunter Jinwoo Sung had planned against the remaining orcs.

Her expectations were high. Her faith in him won out over any logical judgment. Her heart was strangely aflutter.

*Whew. That was close.*

Jinwoo breathed a sigh of relief at Haein's decision. This was just the beginning, and he didn't need any interruptions. He had intentionally let the boss beat Kihoon to within an inch of his life for the sole purpose of taking on all the magic beasts by himself.

*Kihoon's the type to fight until his dying breath.*

Thus, Jinwoo had fought hard against the urge to rip apart that damn shaman and made his move only after the sword finally dropped from Kihoon's hand.

It was all for this moment.

*She's got a good sense for things.*

Jinwoo was glad Haein had caught on quickly. She'd stood down without argument.

He smiled and turned.

"My shadows!" His voice echoed throughout the dungeon, and at his command, every single soldier fell back into battle stances.

*Tmp!*

For a moment, a blanket of quiet settled over the area.

Finally, Jinwoo pointed at the shaman and broke the silence. "Go."

Over a hundred shadow soldiers stampeded toward the trembling high orc warriors.

*Thud, thud, thud, thud!*

The ground, the cave, and the eyes of those watching all shook as the soldiers charged.

* * *

Jinchul dashed through the dungeon as fast as he could.

"Huff, huff, huff!" His breathing was labored from running. Once he caught his breath, he straightened up and saw a woman with short hair standing at the entrance of the boss's lair.

He recognized her at once.

*Haein Cha......*

Was there any other female hunter with that formidable a presence? *But what is she doing just standing there?*

Thinking it strange that she wasn't joining the fight, he approached her. As he did, he was finally able to take in the scene inside the lair.

"Wh-what is...?"

Soldiers in black armor were slaughtering the high orcs.

"G-graaahhh!"

"Gah!"

"Guuuuh!"

Jinchul's ears rang from their screams. It might have been less shocking had there been only humanoid soldiers, but one of them was rather large for a person, quite a few were black bears that seemed to be giving off smoke, and there also seemed to be several high orcs clad in black armor.

"Long time no see, Manager Woo."

"Oh, yes. It's been a while. Do you know what those things are? They don't look like magic beasts......"

"They're minions summoned by that man." Haein pointed out Jinwoo in the fray.

Jinchul took off his sunglasses and watched Jinwoo fight among his soldiers. He was using two daggers to break through the crowd of orcs.

*The more I watch him, the more he appears to be a high-level brawler.*

Yet, he seemed capable of using summoning magic as well. Jinchul's theory was proven right as Jinwoo's lips moved and a few dozen more minions spawned from the ground.

"Good heavens!" Jinchul's jaw dropped.

How many was Jinwoo able to produce?

*If this is Hunter Sung's ability...*

Jinchul couldn't close his mouth. Had President Go already recognized this talent in Jinwoo? If so, Jinchul understood President Go's keen interest in him.

Haein eventually tore her eyes away from Jinwoo to question Jinchul. "May I ask what you're doing here, Manager Woo...? Was the Surveillance Team already contacted by our guild?"

Jinchul worked to conceal his shock from Haein. "No, we happened to be nearby and detected abnormal activity from this gate, so we wanted to evacuate the strike squad..."

Jinchul turned his attention back to Jinwoo. "But I guess we didn't need to."

He was witnessing Jinwoo's abilities for the first time. The hunter was clearing an A-rank dungeon all by himself. The man didn't need anyone's help.

"Yes. I think it's best if we stay out of the way," Haein agreed.

There was no room for anyone else in this fight, not even an S-rank hunter.

"Do you know him?" Haein asked.

Jinchul had asked about Jinwoo's ability, not his identity. Jinchul was also a member of the association, which was currently keeping information regarding Jinwoo under lock and key.

*Maybe Manager Woo knows something about him?*

Haein was correct.

"I know a little bit."

"Who… Who exactly is he?"

Jinchul put his sunglasses back on. "I'm afraid that's classified information."

* * *

The shaman was enraged. When it had first spawned in this place, there had been but a single command in its mind.

*"Hunt humans!"*

But look at what had become of them. For a mere human to destroy its whole tribe? That wasn't possible. No, that must not be possible.

As the shaman watched its warriors being slaughtered, its eyes began glowing red.

*Damn insects! I'll stomp on you all!*

If its curses wouldn't work on the enemy, then it would have to face them after blessing itself.

"Song of Rage! Song of Strength! Song of Giants! Song of Dragon Fire!" With the spells cast, the shaman grew until it was close to ten meters tall. Vigor flowed through its body as its strength, agility, stamina, and confidence all shot up. Soon, the shaman was swiping away shadow soldiers with its huge arms. It then took a deep breath and…

*Fwwwoooo!*

The shaman spewed out a blackish-red flame.

*Fwooshhh!*

The dragon fire vaporized enemies in the blink of an eye. No soldier touched by the flames was spared. If they didn't lose their whole body, they were unable to fight because a limb had disintegrated. A second blast of fire immediately followed the first.

Seeing its attacks mowing down so many soldiers, the shaman roared confidently. "Do you still think I, Kargalgan, am no match for you?!"

The answer came from above its head.

"Yup."

Startled, the shaman hastily erected a shielding spell as it looked up, but Jinwoo was faster. He punched the top of the beast's skull.

*Wham!*

*Krak!*

The shaman's head slammed into the ground. It left a spiderweb of cracks in the cave floor. Jinwoo already had experience in literally sending someone flying with his bare fist—he'd knocked off Vulcan's, who'd been much bigger than the shaman.

**[You have defeated the master of the dungeon.]**

*Tmp.*

As soon as Jinwoo landed lightly on the ground, he got a couple of consecutive messages containing good news.

*Ping!*

**[You have leveled up!]**

"Hell yeah!" Jinwoo pumped his fist. He'd leveled up once when fighting with the Stealth skill activated, once when clearing the high orcs in the lair, and one final time when defeating the boss. He'd leveled up three times for clearing this A-rank dungeon. This result was beyond his expectations.

He felt grateful to Yoonsuk for offering him another job today.

*Awesome.*

Jinwoo cheerfully made his way over to the boss. The shaman's body, which had been enlarged using magic, was now back to its original size.

Jinwoo noted the sizable essence stone lodged in the necklace around its neck but had no desire to keep it.

*I've already gotten all these experience points.*

This was the Hunters Guild's dungeon. If he needed an essence stone from an A-rank dungeon, he could get one from a location he himself had acquired legally. Jinwoo was actually after something else—the black smoke emerging from the shaman's body.

*Gulp.*

Jinwoo swallowed anxiously. His mind flashed back to how he'd failed at extracting Barca's shadow in the red gate.

*But I've changed since then.*

Back then, it hadn't been easy defeating Barca because he hadn't had much experience. He'd struggled even with the assistants from the knight ranks, Igris and Iron. However, he'd finished off the shaman easily.

It was the result of the week he'd spent in the Demon's Castle. This proved that enduring those grueling seven days had been worth it.

Jinwoo uttered the command to the billowing black smoke. "Arise."

He felt a chilly breeze sting his cheeks and instinctively knew that it had worked.

*Success!*

A smile blossomed on his lips.

*Graaaaaaaahhh!*

A hooded mage burst forth from the shaman's shadow with an ear-piercing shriek.

*What?*

Jinwoo sensed something peculiar had occurred and checked the mage's info screen.

### [?? LV.1]
### Elite Knight Rank

*Elite knight?*

Until now, he'd only ever seen three confirmed ranks for the shadow soldiers—regular, elite, and knight rank. This was the first time he'd met one that was an elite knight rank. Jinwoo surmised that this was a level higher than Igris and Iron's knight rank.

*This one's magic power is definitely stronger than theirs.*

It was appropriate for a shadow soldier born of a boss of an A-rank dungeon.

*Ping!*

**[Please choose a name.]**

Like before, the system requested he name the new soldier, as his rank was that of a knight or higher.

*A name......*

Although he couldn't see them because the mage wore a hooded robe that covered most of his face, high orcs were known for their long fangs.

*Fang it is.*

With Jinwoo's decision made, the name automatically registered with the system.

**[FANG LV.1]**
**Elite Knight Rank**

The name replaced the question marks. Considering how narcissistic the shaman had been right up until its death, it would have been absolutely aghast to hear its new moniker. Oh well. It was already dead anyway.

Jinwoo contently recalled his shadow soldiers. He could now store 130 shadows, but that unfortunately meant having to release the rest into the void.

*I've done enough for today.*

When he dropped down from the altar with a smile, many people swarmed around him, including the strike squad hunters, Haein, and some men in black. There was a familiar face among the men in suits.

*When did Manager Woo get here?*

Judging by the look on his face, Jinchul had also been witness to the shadow soldiers.

"Jinwoo."

"Hunter Sung."

"Mr. Luggage?"

Different people called out to Jinwoo at once, and they stopped to eye one another warily.

Since Jinwoo didn't have to hide his powers any longer, he'd enjoyed being able to go all out, but……

*How am I going to slip away from here?*

Jinwoo scratched the back of his head as he glanced around at the people surrounding him.

Jinchul made the first move. While the others were busy sizing up the competition, he situated himself next to Jinwoo and presented his ID to the other hunters.

"I'm from the Association's Surveillance Team."

No matter their rank, the mere mention of the Surveillance Team made hunters nervous, so this was an effective strategy. Everyone from the Hunters Guild, with the exception of Haein, felt a flash of apprehension. Jinchul smoothly took advantage of the situation.

"The association is managing Hunter Jinwoo Sung's case, so all matters relating to him are to be considered extremely confidential."

Jinwoo was impressed by Jinchul's acting. He was half-convinced that Jinchul had rehearsed these exact facial expressions and lines in front of a mirror, but he quickly picked up on what Jinchul was trying to do. In fact, Jinchul's eyes sent a signal to Jinwoo.

*I'll help you out of here.*

Jinwoo had no idea why the Surveillance Team was helping him, but he wasn't about to look a gift horse in the mouth. He nodded. This was what he wanted anyway.

Jinchul's subordinates caught on quickly and wasted no time encircling Jinwoo.

"If you have any questions, please submit them through the association. We will escort Hunter Jinwoo Sung out."

It was heavily implied that Jinchul wouldn't tolerate any opposition. His steely resolve rendered those from the Hunters Guild speechless, even though they had much to say to and ask Jinwoo.

"Please come with us."

The Surveillance Team led Jinwoo past the other hunters.

*I appreciate the help, but......*

It all felt strange. Why was Jinchul doing him a favor he hadn't asked for?

Jinwoo waited until they'd put some distance between themselves and the others before quietly asking, "Why are you suddenly helping me?"

"May I ask if you're planning to join the Hunters Guild?"

Jinwoo shook his head.

Jinchul quickly gave his explanation without missing a beat, as if he'd already known Jinwoo's answer.

"You just demonstrated that you possess powers higher than those of an S-rank hunter in front of members of the largest and richest guild in Korea. This was the best option if you want to avoid a big fuss."

True, no one knew the lengths to which the boundless Hunters Guild would go to in order to acquire another S-rank hunter. Although other S-rank hunters would welcome this opportunity with open arms, Jinwoo wouldn't.

The Hunter's Association was in the same boat. With the association trying to prevent a specific guild from upsetting the balance of power and Jinwoo trying to get a specific guild off his back, their desires aligned. Jinwoo would've been uncomfortable had this put him in the association's debt, but it turned out that both sides were benefiting.

*The association is making my life easier.*

The serendipitous situation brought a little smile to Jinwoo's face. Just as they were about to exit the boss's lair...

"W-wait!"

An urgent yell came from behind them.

Jinwoo inadvertently turned to see Kihoon heading toward him with the help of a bigger colleague. His wounds had been properly tended to, but his face was still pale from the loss of blood.

*He shouldn't even be on his feet.*

Nevertheless, Kihoon stood before him now. He bowed his head to Jinwoo.

"Thank you." He bared his heart. "We're safe because of you, Hunter Sung. I thank you on behalf of the entire strike squad."

If the Surveillance Team was to be believed, there had been a good reason for Jinwoo to keep his identity hidden.

*Considering the extent of his powers, that makes sense.*

Yet…Jinwoo had helped Kihoon and his squad at the risk of revealing himself. What's more, he hadn't asked for anything in return. He could've insisted on the carcasses of the magic beasts or charged a fee for saving their lives, but he'd instead left without a word.

How could Kihoon convey his utmost respect?

"…Thank you…!" Overcome with emotion, Kihoon bowed deeply. His body screamed in pain, but he endured it for the moment. He'd choked up seeing Jinwoo give the magic beast a taste of his own medicine, punishing an orc in the same manner he'd been abused. When he thought back to that moment, Kihoon felt like he couldn't thank him enough.

The other members of the strike squad finally snapped out of their haze as they watched their squad leader bow.

*If it wasn't for Jinwoo……*

*He's our savior, isn't he?*

*We shouldn't be standing here, staring at them like a bunch of idiots.*

They jostled one another in their rush toward Jinwoo and also bowed.

"Thank you so much, Mr. Lugg…I mean, Hunter Sung."

"Seriously, if it wasn't for you……"

"Thanks to you, my wife isn't a widow!"

The young hunter who'd joked about his hands shaking when Kihoon called off the raid approached Jinwoo with tears in his eyes. "Hunter

Sung…because I'm so grateful for what you've done…may I give you a hug?"

"Okay, that's too far."

"There he goes again. Someone stop him, please."

"Then I'll go for a hug from you!"

*Hwoomp!*

"Gah! Let go of me—you're creeping me out!"

"Ha-ha-ha-ha!"

The squad members laughed for the first time since entering the A-rank dungeon.

Jinwoo watched their interactions, content. He hadn't done this for compliments or thanks, but their genuine feelings warmed his heart.

"Oh." Jinwoo walked over to the female healer cheering on the side.

*I almost didn't see her in the back of the group because she's so small.*

He returned the notebook she'd given him earlier. Blushing, she shyly took it with both hands.

"Th-thank you……" As she did, she mentally berated her past self.

*Geez, I wish I hadn't told him anything.*

It was just one more embarrassing incident that would keep her up at night. How laughable she must have seemed for giving a notebook containing her last will and testament to the luggage carrier who'd made easy work of the boss? She peeked up at him and was relieved that Jinwoo wasn't laughing at her.

Instead, he spoke to her in a rather firm voice. "Miss Healer."

"Yes?" She perked up like a kid in class being called on by the teacher.

"Please keep your personal items out of the strike squad's gear going forward. It makes it heavier."

"O-okay?" She stared at him, speechless.

Jinwoo grinned. He'd said everything he wanted to say, and it looked like the hunters had done so as well. He turned nonchalantly and walked away from the dumbfounded healer.

"Let's go." Jinwoo was accompanied out by the Surveillance Team.

There had been one other person, though.

*Oh......*

Haein was the only one who hadn't gotten a chance to talk to Jinwoo. She'd reached out a hand to stop him but had decided against it.

*I wanted to ask for his number, but......*

She only wanted to request a bit of his time. However, talking to him at this point, when his situation seemed unclear, might only lead to further complications.

Just then...a female mage approached her. "Ummm... Vice President?"

"Yes?"

She gestured at Haein's hand. "Why are you holding a pickax?"

Haein grew redder and redder as she stared at the head of the pickax. She set it down and asked, "Do you think that made me look weird?"

The mage cocked her head. "Depends on who you ask, I guess?"

Haein's neck flushed as well.

Just outside the gate, Jinchul looked at his watch and turned to Jinwoo. "We're planning to return to the association... If you're free, would you like to come with us and have dinner with President Go?"

"What time is it now?"

"It's a quarter past five."

*Hmm......*

It'd be close, but he could still make it in time to his meeting with Jinho.

Still, Jinwoo politely declined Jinchul's invitation. "Thank you, but I already have plans."

\* \* \*

*Inhale...exhale...* Jinho tried to keep his composure by taking deep breaths like he'd seen in a movie.

*My destiny will be decided soon.*

Jinwoo's choice would decide his fate. He was antsier and more jittery than when he'd confronted his father regarding Yoojin Guild a few days ago.

*I need to go back to the basics... The basics...*

It was no coincidence that Jinho had asked to meet in the same café where he'd first presented his proposal to Jinwoo.

*If it wasn't for the boss's help, I wouldn't have come this far.*

When he looked around the store with that thought in mind, he couldn't help but feel a wave of nostalgia. He even happened to be sitting at the same table as well.

*Ting-a-ling.*

The door chime sounded, and Jinwoo strode in.

"Boss!" Jinho sprang to his feet, beaming and greeting Jinwoo with a sharp bow.

Jinwoo nodded in greeting, and Jinho waited until the boss sat down across from him before also taking a seat.

"So, what's up?"

Jinho blinked as he looked up. "Boss, your clothes...?"

"Oh, this?" Jinwoo had come straight from the battle with the high orcs, so his clothes weren't the cleanest. There was a tiny splatter of orc blood on his shirt, too.

Jinwoo seemed unbothered. "I came here straight from a dungeon."

*Whoa!*

Jinho was caught by surprise once again. He felt so inadequate compared to this man. After getting his guild master's license, he'd spent his free time drinking. But the boss? Despite how powerful he already was, he continued to train inside dungeons whenever he had the time.

Jinho was ashamed of himself.

*He's really amazing......*

He had an infinite amount of respect for Jinwoo as well. He figured Jinwoo walked around in battle-stained clothes because he was confident enough not to feel like he needed to hide his training process.

*He wears it proudly like a badge.*

Jinho's expression hardened. Whatever Jinwoo ended up deciding, Jinho was prepared to follow him, no questions asked. So he needed to be completely honest.

"Boss, the thing is......" Jinho told him every last detail about what had gone down between him and his father that day. This included Myunghwan Ko's testimony regarding who had saved the hunters of the White Tiger Guild in the red gate.

*Well, that was unnecessary......*

Still, Jinwoo couldn't be angry, since Myunghwan had done it for Jinwoo's benefit. No wonder Jinho seemed pretty excited when talking about the red gate.

In any case, Jinwoo understood what Jinho was trying to say.

"You need me in order to be named the guild master of Yoojin Guild, right?"

Jinho had said his piece, so he awaited Jinwoo's answer with composure. He didn't joke around or attempt any sweet talk like he usually did. He was prepared to accept Jinwoo's decision for what it was.

Jinwoo was lost in thought as deep as Jinho's agony. He eventually raised his head.

"Jinho, I..."

*Gulp.*

Jinho's mouth went dry.

* * *

Jongin, the president of the Hunters Guild, received a phone call. He abandoned the work he had been doing in order to yell in his private office.

"What? Jinwoo Sung was at our raids yesterday and today?"

The newly revealed S-rank hunter... How had Jongin not known that he'd appeared in the midst of his own guild? He'd basically squandered an opportunity that had been handed directly to him.

Jongin was frustrated, but... "Pardon? He was on the excavation team yesterday and the luggage carrier today?"

That explained how he'd slipped under Jongin's radar.

*Putting his motives aside......*

He felt that speculating over Jinwoo's motives would only lead to a dead end and a headache. That wasn't important right now anyway.

*Following the White Tiger Guild, the Hunters also received his help.*

They were deeply indebted to him. Jongin had wanted to be on equal footing with Jinwoo when recruiting him, but now the Hunters were in the same position as White Tiger.

*Still, I'm lucky to have found out about the tenth S-rank hunter before everyone else.*

Right. More important than this debt were Jinwoo's abilities.

"So what hunter class is Jinwoo Sung?"

**"Well......"**

Jongin gradually found himself at a loss for words as he listened intently. The person he was speaking with was Kihoon, the leader of today's strike squad. He wasn't the type of person to make up stories or exaggerate details.

But Jongin had to ask, "Is that the truth?"

**"Yes. That's everything I saw."**

*Everything he saw...? Does that mean there might be even more to Jinwoo?*

If Jinwoo was that strong......

"How would you say he compares to me...?" It was a bit of a childish question, but it was also a good way to measure a hunter's abilities.

Kihoon responded hesitantly.

**"Could you clear a higher-level A-rank dungeon by yourself, sir?"**

"......That would be impossible."

**"But he managed it. He even rejected Hunter Cha's assistance."**

*Haein was there, too?*

Jongin wondered what she'd been doing there, but that wasn't a big concern at the moment.

"Is it possible that it was a lower-level A-rank dungeon?"

**"If so, we should've been able to handle it. That man saved us all."**

"......"

Jongin Choi was the man known as the Ultimate Hunter. What

Kihoon said could have been interpreted as insulting, but rather than angering him, it made his heart pound.

*Haein Cha, Jinwoo Sung, and me.*

Depending on how powerful Jinwoo was, there was an opportunity to finally make the Hunters the most famous guild in all of Korea, all of Asia, and perhaps even the world.

**"President Choi, it's not my place to say anything about how to run the guild, but..."**

Kihoon also wasn't the type of person to step out of line and grumble about the guild. Jongin's curiosity was piqued.

"It's okay. Please go ahead."

**"That man... Please recruit Hunter Sung for our guild. I think he'll be able to help you achieve your dream."**

*Ba-dump.*

Jongin's heart skipped a beat. He attempted to hide the trembling of his voice.

"I'll try my best."

\* \* \*

Outside the headquarters of the Hunter's Association of Korea, a long line of reporters waited to interview Minsung. *Minsung Lee, Asia's superstar, becomes hunter!* It wouldn't be an exaggeration to say that reporters from all over the country were here. They jostled and jockeyed for a position, fighting fiercely for real estate.

"Hello? That's our spot."

"Come on! Do you see how many people are here? There's no claiming spots. Where you're standing *is* your spot."

"Hmph...!"

Reporters spilled onto the road. Minsung watched all this through a window from inside the association building with a huge grin on his face.

"Yeah, that's about the right amount." He'd taken time off to attract more attention, and his tactic was paying off.

"Hey, Minsung, what do you think of the headline for tomorrow's newspaper?" The reporter from the bestselling newspaper in Korea showed Minsung the article that would be featured on the front page.

"It's a bit dull, wouldn't you say?"

"You think so?"

"Hmm... How about this—'Minsung Lee, The Man Who Has it All, Now Has Superhuman Strength in His Grasp'?"

"Won't a headline that bold offend readers?"

"It's not like any of it is a lie. Besides, who in Korea would talk trash about me when my fans and the media have their eyes on everything?"

"Okay, then I'll go with that headline."

"Please and thank you." Minsung politely thanked the reporter but sneered as soon as he left the room.

*Why bother talking back to me when he's just gonna do what I say in the end?*

At that moment, two imported luxury-brand cars pulled into the parking lot of the association.

*Tmp.*

*Tmp.*

Yoonho Baek of the White Tiger Guild and Jongin Choi of the Hunters Guild got out of their cars almost simultaneously.

"Huh? Look!"

"It's Yoonho Baek!"

"Jongin Choi is here, too!"

The reporters who were blocking the front entrance now scurried over to the two guild masters.

They both frowned.

*What are these? Reporters?*

*Why are there so many people here today?*

*Ka-shak, ka-shak, ka-shak!*

Cameras flashed as reporters surrounded the two men and bombarded them with questions.

"Are you two here to recruit Minsung Lee for your guilds?"

"As the hunters who represent Korea, do you think Minsung will retire as an actor?"

"What rank do you think Minsung will get?"

"Please tell us what you think about Minsung!"

Short-tempered Yoonho waved them away, clearly annoyed. "I'm not here for him. I've got nothing to say."

Jongin stated the facts without an ounce of emotion in his voice. "Everyone in the industry knows that Mr. Lee has already signed with the Reapers Guild. I'm here on other business."

The reporters turned around, unhappy they hadn't received the answers they wanted.

*What the heck?*

*There's no story here.*

*I got excited for nothing.*

They couldn't exactly complain in front of the two S-rank hunters, though. Instead, they took their spots again waiting for Minsung.

Yoonho and Jongin eyed each other once they were left alone.

Yoonho spoke first. "I hear the Hunters were also in a spot of trouble." He strongly emphasized "also."

"It wasn't as bad as losing an A-rank newbie."

The tension between the two men was as heated as that among the reporters.

Yoonho, who'd gotten worked up, paused and then sighed. "In any case, he helped out both White Tiger and the Hunters."

"And thank goodness he did. Our guild's entire second elite squad would be dead if it wasn't for him."

Their avoidance of saying his name was yet another unspoken fight between the two.

Jongin took a step closer to Yoonho. "That's why it's my moral obligation to recruit the man for our guild."

Yoonho didn't back down. He leaned in close enough to Jongin that their foreheads touched. "We lost some of our members. Shouldn't we get him as compensation to fill out our ranks?"

"Why do you need an S rank for that? What're you planning to do, invade North Korea or something?"

"And you? Since when do you care that much about morals?"

Sparks flew between the two.

*Huh?*

Taegyu Lim, the master of the Reapers Guild, arrived on the scene right on time for the press conference. He smirked at the sight of two grown men locked in a staring contest. What should he say? Would this be like counting chickens before they'd hatched? Taegyu was feeling giddy because White Tiger and the Hunters always tended to snatch up the talented hunters.

He tried to repress his smile as he walked toward them. "Hey, Mr. Presidents. Are you fighting over our Minsung?"

Yoonho and Jongin both turned toward Taegyu at the same time.

*What's with this crazy old man?*

*I already said I didn't care about Minsung or Mingoon or whatever his name is.*

Taegyu instinctively took a step back at their glowers.

*Sheesh, what's gotten into these two?*

\* \* \*

"What? Jongin Choi and Yoonho Baek are here, too?"

Minsung grinned. He already knew the other man out there with them, President Lim. They'd met when he signed his contract.

There was a reason he'd signed with the Reapers, despite them being on the decline, instead of aiming for one of the top two guilds.

*I want people to think I'm a champion of the weak.*

For entertainers, public image was everything, and Minsung was a pro at managing and cultivating the exact image he desired.

*I can't believe the best guilds in Korea are fighting over me......*

Minsung wasn't planning to be a hunter for very long, but he couldn't help but bask in the moment.

Soon, his manager entered the room. "Minsung, everything's set. Time for the press conference."

"All right."

His manager led the way. Once the glass doors of the association opened, Minsung emerged and basked in the camera flashes.

*Ka-shak, ka-shak, ka-shak!*

Minsung aimed his usual fake smile at the hundreds of lenses focused on him.

That was the precise moment Jinwoo arrived at the association headquarters.

*......?*

He'd returned three days later as directed.

*What's with all these people?*

It didn't look like he'd get inside at this time. Of course, he had other ways, such as using the Stealth skill, jumping over the reporters' heads, or using the back door. He'd made an appointment in advance for his reevaluation, though, and wasn't too keen on the idea of going out of his way to find another entrance when the door was right there.

*It's not like I'm committing a crime.*

There was no reason he shouldn't use the front door. Jinwoo had to push his way through the crowd of reporters on the sidewalk in front of the association. "Excuse me, pardon me..."

"Oh, c'mon!"

"What the hell?"

"What's with him?"

Reporters raised their eyebrows as they were helplessly pushed aside, powerless against an S rank. Jinwoo was able to clear a path in no time and made it onto the steps, but a burly man blocked his way before he could take another step.

"Hey!" It was Minsung's manager. He glared at Jinwoo as he yelled, "Who the hell are you? You an employee of the association?"

Jinwoo shook his head without breaking eye contact.

*Oh-ho, look at the balls on this guy.*

The manager's eye twitched. "Don't you see all these reporters here?"

Jinwoo briefly looked over his shoulder at the reporters. They seemed to be disgruntled at him. Jinwoo deduced they were there for a press conference, but it wasn't like the path to the entrance was a part of the press conference area, was it? It was common courtesy not to interfere with a reporter, but neither should reporters get in a civilian's way.

With so many people watching, Jinwoo wanted to be on his way without causing a commotion. But then...

"Take the back entrance. You can't go this way. Move, asshole." The manager blocked Jinwoo's path again and shoved him.

Jinwoo's eyes changed.

*What's this?*

The manager was startled. He was a D-rank awakened being and a brawler. He shoved Jinwoo, hoping to embarrass him in front of everyone, but Jinwoo didn't budge. The manager had used enough strength to really hurt an ordinary person. Jinwoo could tell this was the case.

"......" He silently stared down the manager, whose face was growing pale.

"What? What are they doing?"

"What's going on? Are they about to fight?"

Sensing the gravity of the situation, the reporters began murmuring among themselves.

The manager broke out in a cold sweat. If no one was watching, he'd simply have backed down and stepped aside, but not only did he have all these reporters' eyes on him, his employer, Minsung, was also watching everything.

Minsung approached with a frown and quietly whispered to him, "Come on—get rid of this guy and wrap it up."

"Uh... O-okay." The manager feared he'd lose his job if he botched this. He scrunched his face up and yelled, "I said you can't go this way! Get out of here!"

"Who told you he couldn't go this way?"

*What?*

The voice came from behind him. The manager turned.

President Go of the Hunter's Association of Korea stood just outside the glass doors. His presence was so surprising that everyone even forgot to get pictures.

"Gunhee Go?"

"President Go?"

The boisterous crowd fell silent at his unexpected appearance. President Go approached the steps and spoke. "This man is a guest of the association."

He looked at Minsung. "Do you remember who authorized this press conference, Mr. Lee?"

Minsung snapped to attention. "O-of course."

What if he fell out of favor with the president of the association and had his press conference canceled on his first day as a hunter? He couldn't let that happen with so many eyes on him. Minsung signaled with a look for his manager to step aside, and he bowed to Jinwoo and the president in turn.

"Please come, Hunter Sung."

The reporters couldn't hide their confusion at the sight of President Go leading Jinwoo into the building.

"What was that?"

"Who was that man? Why is the president of the association helping him?"

"Does anyone know anything about him?"

No one had any answers for the increasingly loud and frustrated reporters.

Minsung was fuming. First, there was the man who'd made a huge deal of shoving through the reporters; then, there was President Go himself, who'd personally escorted the man inside.

"What's on the president's agenda today?"

"I heard he cleared his morning schedule!"

"Did he do it for that guy?"

Two surprise appearances in one morning threatened to plunge everything into chaos, making things hardly conducive to a successful press
conference. But Minsung had gone out of his way to set this up today.
He gritted his teeth at his manager.

*That fucker can't do a single thing right.*

The manager dropped his head, not daring to look at Minsung. Since
Minsung had become an A-rank awakened being, he outclassed the
manager in the physical strength department, so the weaker man had
no choice but to prostrate himself.

......

Minsung glowered at him for a bit before finally turning away.

"And action!"

*Gah!*

To add insult to injury, a TV camera was about to roll—and for a
live broadcast, no less. All his work to boost his image by becoming an
A-rank hunter would end in vain if this chaotic scene was broadcast live
to the people of Korea. President Go's appearance had shattered any
interest in his proper press conference.

Why did he have to show up at such a critical moment...?

*Isn't there a way to turn this all around?*

His sly brain began to spin.

*That's it. Flip the script by giving them something even bigger to talk
about.*

The reporters weren't here because they were curious about how
Minsung felt before the evaluation. They'd come to find out superstar
Minsung's hunter rank and what his first move would be after getting
his license. If Minsung provided them with the answers they were looking for, everything would get back on track.

*I need to get the evaluation sooner than I planned.*

There was a cunning smile on his face. People who knew him would
say this type of quick thinking was his forte.

"Ummm, please stand by. I'm going to talk to the association about
today's schedule."

He excused himself to the reporters and walked toward the association building to notify those in charge about a change in the schedule. He had no intention of discussing things with them.

*Considering how much money my father gives the association, they should be accommodating me.*

But...

*Huh?*

Right before Minsung could push open the glass door, a group of Surveillance Team hunters exited the building and pushed him back. They stood in a row, blocking the entrance to the building.

*What's all this now?*

Minsung's brow furrowed. He read the name tag on one man's chest.

*Jinchul Woo, Korean Hunter's Association's Surveillance Team Manager?*

Minsung addressed him. "What's going on? Why are you blocking the entrance?"

Jinchul looked down at Minsung, sunglasses perched on his face.

"Another awakened being's rank reevaluation is in progress. No one is allowed inside the building until the reevaluation is completed at around eleven o'clock."

"What?!"

Was this other awakened being the man who had gone inside with the president of the association? Minsung checked his watch. It was ten thirty in the morning. His appointment for the evaluation was at eleven.

No one was allowed inside until then? His plan to turn his situation around by getting the evaluation earlier was now ruined.

At first, he spoke to them politely. "Please, sir, if you could be so kind as to let me in, I have something to discuss with the person in charge."

"Sorry." Jinchul gave a curt response.

Minsung was frustrated. He couldn't stand it any longer, and his true colors began to show. "Do you know who I am? I'm Minsung, Minsung Lee." Minsung's tone was rude, but Jinchul didn't budge.

"Haaah..." Jinchul exhaled.

"Hey, do you know who the biggest sponsor of the Hunter's

Association is? Yoojin Construction! That's who!" Minsung sneered. "Wongyu Lee, the vice president of Yoojin Construction, is my father. And you see those people over there?"

He pointed at the reporters all along the bottom of the steps. "How can you treat the son of the vice president of Yoojin Construction like this with so many reporters watching? Are you prepared for the consequences?"

Jinchul's answer was simple. "Yes, I am."

"What?" Minsung was floored.

Who the heck was that man who prompted a mere managerial employee to be so resolute? Why had the president of the association escorted him into the building, and why was the association sealing off the building for his rank evaluation?

Minsung placed his hands on his hips and interrogated Jinchul. "Who's that other awakened being? Why is the association so protective of him?"

Finally, Jinchul took off his sunglasses. "If I told you that…"

*Shudder.*

Jinchul's big, bright, beast-like eyes caused Minsung to step back instinctively. He continued in a low voice, staring Minsung right in the eyes the entire time.

"…would *you* be prepared for the consequences, Mr. Minsung Lee?"

* * *

It was quiet inside the building. There was no one in the waiting room save for the occasional staff member passing through. This appeared to be for the same reason all those reporters were gathered outside.

"This way, please."

"All right."

Inside the special evaluation room, Jinwoo was met by a couple of familiar faces.

*Huh?*

Yoonho and Jongin were sitting in the lounge across the way, the same area where the guild scouts had been clustered three days ago when he'd first come to be reevaluated.

The two men trained their eyes on Jinwoo, simultaneously standing and nodding. Jinwoo nodded at them as he passed by.

President Go had a slight smile on his face as they made their way down the quiet hallway. "The two of them have been waiting over an hour for you, Hunter Sung."

The guild masters of the two representative guilds of South Korea had come an hour in advance to await the result of his reevaluation?

President Go continued mildly, as if he'd read Jinwoo's mind. "You're the first S-rank hunter to come around in two years. Plus, Jongin knows about your abilities, so he's probably more anxious."

Jinwoo nodded his understanding.

"Oh my."

"Mr. President."

The employees of the association marveled at Jinwoo as they greeted President Go.

*Who's this man with the president? Why is the president personally escorting him?*

*Is he someone powerful?*

*How does this young man know President Go?*

The employees were taken aback, as President Go had never been a guide for any guests before, not even governmental ministers who had visited the association.

The elder hunter looked straight ahead as he talked with Jinwoo. "I heard about what happened yesterday."

President Go spoke about the incident with some relish. He was genuinely excited. He'd rightly predicted that Jinwoo would be different from other hunters. When Jinchul had described Jinwoo's performance, it had thrilled him as much as if he'd been there. He was impressed by Jinwoo's abilities, but more than that, he liked how Jinwoo had handled the whole situation.

Even though Jinwoo had cleared the entire dungeon, including the boss, mostly on his own, he hadn't asked for any rewards. If Jinwoo's real purpose was to fight against magic beasts rather than gain money and fame, the association was ready to support him wholeheartedly. After all, his purpose aligned with the reason behind the establishment of the association.

*I'll do everything in my power to recruit him.*

But how could he? By joining the association, Jinwoo would forgo the opportunity to battle magic beasts.

President Go had learned about Jinwoo's power only yesterday. His abilities were too good to be wasted outside of dungeons.

Finally, they arrived at the evaluation room located deeper inside the building.

"Before the reevaluation, we are going to classify you based on your abilities."

Jinwoo had been expecting this. Hunters were separated among brawler, mage, healer, support-type, and countless other categories depending on their abilities and were assigned jobs accordingly.

Another employee was waiting in the evaluation room. He bowed at President Go before directing Jinwoo. "This way, please."

Jinwoo stood in the middle of the evaluation room, which was pretty much a spacious gymnasium that could be observed easily and had walls and flooring protected by powerful magic. It had been built this way in case of accidents.

The evaluators began their assessment. "What kind of abilities can you use?"

President Go watched with interest from a corner of the room. This was why he'd personally escorted Jinwoo. He wanted to see Jinwoo's abilities with his own eyes as soon as possible.

"I can do this..." Jinwoo summoned one of his shadow soldiers.

"Whoa!" The evaluators flinched.

Who wouldn't have, seeing a soldier in black armor suddenly spawn from the ground? Jinwoo had called on the lowest level among his regular-rank soldiers, but even it was too much to handle for the average person.

"Is that...a minion? You can command minions?" The evaluator's voice was shaky.

Jinwoo wanted to explain that his soldier wasn't dangerous. He felt bad for the evaluator.

"......Well, I guess they're similar to that?"

"Th-then how many minions can you summon?"

*I guess I can't lie.*

There were more than twenty witnesses who'd seen all of Jinwoo's shadow soldiers when he'd summoned them in the A-rank dungeon. Jinwoo underreported the number of shadow soldiers he had stored.

"About a hundred..."

The evaluator's eyes grew huge at the number. "A h-hundred?"

"Yes." Meanwhile, Jinwoo remained calm.

President Go's eyes twinkled as he examined the shadow soldier.

*A hundred more like that one......*

The soldier seemed to have a level of magic power similar to a B-rank hunter. A person with a hundred of these would be powerful enough to best a large guild. This was a fantastic ability.

Jinwoo could feel Go's fiery gaze on him. He was relieved by everyone's reactions.

*If this is how they respond to just one regular-rank soldier......*

It was a good thing Jinwoo hadn't summoned Igris, his highest-rank soldier, or Fang, whom he had captured only yesterday. This was enough to prove what kind of ability Jinwoo had.

"Then...Hunter Sung is a mage." The evaluator looked satisfied as he took down a few notes. "Now, please step inside the measurement room."

\* \* \*

Jinwoo was handed a new hunter's license.

\*   \*   \*

JINWOO SUNG, S RANK, MAGE CLASS

Jinwoo couldn't believe it, despite seeing his own picture on the license.

*Nice. Everything's working out for me.*

He tucked away the hunter's license in his wallet.

When he got to the end of the hallway, Yoonho and Jongin were waiting for him.

"Jinwoo, a moment of your time?"

"Hunter Sung."

"I'm sorry. I've got some errands to run." Jinwoo brushed past them and walked toward the door.

"Um, Jinwoo?" Yoonho sounded worried. "If I were you, I wouldn't go out that way."

*Because you have an offer I can't refuse?*

Jinwoo wasn't interested, so he pushed open the glass door despite Yoonho's warning.

As he did…

*Ka-shak, ka-shak, ka-shak, ka-shak, ka-shak, ka-shak!*

Reporters were at the top of the steps arguing with the Surveillance Team hunters while taking pictures.

*What the hell is going on?*

Jinwoo was at a loss for words as his eyes were blinded by camera flashes.

\* \* \*

Jinah bought some banana-flavored milk from the cafeteria right after third period as per usual. There was still about an hour left until lunchtime. She wouldn't be able to focus in class on an empty stomach, so a drink was better than nothing.

Right on cue…

*Rrrumble.*

Her stomach was screaming at her for some fuel. As Jinah approached the classroom rubbing her empty stomach, one of her friends excitedly called out to her.

"J-Jinah!"

"Huh? What?"

Her friend's excitement was infectious.

"Your big brother! He's on TV!"

"What? Why is he on TV?"

Jinah's heart sank. Did he get hurt again? If not that, then...

Her friend grabbed her by the wrist and dragged her into the classroom with no further explanation.

Jinah's eyes landed on the big TV next to the blackboard.

"J-Jinwoo?" The banana-flavored milk fell to the ground as she read the flashing caption.

# 7

## THE TENTH
## S-RANK HUNTER

# 7

## THE TENTH
## S-RANK HUNTER

Ten minutes earlier, outside the Hunter's Association, panicked at his inability to get an earlier rank evaluation slot, Minsung dropped a bombshell.

"I, Minsung Lee, will retire from acting and serve you as a hunter regardless of the evaluation result!"

This was a Hail Mary pass to try to get the press conference (that had fizzled out on the heels of President Go's appearance) going again. It was an effective gambit.

"What?"

"Minsung is going to retire?"

"No matter what his rank is?"

The press conference was back on track.

*Ka-shak, ka-shak, ka-shak!*

Countless cameras were trained on Minsung as excited reporters hit him with a barrage of questions.

"Minsung, over here!"

"Are you saying you'll turn your back on your standing as Asia's superstar even if you're a low-level hunter?"

"Can you give up all you've worked for as an actor?"

*Awesome!*

Minsung was thrilled that everyone was paying attention to him again. "Even if I get a low rank, I will battle magic beasts to repay all the love you've given me up to now!"

Of course, that was a big fat lie. He was contracted for exactly two years. He was going to help the Reapers promote their guild for two years while being paid a handsome annual salary. Additionally, this was the best way to make certain small controversies went away, like his father pulling strings to get him out of the mandatory Korean military service.

Sacrificing his superstar status to protect people's lives! Talk about a golden opportunity to become immune from criticism.

Minsung continued the press conference, excited that everything was going his way. "Guild Master Taegyu Lim, the president of the Reapers Guild, shares my conviction that..."

As the reporters hung on his every word...

*Riiing, riiing, riiing!*

A cell phone rang. The reporters around the ringing device shot dirty looks at its owner, who quickly turned it off and bowed profusely in apology. The press conference had been interrupted but, thankfully, hadn't been brought to a halt. Minsung pretended not to have heard anything and pressed on.

Then another person's phone rang.

"Oh, come on."

"Whose cell is that?"

"Silence your phone during a press conference. It's common sense!"

"Please turn it off already."

Minsung smiled and took the opportunity to look good in front of the press. "That's okay. Maybe we should all take a call before continuing?"

"Ha-ha-ha-ha-ha!"

Everyone laughed at his quick wit. Who could have foreseen that this was only just the beginning?

*Vrrrr, vrrrr.*

*Vrr, vrr, vrr.*

Phones started going off everywhere.

"What?"

"What, me too?"

The reporters who'd hastily turned off their phones earlier realized something strange was going on and checked their messages.

"An alert from the association?"

"Why didn't anyone say so before?!"

The reporters scrambled to check the association's website. The new S-rank hunter's picture and name had been posted as if it had been scheduled in advance. Today was the day Jinwoo's evaluation was to be announced.

*Wait, didn't they say no one could use the evaluation room this morning?*

*It wasn't for Minsung, then?*

*The association cleared Building B for that S-rank hunter?*

The face of a certain man popped into the reporters' minds in that instance.

Could it be?

It had to be the guy who'd followed President Go inside the association! That man was the only one who'd used the evaluation room today. Would they be able to get a picture of him if they followed him in now?

"H-hello…?"

The reporters had eyes like starving beasts as they ignored Minsung and stampeded toward the building. Jinchul gave a signal, and the Surveillance Team hunters spread their arms to form a barricade.

"Let us in!"

"We heard there's a new S rank! Why weren't we informed in advance?"

"Please get out of our way!"

The civilian reporters aggressively tried in vain to get past the Surveillance Team hunters.

"Wh-what?" Left out in the cold, Minsung dashed to his manager, who'd been checking his phone. He held it up for Minsung to see.

"S rank?" Minsung was dazed. "An S rank had to emerge today of all days?"

He'd wanted to capture everyone's attention by becoming an A-rank hunter, but this S rank had come out of nowhere and ruined everything. He shook his head.

*No, that can't be right.*

An S-rank hunter wasn't like a snack from a vending machine that popped out easily once coins were entered.

Did the reporters perhaps know something about this? Minsung spotted one still on his phone as he brought up the rear of the throng. It was same the newspaper reporter who'd asked for Minsung's opinion about a headline earlier.

"Excuse me, Reporter Lim!"

Lim only gave Minsung a passing glance despite the urgency in Minsung's voice. "Oh, Minsung. I'll get back to you later."

"What? Reporter Lim. Reporter Lim!" Minsung could hear the reporter's conversation as he drew farther and farther away.

".......That's right. The headline for tomorrow should be, 'The Tearful E Rank Becomes Joyful S Rank.'"

Minsung's eyes darted around hopelessly. He was all alone. He fell to a heap on the ground.

"What...the hell is this?" As he feebly muttered to himself, the door of the association swung open to reveal the tenth S-rank hunter of Korea.

*Ka-shak, ka-shak, ka-shak, ka-shak, ka-shak, ka-shak!*

Jinwoo's eyes widened in surprise.

*What the hell is going on?*

Jinwoo's full-portrait shot was caught on camera...as well as the vexed look and wry smile on Yoonho's and Jongin's faces, respectively.

\* \* \*

It was lunchtime for the excavation team as they wrapped up the morning's work. They were sitting together and eating lunch. Although mining was their main duty, they were rather carefree, as they didn't have to worry about cave-ins or collapses.

Some hunters lay down for a rest after inhaling their lunch, while others chatted on their phones, and some enjoyed sharing a drink over snacks.

"Huh?" One of the hunters on their cell phone sat straight up in shock. "Isn't this Sung?"

This got Seonggu's attention.

"Oh, it is."

"Sung is on the news?"

Seonggu wasn't hearing things. "I knew it." Seonggu's face was red from the three glasses he'd drunk with his lunch. He ran to where his colleagues were gathered. His mouth wouldn't stop moving. "I knew it from the moment that bastard glared at me! Let me see what horrible thing he's done!"

Maybe he'd said that a little too loudly.

"Sung did what?"

"Did Sung commit a crime?"

The excavation hunters nearby, including the foreman, all rushed over.

Jinwoo's face filled the cell-phone screen, and the scrolling caption beneath it read...

**"...Jinwoo Sung, the tenth S-rank hunter after Dongsoo Hwang and Haein Cha, has just..."**

"What?!" Seonggu's eyes twitched as soon as he saw Jinwoo's picture.

\* \* \*

Outside the chairman's office at Yoojin Construction, Jinho stood at the door and exhaled. "Hwoo."

*Click.*

He cautiously opened the door to find his father inside. Chairman Yoo didn't bother looking up from the document he was reading. "Come in." He signed the papers as he spoke.

Jinho stood right next to his father, who briefly checked that it was his son.

*Father hasn't changed.*

In the past, Jinho would've been intimidated by his father's attitude and run away, but things were different now.

"I have something I'd like to say to you."

"Is this about Hunter Sung?"

"Yes."

Chairman Yoo finally looked up. "Good. How did—?"

At that moment, the chairman's phone vibrated.

*Vrr, vrr, vrr.*

"Hold on." He raised his hand to stop Jinho. Chairman Yoo's eyes grew bigger as he read the message.

*Something can actually take the old man by surprise?*

Jinho cocked his head.

"......You need to see this."

"Excuse me?"

Instead of replying, his father hastily grabbed a remote to turn on the huge TV mounted on the wall.

Breaking news came on the screen.

**"Yes, it's just been confirmed. The hunter who has received an S rank today is a reawakened being who used to be an E-rank hunter working under the association. His name is Jinwoo Sung."**

The reporter's excited voice matched the energy of the people on the screen.

Jinho nearly jumped out of his own skin when he heard Jinwoo's name being mentioned.

*Whoa!*

Then the image on the screen changed. A person Jinho knew very well was staring coolly ahead. It was the boss.

*He's definitely miffed right now.*

Since they had been working together for some time now, Jinho could sense how his boss was feeling at that moment despite his blank expression.

But never mind that. The boss was an S rank? Jinho had known how awesome Jinwoo was, but this exceeded all his expectations. At the same time…

*Did he train in dungeons every day despite having all this power?*

Jinho was overwhelmed with respect for Jinwoo. Having worked alongside him, Jinho felt his heart fill with pride each time the reporter uttered Jinwoo's name.

*Blip.*

Jinho pouted when the boss's face disappeared as the TV was turned off.

"Continue." His father meant for him to continue what he'd come here to say.

"I'm sorry, Father. I couldn't change the boss's mind."

Chairman Yoo stiffened. "……I see. What was Hunter Sung's reason for rejecting our offer?"

"The thing is……" Jinho hesitated, then peeked at his father. "He told me he was going to form his own guild and offered me the vice presidential position…"

He paused, thinking his father would ignore him or get angry, but instead, his father looked stunned. Then finally…

*Heh.*

Yoo silently laughed. Chairman Yoo, well-known for his poker face, had shown emotion in front of his son.

*Why's he laughing?*

Jinho didn't dare ask, so he just averted his eyes.

Yoo finally stopped laughing and asked, "Do you know why I want to form Yoojin Guild?"

"Isn't it because…there's good money to be made?"

"No," Chairman Yoo said firmly. "I already have plenty of money to burn. Do you think I'd work on something that would cause trouble with large guilds just to make money?"

*So it wasn't about the profit?*

Jinho blinked. "Then…why?"

Chairman Yoo quietly set down his pen. "To protect us."

The grave look on his father's face made Jinho swallow hard.

"The power of hunters continues to grow. It's not unheard of for one of them to wield as much power as an entire country's military force."

Yoo was referring to the world's strongest hunters, the aptly named national-rank hunters.

"I've heard hunters already rule like kings in some small countries. How long do you think law and order can protect us from that scenario?"

His voice sounded somber, but Jinho suddenly realized that he felt happy listening to his father. Why was that?

*Oh......*

He'd said "us," which included Jinho. He was giddy he'd caught this glimpse of his father's love for him.

Chairman Yoo continued with his explanation. "I want to gather reliable hunters to form a guild. I want hunters I can trust and rely on, not ones interested in money or connections." He had a little smile on his face again. "It looks like you already found someone like that."

"Yes." Jinho responded right away.

It was hard to tell what exactly his father was saying, but that at least was something about which Jinho could be certain.

Yoo nodded. "All right."

"Huh?"

"You passed."

*Passed what?* Jinho, who'd been listening with his head down this whole time, looked up.

"I leave Yoojin Guild to you."

"Sorry?"

"Grow Yoojin Guild. Recruit strong hunters you can trust and rely on. They will be more valuable to you than any kind of fortune." Chairman Yoo spoke with a voice filled with confidence. Jinho's ecstasy matched his father's confidence. This may have been the first time Jinho had been validated by his father ever since birth.

"Thank you, Father!" Jinho smiled widely and gave his father a ninety-degree bow.

Yoo regarded his son proudly but didn't expect to hear what came out of Jinho's mouth next.

"However, I don't think I can do that."

"What?" Chairman Yoo's eyebrow twitched.

Yoojin Construction's financial power could buoy Yoojin Guild once it was established. They were already in talks with a few S-rank hunters. Yoojin Guild was primed to become one of the most prominent guilds in Korea. Jinho had to know all this.

*Isn't that why he wanted to be the guild master?*

So why would he decline the opportunity his father had just presented him? Had he grown scared? The chairman suppressed his disappointment and anger enough to ask...

"...For what reason?"

Jinho raised his head and cheerfully replied to his father without a moment's hesitation. "I'm going to join the boss's guild."

\* \* \*

Jinwoo was surrounded by reporters and didn't know what to do.

*What are these people doing in front of me instead of taking pictures of Minsung Lee?*

He looked over his shoulder to see if Minsung was perhaps standing behind him but saw only Yoonho and Jongin.

Just then, his thigh began to vibrate.

*Vrr, vrr.*

He fished out his phone from his pocket.

*Why is Jinah calling me at this time of day?*

His sister's urgent voice came over the receiver as soon as he pressed Talk.

**"Jinwoo! You're on TV!"**

Of course he was—just look at how many cameras there were. Every station was probably broadcasting the same thing. Jinwoo had been worried that Jinah was calling because something had come up at school, so he was relieved that wasn't the case.

"So…what's up?"

**"What's up? What do you mean, 'what's up'? You're reawakened? And an S rank!"**

Jinah must've gotten quite a shock, but he wasn't exactly in a position to explain everything to her at his leisure.

"I'm a little busy, so…I'll talk to you at home."

**"Wait, Jinwoo—"**

He hung up on his sister despite how desperately she pleaded with him.

*Beep.*

He then discovered how he'd gotten into this mess.

*……I've got a message.*

The Hunter's Association sent out notifications through an app. Typically, they sent alerts about A- or S-rank dungeons or dungeon breaks, but this wasn't a typical day.

*Huh.*

Jinwoo read the message and quickly pulled up the association website. Sure enough…

The ink on his S-rank license hadn't even dried yet, but the list of highest-ranked hunters had already been updated.

## Jinwoo Sung, S rank, mage class

It was written the same way it was on his hunter's license.

*……Why can't they be this quick about everything they do?*

Jinwoo stuffed his cell into his pocket and looked up again.

"Mr. Sung! Are you the same Jinwoo Sung who used to work under the association as an E rank?"

"You're one of the rare few reawakened beings! How do you feel about this?"

The reporters did everything they could to keep Jinwoo's voice or face on camera a little while longer. Unfortunately, Jinwoo wasn't happy about this frenzy of attention.

*I should get out of here.*

He didn't think they'd listen if he politely asked them to let him by. He raised an eyebrow. Should he just summon his shadow soldiers to clear the way for him?

"Over here, Hunter Sung! Look this way, please!"

"Hunter Sung, the entire nation is watching, so please give them a smile!"

As the camera lenses got closer, Jinwoo seriously debated for a brief moment about summoning Tank or Fang.

Behind him, Jongin noted that Jinwoo was stuck because of the throng of reporters. He approached President Baek.

"It looks like my new hunter is having a hard time thanks to all this attention."

"Who says Hunter Sung is your new hunter?"

"It's a joke. Can't you take a joke?"

They locked eyes in a staring contest again. Jongin was the first to eventually back down.

He sighed and continued. "Anyway, keeping Hunter Sung here any longer is just giving other guilds a shot at him."

President Baek agreed. Taegyu Lim, the guild master of the Reapers Guild, was already here because of Minsung, and the other two large guilds would soon be frantically trying to get in touch with Jinwoo.

Baek glanced at the reporters. "So what're you suggesting…?"

"I'm suggesting we escort Hunter Sung home before the other sharks smell the blood in the water. We can also use the time to talk to him."

Jongin was suggesting they team up to keep other rivals away from Jinwoo. Regardless of how powerful Jinwoo may be, he'd need to join a guild to tackle high-rank dungeons, so if they played their cards right, an S-rank hunter would be joining either White Tiger or the Hunters today. Jongin, as the leader of the Hunters, was confident in his guild.

"Fine." It wasn't a bad proposal for Yoonho, either. White Tiger wasn't as big as the Hunters, but they had plenty of potential for growth. Not to mention…

*Our Manager An and Jinwoo have known each other for quite some time.*

He was certain his guild had a better relationship with Jinwoo.

Having reached a cease-fire, they eyed each other warily as they headed toward Jinwoo.

President Baek was quick to call out to him. "Hunter Sung."

Jinwoo turned back to look at him. "Yes?"

Jongin was a little frustrated that Yoonho had taken the lead, but in the interest of cooperation, he didn't interrupt.

President Baek pasted on his most winsome smile. "Having trouble with all these reporters? Please come with us, and we'll escort you home. We're experts in dealing with this sort of thing."

His words were a little exaggerated, but they weren't empty by any means. Not only had the two guild masters experienced the same thing as S ranks, but running large guilds had also taught them how to handle the attention.

Jongin joined in. "Yes, come with us, please. We have something we'd like to discuss with you on the way."

Jinwoo declined their kind offer with a polite smile. "That's okay." He pulled the hood of his sweatshirt over his head. "I have somewhere else to be."

"Pardon? How do you expect to get out of here with all these repor—" Jongin didn't get to finish his sentence.

*Hup!*

Jinwoo swiftly turned to go and launched himself several meters over the reporters' heads, landing safely outside the swarm.

"What the—?"

Before the flustered reporters could react, Jinwoo disappeared into the crowd of people on the street.

Jongin was at a loss for words. Even an S rank like himself had barely had time to react, so it was a lost cause for the reporters, all of whom were average civilians.

Jongin laughed in spite of himself.

*He was just registered as an S rank, and he's already playing Superman!*

For Jinwoo to hold that kind of physical prowess as a mage hunter…

As a fellow mage, Jongin had to admit he was a bit jealous. So then what was the reaction of a brawler?

"Just now, he…" Jongin turned to discuss what they'd witnessed with Yoonho but recoiled at what he saw.

"Baek? Your eyes!" In his shock, he forgot to address President Baek by his full title.

"Oh…! S-sorry about that."

Yoonho covered his eyes with one hand and turned away. After a beat, he reopened them, and his pupils had gone from a beast's to a regular human's. He was still rattled, though.

*How is that……?*

He was trembling. When Jinwoo had focused energy in his legs to jump just now, for a short instant, his hidden magic power was exposed. Normally, it'd be nearly impossible for even high-level hunters to detect, but President Baek instinctively used his ability, Eyes of a Beast, to get a sense of Jinwoo's power level.

*He's powerful.*

He'd already known that Jinwoo was strong. However…

*That's not the issue, though.*

Back at the red gate, he'd unintentionally activated Eyes of a Beast during a confrontation with Jinwoo, so Yoonho had a frame of reference for Jinwoo's power level back then as well. The other man had certainly been strong—so much so that Yoonho hadn't thought he'd win a fight against Jinwoo without losing an arm or two.

And there it was. Jinwoo was the type of opponent Yoonho couldn't hope to defeat without some kind of sacrifice. Even so, there seemed to be a difference in the level of magic power that Yoonho had just sensed. Jinwoo's current level was incomparable to what he'd felt in the past.

Jinwoo had somehow gotten stronger—much stronger than before, but his reawakening had to have occurred some time ago. So how had his powers increased?

An impossible theory popped into his mind.

*Is he…able to increase his power level?*

Maybe instead of a second reawakening, he'd somehow trained......

He was interrupted just as he was about to reach a conclusion.

"Hey, President Baek, are you okay? You don't look good...," Jongin said out of concern.

Yoonho rubbed his face with both hands and shook his head vigorously. "I suddenly felt a little dizzy. I'm fine now."

"You're still young... You have to take care of yourself." As Jongin blathered on, Yoonho's eyes were fixed in the direction Jinwoo had gone.

*He's already far beyond a normal S rank. But if he can increase his power even more...*

Yoonho shuddered at the thought.

\* \* \*

"Taxi!" Jinwoo successfully eluded the reporters and caught a cab on a quiet street.

He clutched his S-rank hunter's license, delighted to finally have it in hand. Leveling up and raiding dungeons was great and all, but the most important thing now was curing his mother.

*The elixir of life...*

He wasn't sure if it could actually heal her.

*But even if there's a one-in-a-thousand, or even a one-in-ten-thousand chance......*

He wanted to clear the Demon's Castle and gather all the ingredients as soon as possible. In order to do that, Jinwoo needed an artifact that could protect him from the heat inside.

He told the driver his destination. "The Hunter's Auction House of Korea, please."

The taxi driver glanced at Jinwoo through the rearview mirror and smiled. "Going there to sell something good? I hear they deal in items worth at least several million won."

Jinwoo gave a tight-lipped smile.

*Gulp.*

His silence made the driver nervous. His passenger was going to the auction house, so he had to be a hunter, and one had to be extra careful when dealing with those. Many hunters were as eccentric as they were powerful, and they weren't people who should be crossed.

*This young man doesn't look like trouble, but better safe than sorry.*

The driver read Jinwoo's mood and shut his mouth, so it was quiet inside the taxi. Jinwoo used the time to check the Web. Social media, the blogosphere, and every single news site was abuzz about the new S-rank hunter. Until this morning, Minsung Lee had been the most widely searched topic on the Internet, but now his name wasn't even in the top ten.

*Tsk.*

Jinwoo clicked his tongue.

*I wasn't expecting this much attention...*

He knew people would be interested in him, but he didn't think it'd cause this much of an uproar. Thinking about it, though, there had only been exactly ten of them to ever appear in Korea. With one dead and one overseas, there were just eight other S ranks in the entire country, so how could he not be trending?

*But why had the media been so quiet in Haein's case?*

He thought he'd maybe catch a break, since Haein, the ninth S-rank hunter, hadn't received that much media attention. He did some digging and found she'd requested the association keep her information classified after she'd been confirmed as an S rank.

*If I'd done the same, the media or guilds wouldn't have found out about me.*

Why hadn't President Go told Jinwoo about this convenient option?

Ah, that's right. Jinwoo remembered the question President Go had posed while the two walked to the evaluation room together.

*"Do you have a guild in mind?"*

*"No, not yet."*

Had this been why he'd asked? President Go might not have mentioned it so guilds could access him.

*Well, then.*

Jinwoo sent in an online application to have his information classified and then called the auction house.

*Click.*

**"This is the Hunter's Auction House of Korea."**

"I'd like to get an artifact appraised. I'm already on my way, if that's okay?"

**"Of course, sir. What kind of artifact would you like appraised?"**

"It's a sphere that amplifies the effect of magic."

**"Ah, a magic sphere with an amplification effect... It sounds like you've already had it appraised elsewhere if you're aware of what it can do?"**

"Yes, but they weren't a credible source, so I would like an auction house appraisal."

**"Ha-ha. You've made the right choice. We are known to be the best in the business."**

The conversation paused for a moment as the person on the other end took down some notes.

**"How much was the amplification effect based on the last appraisal?"**

"A hundred percent."

**"Pardon?"**

"The sphere amplifies magic by a hundred percent."

"......"

There was another pause.

**"I'm sorry, sir, but are you a hunter?"**

"Yes."

**"We require your personal information for the official appraisal process. May I have your rank and name please?"**

The ends of Jinwoo's lips curled up.

*I knew it.*

If he'd tried to sell this item as an E-rank hunter, would the Hunter's Auction House have even bothered hearing him out? It was precisely for this reason that Jinwoo had gone through with a reevaluation.

He answered coolly, "S rank. Jinwoo Sung."

\* \* \*

Jinwoo arrived at the auction house. The building wasn't very tall, but it was somewhat wide and more reminiscent of a museum or an art gallery than a commercial building. The parking lot was huge and looked like it could accommodate events with over a hundred guests, maybe even a thousand. It was obvious that the Hunter's Auction House made a ton of money from commissions.

As Jinwoo got out of the taxi and headed toward the doors, a formally dressed man ran out to greet him.

"Are you Hunter Jinwoo Sung?"

"Yes, I am."

The man was astonished after looking up at Jinwoo's face.

Then he remembered where he was and greeted Jinwoo with an upbeat voice. "We spoke on the phone. I'm Junggi Kim of the appraisal team. Please follow me."

Jinwoo gave a short nod.

A myriad of thoughts ran through Junggi's mind as he walked Jinwoo to the appraisal room.

*I can't believe the new S-rank hunter who vanished in front of all those reporters is actually walking behind me.*

He'd initially thought Jinwoo's call was a prank. First, the item's effect was implausible. Second, he was claiming to be the S-rank hunter who'd just been announced today.

*I almost cussed out an S-rank hunter......*

His blood had run cold when the Hunter's Association confirmed Jinwoo's phone number. He was extremely relieved he'd gone by the book and hadn't been rude.

* * *

*"...Hunter Jinwoo Sung was newly registered as an S rank, hav-*
*ing gone up from an E rank through a reawakening. He jumped five*
*ranks and has been registered as a mage class..."*

TVs scattered throughout the auction house were still broadcasting Jinwoo's face. Bothered by this, Jinwoo pulled his hood down farther. Despite not being the actual person featured, Junggi couldn't help but puff out his chest in pride.

*Should I ask him to take a selfie with me?*

He shook his head. If he wasn't at work, he would've asked for a picture or an autograph. However, it would be rude to bother a customer on important business with such a request. He had to keep it professional.

*Oh, we're here already?*

They'd arrived at the appraisal room while Junggi had been lost in thought. He looked somewhat disappointed. "Right this way."

In the huge room, the appraisal team manager and the head appraiser, who'd given up their lunch hours to be here, anxiously awaited Jinwoo. The manager's eyes widened when he saw the S-rank hunter.

*It really is the man from the news, isn't it?*

The head appraiser struggled to tamp down his nerves.

*So the magic amplification sphere is really......?*

No, he couldn't be sure. Just because the person was real didn't mean the item was, too. The head appraiser repeated this mantra to himself in an attempt to calm his nerves.

Even the world's leading craftspeople pouring all they had into making the most powerful magic amplification artifact with top-grade materials would only be able to produce one with a 50 percent amplification. That particular project would also take years to gather all the resources, not to mention the countless number of people involved.

Mage hunters across the planet would line up to buy such an artifact, so the lack of said item wasn't due to lower demand, either. Even in Korea, Jongin Choi, the mage hunter also known as the Ultimate Hunter, was said to be searching for a magic amplification sphere that provided a buff of over 50 percent. And along came a brand-new S-rank hunter with a magic sphere that could amplify magic by 100 percent?

*Ridiculous......*

The whole thing was incredible enough to warrant throwing Jinwoo out onto the street if not for his rank. But they couldn't turn away an S-rank hunter. Even if this ended up being a big hoax, he'd be an important client for years to come.

*We have nothing to lose here.*

The head appraiser spoke to Jinwoo, half-suspicious and half-expectant. "Could you...please show me the item?"

Junggi and the manager also stared restlessly at Jinwoo.

"Sure." Jinwoo called up the Sphere of Avarice from his inventory while pretending to take it out of his pocket.

"So this is..." The head appraiser adjusted his glasses.

It was a beautiful bloodred sphere, one that compelled people to admire it. Junggi and the manager let out quiet sighs of appreciation.

"Hmm..." The head appraiser tilted his head while fidgeting with his glasses. "This isn't made from an essence or a mana stone, is it?"

"That's right."

The head appraiser nodded.

*I knew it.*

He'd been working in this profession for seven years now. He'd inspected many artifacts in his day, but this was his first time seeing a red sphere. Spheres were typically a clear blue in color, and they turned blacker as the quality went up. But a red one?

The head appraiser was still unsure as he took the sphere. As he held it in his hands, though...

*Wh-what's this?*

A chill ran up his spine as he felt a mysterious force radiating from the sphere.

*It can't be......*

He was astonished as he inspected the item. The head appraiser was a B-rank mage. He knew intuitively exactly what kind of item it was. His entire body broke out into a cold sweat.

*Oh my God!*

The power emanating from the sphere unnerved him, and his eyes shot up to see Jinwoo calmly watching him.

*If only he were a low-rank hunter......*

He was overcome by a feeling he had never felt before. People had brought in countless items in the past, but this was the first time he'd ever wanted to knock out the client and rob him. But this customer was an S rank.

*......?*

Jinwoo stared silently at the head appraiser, who barely suppressed his desire under Jinwoo's gaze.

*Rob an S rank?*

Jinwoo was so powerful, the head appraiser could barely stand to entertain the idea, let alone try it.

Jinwoo cocked his head and studied the appraiser.

*What's wrong with him?*

Was he feeling ill, perhaps? The appraiser wiped the sweat from his forehead before speaking to the manager.

"Please turn on the camera."

"Oh! Yes, of course."

Turning on the camera was a sign that what the appraiser held in his hand was the real deal. Both the manager and Junggi couldn't wait to see the results.

"Rolling." The manager turned the camera toward the appraiser, who stood in front of a circular mana meter. He placed the sphere on the meter.

*Beeeeeep.*

A number came up. The appraiser held the sphere in his hand and measured it again. The number doubled instantly.

*Beeeeeep.*

Junggi's face paled as he read the number. "Incredible......"

The manager quickly leaned in to check the result.

*One hundred percent? This magic sphere actually amplifies magic power by 100 percent?*

On average, the auction house received a 5 percent commission per artifact handled. If an artifact was worth 100 billion won, they would earn a tidy 5 billion. However, despite his many years of experience, the manager couldn't even begin to estimate how much the red magic sphere was worth.

*We're gonna be rich! Rich, I say!*

Had they been alone, he would've screamed for joy and hugged his employees. What would their cut be if this deal went through? He found his excitement made it difficult to breathe.

Junggi's reaction wasn't much different. He ecstatically pumped his fist.

*Yes!*

If everything went well, his promotion was in the bag.

"I… I'm going to test the sphere now." The appraiser could barely get the words out in a shaky voice.

The two men from the appraisal team took a step back. Jinwoo did the same.

The camera kept rolling. Video evidence was much more effective than numbers on a piece of paper to convince potential buyers.

The appraiser looked right at the camera. "Let's begin."

A flurry of snow about the size of a truck tire swirled around the appraiser's right hand.

"I will now touch the magic sphere while continuing to use magic."

As soon as his left hand made contact with the Sphere of Avarice…

*Hwoooooo!*

The dancing snowflakes turned into a blizzard that shook the entire room.

"Whoa!" Had the alarmed appraiser not ceased his magic when he did, the whole room would've been encased in ice.

"Please turn off the camera."

"Right."

The team manager ran to turn off the camera, nodding as he went. The appraisal process for the item was complete.

*Whew.*

Jinwoo had been anxious when the snowstorm exploded from the appraiser's hand, but he could relax now. Jinwoo wasn't the only one, either—everyone exhaled deeply to calm their nerves. For a moment, the room fell silent.

Jinwoo broke the silence. "So how much is the sphere worth?"

Would he be able to afford the artifacts he needed? While he was excited about buying new items, more than anything, he was genuinely curious about what he could get for the sphere.

The appraiser looked incredulously at the Sphere of Avarice.

"How… How could I put a price on such an item…?"

His eyes turned to Jinwoo.

*Gulp.*

He swallowed nervously. Where had Jinwoo found an artifact like this? This had nothing to do with the appraisal, but he couldn't help himself. "Where did you get this?"

Jinwoo turned to Junggi instead of the appraiser. "Do I need to answer that for this deal to go through?"

Junggi shrugged and awkwardly avoided Jinwoo's eyes.

The appraiser shook his head. "No, you don't. I was just…taken aback. But everyone will be curious when they find out this kind of magic sphere exists."

Naturally, the other two men looked like they were dying to know as well.

*Well, I guess it doesn't matter, does it?*

There was no reason not to answer. It wasn't something he'd acquired unfairly or an item other people could get their hands on even if he told the truth.

Jinwoo slowly opened his mouth. The others waited with bated breath to hear what he had to say.

Jinwoo smiled as he said, "I picked it up in a dungeon."

\* \* \*

President Baek strode into his office while calling to his secretary. "I'd like to be alone, please. No visitors."

He also went so far as to lock the door before turning on his computer and starting a search for information using the clearance level he held as an S-rank hunter and a guild master.

*Is it even possible?*

He couldn't stop thinking about Jinwoo. A hunter who could upgrade his abilities didn't sound plausible, yet what other explanation was there to explain the discrepancy he'd noticed in Jinwoo's power?

President Baek's fingers moved quickly. He pulled up information from the website for the world's top-ranked hunters, but it proved to be a waste of time.

*Nothing......*

There had never been a hunter who could increase their abilities on their own. Hunters could increase their power only through paranormal phenomena such as an awakening or a reawakening. That was why some people considered hunters to be those chosen by the heavens.

Numerous browser windows were opened and closed. Countless words moved endlessly across the screen. Three hours later, tired from all his research, President Baek leaned back in his chair.

*Am I being too paranoid?*

Maybe he was. Perhaps the shock at how strong Jinwoo was had addled his brain.

"Ha-ha." What was he doing at this crucial moment? He should've been texting Jinwoo instead of wasting time like this. What if that sly President Choi had presented Jinwoo with a contract already?

Yoonho laughed in spite of himself and began closing all the browser windows one by one until only one remained.

*Wait......*

Just for fun, he typed *hunter upgrade ability* into a search engine.

Nothing came up, of course. Not that he really expected anything. He just happened to still be in research mode.

*I just realized...I haven't eaten lunch today.*

President Baek rubbed his stomach and licked his lips as he realized how hungry he was. He was about to close the search engine when something caught his eye.

......?

There was a post on the fifth page of results that linked to a website. He would've ignored it if the link didn't lead to the hunter-exclusive forums. Yoonho moved the cursor over.

### [Title: Something strange happened.]

[Contents: I started seeing my stats on a floating screen like in a video game, and I can even upgrade them. Has anyone else experienced this?]

It was an anonymous post, but for some reason, Yoonho felt his breathing quicken as he read.

*If anyone could see me now, they'd think I was crazy.*

Still, he had nothing to lose by looking into it. He picked up the phone.

"Yes, Mr. President."

Manager Sangmin An from the second administration team answered the phone.

"There is something I'd like you to look into, Manager An."

Yoonho wanted to know what Jinwoo had been up to the day that anonymous post had gone up.

"Understood. I'll look into it."

With that, Sangmin hung up the phone. He was an extremely capable employee. He'd get an answer for President Baek using any means necessary, no matter how long it took.

The answer came much sooner than expected.

*Already?*

President Baek answered his ringing phone.

**"There were official records, so it didn't take long."**

"Really?" President Baek was very pleased. Now that he thought about it, he'd heard the second administration team had already collected as much information about Hunter Jinwoo Sung as they could under Manager An's orders. Hence the quick reply.

**"Yes. On that day, Hunter Sung was... Oh, looks like it was around that time. There was that double dungeon incident from several months ago, no?"**

"Right."

**"Hunter Sung was a survivor of that double dungeon affair. I believe he was hospitalized and comatose during his stay."**

"Oh...I see." President Baek was disappointed. A person in a coma couldn't post on the Internet.

*Increasing abilities... Guess that's not possible.*

He couldn't even laugh. He just felt tired. He thought about going home and taking a nap.

**"Huh? Wait. He was unconscious for a while..."**

Sangmin sounded like he was invested in Jinwoo's story.

**"...and then Hunter Sung woke up on the day you mentioned earlier."**

Hearing this, President Baek shot up straight.

*He woke up on that day?*

**"Oh, to be exact, it says he came to the day before."**

Although Sangmin quickly corrected himself, a difference of one day wasn't significant in Yoonho's opinion. The important thing was whether it had been possible for Jinwoo to have written that post.

"......I see. That's enough for now. Good work." President Baek hung up the phone and opened a report he had saved in his files. It was the report about Jinwoo from the second administration team's investigation.

*Click, click.*

He was most interested in Jinwoo's current activities. Until relatively recently, Jinwoo hadn't been particularly special. He had lived as a typical E-rank hunter who'd gotten more injuries than money.

But...

*The double dungeon incident.*

President Baek had also been at the scene on that day. The association had asked the nearest large guild, the White Tiger Guild, for their help. President Baek had gladly gone with his elite strike squad.

*Wee-ooh! Wee-ooh!*

He had seen an unconscious man being carted away by an ambulance.

*I didn't know that was Jinwoo......*

What exactly had happened in that dungeon? Whatever had gone down in there, Jinwoo had completely changed after that day. The man who used to quietly take on jobs from the association joined a freelance strike squad and cleared multiple C-rank dungeons in a single day. Something had changed inside him for sure.

Baek was fully convinced.

*It wasn't an ordinary reawakening.*

Manager An had proposed a theory that Yoojin Construction had gotten Jinwoo reevaluated when he had reawakened.

*No, that's not possible.*

If so, there was no way to explain how Jinwoo's power had increased even after the reawakening finished.

*What if a hunter who can increase his power actually exists?*

Moreover, what if that growth occurred so quickly that he'd gone from an E rank to an S rank in several months?

"......"

A moan spilled out from Yoonho's mouth. He got chills just thinking about it. Of course, there was no evidence that whoever had written that post and Jinwoo were one and the same. But imagine how much stronger Jinwoo could become if he actually could upgrade his abilities like the post suggested.

*How foolish I was...*

President Baek now understood why Jinwoo wasn't interested in joining any guild.

*If I were him......*

Would Yoonho have wanted to join someone else's guild if he could grow his power exponentially? He shook his head.

*I would rather make my own guild.*

It didn't matter whether the current number one or two guilds wanted Jinwoo when whichever he went with would end up being the best.

*It looks like President Choi and I were dreaming in vain.*

He couldn't stop laughing at the thought of Jongin going to great pains to locate Jinwoo even now. But...

*If my theory is true, this is no laughing matter.*

Jinwoo would be the one to rock the world of Korean hunters. He'd be the center of international attention. It was time to rethink the way he was approaching Jinwoo.

But first...

*I have to meet with him and get some confirmation.*

Yoonho nodded. The more he thought about it, the more he was certain his priority should be to speak to Jinwoo. But...

*...How should I ask him to meet with me?*

Yoonho ran his hand through his hair. "......"

He had a migraine thinking about how best to get the attention of a man who'd left him hanging so many times before.

* * *

The appraiser was astonished. "Did you say you picked it up from a dungeon?"

Jinwoo nodded. Technically, he'd picked it up after defeating Vulcan in the Demon's Castle dungeon.

*You can pick up that kind of thing in a dungeon?*

*It's true that no craftsman can make something like this...*

Neither the appraiser who asked the question nor the two other auction house employees who'd heard the answer looked like they believed it. However, there was nothing to do but trust their client. Either way, where Jinwoo got this red magic sphere wasn't important.

*What's important is what Hunter Sung plans to do with it.*

The manager stepped forward. "Well, this is the real deal." He gazed at the sphere in Jinwoo's hand. "Would you like us to auction it? We'll do our level best to get the top price."

What should he do? Jinwoo had one question before he could decide what to do with the Sphere of Avarice. "Can I buy any flame-resistant artifacts here?"

The team manager and Junggi looked at each other, then awkwardly back at Jinwoo.

Jinwoo was puzzled. "Did I say something wrong?"

"No, not at all."

"Then are they difficult to get?"

"Actually..." The manager smiled. "Just the opposite. That type of gear is extremely easy to acquire."

"Then why couldn't I find anything online?"

"Weapons or protective gear with applied attributes are quite expensive, so they're not normally sold online. But they're still easy to acquire, since fire magic is the most common type of attack magic."

Now that he thought about it, most of the mage hunters Jinwoo had come across thus far had used light or fire. He'd heard that S-rank hunter Jongin's specialty was fire magic. Even Jinwoo's shadow mages used it, including Fang, who could breathe fire. It was clear this type of magic was extremely common.

*I'm glad fire-resistant things are easy to get.*

He'd flinched when they mentioned that fireproof artifacts were expensive, but since his mother's cure depended on this, he was willing to pay whatever the price if that meant he could get his hands on them faster.

If it came down to it, he could sell the Sphere of Avarice.

"Could you look into that for me?"

"Of course. I'll get right on that." The manager turned to leave but then stopped to talk to his employee. "Junggi, why don't you give Hunter Sung a tour instead of making him wait here?"

"With pleasure." Junggi led the way. "Please follow me."

Junggi and Jinwoo went into the VIP-only exhibition room filled with the auction house's most expensive items that hadn't been bought yet or were due to be put up for auction soon. Weapons, protective gear, rune stones, and more were displayed in transparent glass cases.

Jinwoo stopped in front of a display with a sword inside.

Junggi approached him. "Do you see anything you like?"

"No, that's not it." Jinwoo knocked on the glass case. "Is this thin glass enough to protect it? I can't see any other security measures."

Junggi assured him. "It may be thin, but it's magically enhanced tempered glass crafted by the best glassmakers. It can withstand the full-force punch of an A-rank brawler with no issue."

"An A-rank brawler, really?"

Junggi grinned at Jinwoo's doubtful expression. "If you don't believe me, would you care to give it a go? If the box breaks, we'll give you the item inside for free."

"Hmm......" Was this tempered glass really that strong?

*I can sense its magic power, but...*

With his curiosity piqued, Jinwoo focused energy in his right arm.

*Hwoooo.*

The muscles in his shoulder and arm bulged, and the air around him seemed to settle.

"H-hold on!" Junggi hastily stopped Jinwoo. "That was just an example. I didn't mean for you to actually smash it."

"Oh, I see."

"If it broke, elite hunters from the Hunters Guild would rush over here. We have a security contract with them."

"Ah…"

It'd been hard to tell whether Junggi had been joking or not. Jinwoo powered down.

When the energy around Jinwoo subsided, Junggi sighed in relief.

*Isn't he supposed to be a mage hunter?*

How was a mage hunter's energy so imposing…? Junggi hadn't actually been kidding when he'd told Jinwoo to strike the glass. Though Jinwoo was technically an S rank, he was also a mage hunter, so Junggi had thought it would be fine. However, Junggi had gotten an ominous feeling when Jinwoo focused his energy.

Luckily, Jinwoo had agreed to back down.

*Which is good, because Hunter Sung could've gotten hurt if something had gone wrong.*

Junggi convinced himself of that as he showed Jinwoo some more artifacts.

Jinwoo glanced around the room. "Could I take a closer look at any of these? Preferably daggers."

Not really being the type to rely on weapons, Jinwoo hadn't paid much attention to them until now, but seeing these weapons on display had piqued his interest.

Junggi's face lit up. This was why the auction house gave hunters the tour. Hunters were sellers, but they were also valuable customers.

"Of course." He used the walkie-talkie around his neck to call for the person in charge of weaponry. The employee appeared in a flash, as if worried Jinwoo might change his mind in the meantime.

"Is this the gentleman?" He indicated Jinwoo with his gaze, and Junggi nodded. "Ah yes, nice to meet you. I'm in charge of weaponry. Please come with me." He led Jinwoo out of the VIP exhibition room.

Junggi let out a sigh once they were gone.

*Hunter Sung has a certain knack for surprising people.*

Junggi wandered aimlessly around the room to calm his nerves and found himself in front of the sword in which Jinwoo had shown an interest. They'd been standing pretty close to the display, so Junggi was checking the glass for any fingerprints to clean off when he noticed something.

"Huh?" There at the top of the case. "What?"

In one corner was a tiny, hard-to-see crack.

"When did this happen?" He took out his handkerchief and rubbed at it, but it wouldn't go away. It was definitely a crack and not some dirt.

"Oh boy." Junggi frowned. Had Hunter Sung spotted this, it might've cost them the trust of a potentially big client. Good thing the crack was in a corner and hard to see.

*Tsk, tsk.*

Junggi clicked his tongue and called the maintenance team before leaving the VIP exhibition room.

* * *

Jinwoo picked up the dagger he was being shown. To be honest, it was awful.

*Knight Killer has a B-rank acquisition difficulty, but it's better than this.*

Its attack power wasn't even half that of Knight Killer. He returned the sword with a dissatisfied look on his face. "How much is this?"

"It's thirty million won."

Jinwoo was startled. That piece of junk cost how much? "Could you repeat that?"

"Thirty million won, Hunter Sung."

"Hold on." Jinwoo turned around and pretended to look for something inside his jacket as he produced Knight Killer in his hand. "How much would this be worth?"

The employee's eyes bulged. "Is this yours, Hunter Sung? Wow, the intricate work of a master craftsman is apparent in it!"

No, this was just an item from the system shop...

The employee hesitated a little bit, then smiled. "It's hard to give you an exact appraisal, since I'm not a professional, but...this looks like it's worth at least one hundred million won."

Jinwoo was stunned.

*I bought this from the shop for around 3 million gold.*

It had cost 2.8 million gold to be exact.

After seeing the expression on Jinwoo's face, the employee scratched the back of his neck in embarrassment. "Was it something I said? I'm not an expert at appraisal, so I may have misspoken."

"No, it's nothing." Jinwoo was flabbergasted at how ridiculously expensive everything was. Then again, the first weapon Jinwoo had owned had been Kim Sangshik's steel sword with its ten attack power, which he'd heard was worth 3 million won. And there was Jinho's armor, which had apparently cost over 100 million won, though he hadn't gotten much use out of it. He supposed it shouldn't be surprising that high-level items from the shop could be sold at very high prices.

*I just hadn't been paying attention.*

After all, he hadn't been too interested in making money while leveling up.

*Wait......*

He had tons of gold saved in his inventory. What if he bought items with gold and sold them at the auction house at a premium? The gears in his mind started to turn.

*Then I wouldn't necessarily need to sell the Sphere of Avarice, would I?*

As soon as he thought this...

*Whoo-hoo!*

Was he imagining things? Jinwoo thought he heard the shadow mages cheering from the shadow beneath his feet.

# 8
## DEMON'S CASTLE, ROUND TWO

# 8

## DEMON'S CASTLE, ROUND TWO

"Whoa! Jinwoo, the reporters are still there." Jinah was looking out their window.

It was late at night. Reporters were camped near the entrance of their apartment building.

"Up there!"

They spotted Jinah's silhouette in the window and, mistaking her for Jinwoo, quickly started taking pictures.

*Ka-shak, ka-shak, ka-shak!*

Startled by the flashes, Jinah closed the curtains.

*Shhhk!*

She turned around, eyes wide like a puppy's. "Whew."

Jinwoo had been planning to get some rest after coming back from the auction house, but his face showed his displeasure. "Should I go down and tell them off?"

He didn't mind them interrupting his rest, but he was concerned they might be disrupting his sister's studies. Jinah was a college applicant in her senior year of high school. Some touchy students would complain about so much as the sound of footsteps outside their rooms.

*Jinah's not the type to be bothered by much, but...*

How could she concentrate on her work if her surroundings were this chaotic?

"No, it's fine." She waved her hand dismissively. "People are already bad-mouthing you on the Internet. What would they say if you kicked those reporters out?"

"Bad-mouthing me?"

What had he done to deserve that? Jinwoo cocked his head, confused, as Jinah pulled up an article on her phone and handed it to him.

......

On the screen was a picture of Jinwoo on his phone, ignoring the throng of reporters surrounding him in front of the association building. He scrolled past the article to the comments.

—His attitude is trash.
—He already thinks he's too good for the reporters.
—How cold.

The one with the most likes was "Look, Mom, I'm an S rank now!" Jinwoo laughed at how well it suited the photo.

Jinah couldn't believe his reaction. "You think this is funny?"

"But it is."

"......" When Jinwoo showed her his favorite comment, she visibly had to restrain herself from laughing. In fact, it had the opposite effect. "That's not the point!"

Jinah's face was a little red as she raised her voice. "Why did you have to pick up right then and there in front of the reporters? Now everyone in Korea knows my name, too."

Jinwoo answered mildly. "Do I have to ask permission before answering a call from my own sister?"

"Ngh!" Jinah was at a loss for words. Try as she might, she couldn't think of anything wrong with his point.

......*I really can't beat him in an argument.*

He returned her phone. "Here."

Jinah still looked miffed as she took back her cell. "Anyway, I'm fine, so never mind those reporters."

"Gotcha." He nodded in understanding. It would've been a bigger problem if this was going to continue, but the association had informed him that there would be a restraining order issued against the reporters within a day or two.

*I can be patient.*

It wasn't like he wanted things to blow up any more than they already had anyway.

"I can't believe this is happening." Jinah stared at Jinwoo in disbelief. "My older brother is now an S-rank hunter, and reporters are stalking him..."

Most people would've been similarly astonished. She'd adjust to the new reality soon enough.

*I was the same.*

In an attempt to comfort her, Jinwoo gently pinched his sister's cheek. As usual, Jinah responded with a swift kick to his leg.

"Owww!" She clutched her foot. "That hurt..."

Jinwoo just shrugged as she pouted at him. It looked like it would take a while for her to adjust to her brother being an S-rank awakened being.

"You'll only get busier, won't you?" she asked cautiously.

"Yeah." Jinwoo nodded.

He had many things on his to-do list, but the first was the Demon's Castle. He'd already purchased fire-resistant artifacts for raiding higher floors.

His heart had sunk when he hadn't had enough money to pay for the items, but the auction house had thankfully given him a loan when he offered to leave an A-rank item from the system shop with them.

*I can't believe I got plunged into debt as soon as I became an S-rank hunter...*

The irony wasn't lost on him. At least he'd be able to pay off the loan sooner than later, as long as the items from the shop went for high prices during their auctions.

"Then it'll get harder to see you." Jinah looked a little saddened by the fact.

She must have felt lonely when she was home alone. Jinwoo wordlessly placed his hand on her head. Just a few more days, and as soon as he cleared the Demon's Castle, she wouldn't have to be alone at home.

*I'll make it happen no matter what.*

Suddenly, Jinwoo's eyes narrowed and snapped to the door.

*Someone's coming.*

Jinah noticed her brother's odd behavior and fearfully asked, "Jinwoo?"

"Go to your room."

"What's wrong?"

Someone had gotten off the elevator and was making a beeline for their unit.

*A hunter......?*

The stranger possessed magic power, however weak. Jinwoo couldn't sense any hostile intentions, but he was nonetheless displeased about an uninvited guest. Was this someone from a guild? Or perhaps a naive reporter making a bold choice? Whatever the case, Jinwoo did not look kindly upon an unannounced visitor showing up at his door at ten o'clock at night.

He stood in front of the door.

*For that level of power......*

There was no need to bring out a weapon. He did a couple light stretches and cracked his neck. Then, as he expected...

*Knock, knock.*

Whoever it was knocked twice and, alarmed, Jinah rushed into her room.

Jinwoo calmly opened the door.

*Creeeak.*

Through the open gap, he saw a familiar man.

He opened his mouth and sniffled...

"Boooss..."

Standing in front of the door was Jinho, his nose red and runny.

"......" As Jinwoo stared at this ridiculous sight, Jinho cried to him.

"Boss, I got kicked out. My father tossed me out."

"......" Jinwoo then noticed that Jinho was carrying a huge backpack practically as big as he was. Both his hands were full as well.

"......I thought you had your own place?"

"The thing is......"

*Sniff.*

"My dad owns that town house, so he kicked me out and cut off my access to all my bank accounts."

A father cutting off his son like that? Jinwoo had only seen stuff like that in movies, but it sounded plausible for Chairman Yoo, the richest man in Korea. So what the heck had Jinho done to piss off his father?

As Jinwoo continued to stare, Jinho desperately begged, "May I ask you a favor, boss? Can I crash here for a while?"

*Creeeak.*

*Slam!*

Jinwoo closed and locked the door without a word.

*Click.*

Jinah, having kept a worried eye on the situation from afar, beelined out of her room. "Who was that? Someone you know?"

Jinwoo shook his head. "Nope, I've never seen him before."

"You don't know him? Then why did he come here?"

"Don't worry about it. He got the wrong place."

"......Really?" That wasn't what it looked like.

*Knock, knock!*

As Jinwoo shoved his unconvinced sister back inside her room, a sad voice called out from behind him.

"Booooooooooss? Booooss!"

* * *

"Honey, don't you think you were too harsh on Jinho today?"

"Hmph." Chairman Yoo tugged roughly at his tie.

That impudent boy. Myunghan had been trying to hand his son a core part of Yoojin Construction's future, and that's how he showed his gratitude?

*"I'm going to join the boss's guild."*

What? Join his boss's guild?

"That boy deserves it." He snorted.

If Jinho wanted to be independent, then he'd have to do it by his own strength. Chairman Yoo wanted his son to learn firsthand that his choices came with consequences.

Was it because he was angry? He was having trouble untangling his tie. The more he tugged, the more knotted it became, and eventually, the first lady of Yoojin Construction reached out to him.

"Let me do it for you."

The tie was quickly taken care of. Myunghan quietly left it to his wife. She giggled as she held the untied piece of fabric in her hand.

"Why are you laughing, dear?" He was curious.

She'd been tying and untying his tie for him for years. There was no reason to laugh about a tangled tie after all this time.

"Honey, are you sure you're mad at Jinho?"

"Hmm...?" What was she going on about? What nonsense.

Chairman Yoo inspected himself in the mirror.

*Odd......*

He was surprised by what he saw. Why did he look happy despite all his grousing just now? Embarrassed, Myunghan rubbed at his cheeks and chin.

"Today was the first time, right?"

"First time for what?"

"The first time he's gone against you."

"......"

That was why Yoo was mad. Just as water flowed from the top to the bottom, so a company was run from the top down. The same went for a family. He'd managed his family the same way he managed the company, and he wouldn't allow anyone to go against his decisions.

Today's events had made him angry, but he wasn't upset about it for some reason.

*Shouldn't I be?*

He couldn't make sense of his own feelings. His wife, however, understood how his mind worked and talked to him soothingly like she would a child.

"For the first time, Jinho is trying to do something for himself. How about cheering him on instead of jeering at him?"

"......" Myunghan didn't respond. It was hard even for him to know his own heart.

"I'll...keep an eye on him for now."

"Of course." His wife smiled and accepted the suit jacket he handed her. That was when...

Myunghan stared at his wife's face. "It's strange."

"What's strange?"

"There seems to be two of your face..."

"What?"

As her eyes widened, Myunghan staggered and lost his balance.

"Honey?" Startled, she rushed to his side.

He shook his head hard to try to clear his mind, breathing heavily. "Huff, huff."

There was panic in his wife's eyes.

*Why is he sweating so much?!*

Chairman Yoo tried to fight the sleepiness by forcing his eyes wide open, but he eventually lost consciousness.

\* \* \*

Chairman Yoo woke up in the VIP hospital room of the best university hospital in Korea. One of the doctors who'd been on rotation to watch him around-the-clock hurried into the room to check on him.

"How are you feeling, Chairman Yoo?"

"......" After surveying the room, Chairman Yoo worked out the situation. "How long have I been here?"

"You've been asleep for two whole days."

Two days? He was known for being a workaholic. Even if he was tired, he had never slept for more than five hours.

"......" He didn't speak for a time but eventually shrugged it off. "I guess I was quite tired."

He'd been very busy of late, so he figured that dizziness and fatigue were consequences of his lifestyle. However, the expression on the doctor's face indicated that it was something more serious.

As the head of a company with several hundred thousand employees, he had a knack for reading people's minds.

He took in the doctor's somber expression and asked, "......Did you find something?"

"Do you spend much time with any hunters or other awakened beings?"

What a strange question. Myunghan had asked if something was wrong, so why was the doctor bringing up hunters?

Yoo answered with a question of his own. "What are you talking about? What's this got to do with hunters?"

"Have you heard about the Eternal Sleep Disease?"

Chairman Yoo's calm demeanor finally crumbled, and his eyes twitched.

The Eternal Sleep Disease. The strange sleep from which no one had awoken yet. Not only did patients not wake up, but their bodies also quickly deteriorated, necessitating they be put on life support powered by magic. The disease had been first diagnosed after gates began appearing. It was a horrible affliction that had taken the lives of many people who couldn't afford to pay for a life-support machine.

"It's a disease where, at first, you are simply drowsy but eventually end up unable to awaken."

The doctor looked torn. There was yet to be a single case of a patient coming out of it. Although their life could be extended, they were basically in a coma. It was, to be blunt, a death sentence.

"......" Myunghan waited for the doctor to finish before speaking. "So what do hunters have to do with it?"

"It's widely believed there's a connection between Eternal Sleep Disease and mana."

Some people were born with a lower tolerance to mana. Those types of individuals were found to be more susceptible to Eternal Sleep Disease, particularly anyone with prolonged exposure.

"Didn't you say that the life-support machines used are powered by magic?"

"Yes, however…" The doctor explained that, similar to nuclear energy, while magic power itself was harmful, its by-products were harmless. "What you need to be careful about is exposure to essence stones, magic gems, and people with magic power."

*"People with magic power"……*

Chairman Yoo thought of Jinho, the only awakened being in his immediate family.

The doctor proceeded cautiously. "Isn't your youngest son a hunter, Chairman Yoo?"

Yoo's expression hardened at the mention of Jinho. "So…you're telling me to avoid my own son?"

"Well, as much as you can—"

"That's ridiculous!" Myunghan firmly cut him off. "That's nonsense." Annoyed, he gestured for the doctor to leave the room.

"Chairman Yoo…" The doctor hesitated, unsure what to do, but hastily exited the room at Myunghan's glower.

Myunghan was livid as he stared at the door.

*Stay away from my own son if I don't want to get sicker? Who says that to a father?*

Even if it was the truth, what would Jinho think if he found out? Myunghan couldn't put such a burden on his son.

*Furthermore……*

Over time, magic was being relied upon more and more, and the number of people with magic powers was steadily increasing. Then were the people who were intolerant to magic being forcibly expelled from this world?

He snorted.

*Expelling me, Myunghan Yoo?*
He couldn't let that happen.
*I won't lose to this.*
He'd accomplished countless things people had told him were impossible. When he'd inherited Yoojin Construction, it was barely a Top Thirty company, but he had been the one to grow the firm to be the largest in Korea.
*I will not surrender to something like this damn disease.*
He would be victorious.
Myunghan repeated this mantra in his mind over and over again.

* * *

Jinwoo carefully opened the door to Jinah's room. It was early in the morning, and she was in such a deep sleep that she wouldn't have woken up if someone whisked her away.
He was suddenly struck with worry.
*People may try to approach Jinah while I'm away.*
No one really had the balls to harm an S-rank hunter's sister, but one never knew with humans. He needed some kind of safeguard.
*Wait. Come to think of it, my soldiers can hide in shadows, can't they?*
Jinwoo remembered how he'd had his shadow soldiers patrol the neighborhood to keep an eye out for that serial killer on the loose. The soldiers moved about by hiding in the shadows. He could have them do something similar to protect his sister without anyone noticing. And he knew which ones would be perfect for the job.
*Come forth.*
Jinwoo summoned the shadow soldiers who had been Fang's bodyguards.
*Fwssssh.*
These three shadow soldiers were especially brawny, even for high orcs, so his sister's room suddenly felt super cramped with their additional presence.
Wait...
*Huh? Why are there only three?*

He was certain there'd been four guards. Jinwoo then remembered.

*Oh.*

He'd forgotten to extract the shadow of the guard he'd smashed into the ceiling.

*I need to pay better attention next time.*

He smirked as he assessed the three shadow soldiers. They were all of elite rank, which put them on another level from the other regular-rank high orc warriors. This trio would have no problems dealing with even an A-rank hunter.

This wasn't a random guess; Kihoon, the leader of the Hunters Guild strike squad, had been an A rank, but he'd had a tough time dealing with three regular high orc warriors. These three would be more than able to hold their own.

Jinwoo pointed his chin toward Jinah. As he did...

*Vwoom...*

The guards returned to shadow form and glided across the floor to merge with Jinah's shadow.

*Perfect.*

*Lie low, and if anyone tries to hurt her, don't hold back.* After relaying that order to the guards, Jinwoo left her room and carefully closed the door behind him.

*I can relax now.*

His heart felt much lighter.

Jinwoo locked the door as he left and went downstairs to the entrance of the apartment building to find Jinho waiting for him as discussed.

"Boss!" Jinho greeted Jinwoo with his usual cheer.

"You sleep okay?"

"Yes, boss. The motels these days are pretty decent."

With Jinah at home, Jinwoo had put Jinho up in a motel nearby. Luckily, Jinho didn't seem to mind.

"You'll only be there until I get an office space for the guild."

"Yes, boss." Jinho kept smiling inexplicably.

Jinwoo had heard the summary of what had happened from Jinho yesterday. Jinwoo hadn't expected him to throw aside the position of guild master to come here. When Jinwoo questioned him in disbelief, Jinho had gotten offended.

*"Why would you do that?"*
*"You're the one who told me to join you, boss!"*

Jinwoo couldn't exactly talk badly about a guy who had declined the position of guild president simply because he liked Jinwoo so much.

"Let's go."

"You got it, boss."

Jinho got in the driver's seat, and Jinwoo sat in the front passenger seat. Their van headed for Daesung Tower.

Jinho kept glancing at Jinwoo.

*Why does he need to go to Daesung Tower so early in the morning?*

He was dying to ask, but Jinwoo wasn't fond of getting peppered with questions, so Jinho kept his thoughts to himself.

*Skrrrrch.*

As the van came to a stop in front of Daesung Tower, Jinho worked up some courage. "Um, boss, why are we—?"

"I'll be right back."

"What?" Jinho quickly turned to the passenger seat, but all he saw was the open van door. Jinwoo was already gone.

Jinho had a strong case of déjà vu.

He rubbed the back of his neck.

*He always comes and goes so quickly.*

\* \* \*

**[You have entered the Demon's Castle dungeon.]**

Jinwoo deactivated the Stealth skill.

*I'm finally back.*

He was happy to have returned to a place where he could fight to his heart's content. As soon as he passed the castle's gate, the electronic sound rang.

*Ping!*

[A new quest has arrived.]

Unlike his first visit, he wasn't caught by surprise this time.

That time, he'd received the quest Collect Demon Souls (1), so though he hadn't known when, he knew he'd receive the next part of the quest someday.

Jinwoo opened the message window.

*Ping!*

**[QUEST: COLLECT DEMON SOULS (2)]**
The Demon Monarch Balan resides on the highest floor of the Demon's Castle. Defeat Balan and collect his soul. Marvelous rewards await should you succeed.

**Quest Activation Requirement**
—The completion of Quest: Collect Demon Souls (1)
—Reentry of the Demon's Castle

**Quest Clear Requirement**
—Defeat the Demon Monarch

**Rewards:**
1. Rune stone of the highest rank
2. Ability Points +30
3. Mystery Reward

*The goal of the quest is to defeat the Demon Monarch.*

Jinwoo's face lit up. He could head straight to the top without having to go back to a lower floor. On top of that, the rewards were great, too.

*Thirty bonus ability points!*

The last quest had been extremely labor intensive, having to collect ten thousand demon souls, and he'd gotten twenty ability points for all that work. Yet the system was going to award him thirty points for killing a single demon boss this time. Usually, it would've taken him ten daily quests or leveling up six times to receive that many, so the unexpected reward elicited a smile.

*But what's this rune stone of the highest rank?*

Jinwoo selected the first reward.

*Ping!*

**[RUNE STONE OF THE HIGHEST RANK: SHADOW EXCHANGE]**
**When you crush the rune stone, you may obtain a job-exclusive skill.**

*I can learn a job-exclusive skill?*

Jinwoo's eyes popped out of his head. He'd acquired three job-exclusive skills so far: Shadow Extraction, Shadow Storage, and Monarch's Domain. All of them were incredible, so the thought of picking up another excited him to no end.

*What'll it be this time?*

Jinwoo tried to call up more information, but all the system would show him was the name. Jinwoo pursed his lips.

*Well, I'll find out after completing the quest.*

A job-exclusive skill and thirty extra points. These were truly marvelous incentives even without the mystery reward. He had the impulse to bolt for the highest floor right away, but…

*Before I start……*

For the first time in a while, he called up his stat screen.

*Ping!*

*   *   *

# 【Name: Jinwoo Sung】  【Level: 80】

[Class: Shadow Monarch]

[Title: The One Who Overcame Adversity (and 1 other)]

[HP: 24,406]

[MP: 5,019]

[Fatigue: 0]

## 【Stats】

| Strength: | Stamina: | Agility: | Intelligence: | Perception: |
|-----------|----------|----------|---------------|-------------|
| 186 | 145 | 175 | 189 | 126 |

(Available ability points: 0)

Physical damage reduced by: 46 percent

## 【Skills】

Passive skill: (Unknown) Lv.Max, Willpower Lv.1, Advanced Dagger Wielding Lv.2

Active skill: Dash Lv.Max, Fatal Strike Lv.Max, Murderous Intent Lv.1, Dagger Throw Lv.2, Stealth Lv.2, Ruler's Hand Lv.2

## 【Job-Exclusive Skills】

Active skill: Shadow Extraction Lv.1, Shadow Storage Lv.1, Monarch's Domain Lv.1

* * *

## [Craft]
Consumable: Elixir of Life (2/3)

## [Item Equipped]
Crimson Knight's Helmet (S), Demon Monarch's Earrings (S), Demon Monarch's Necklace (S), High-Rank Knight's Chestplate (B), High-Rank Knight's Gauntlets (B), High-Rank Mage's Ring (B), Mid-Rank Assassin's Boots (C)

His level had jumped to 80, and because he'd been investing all his recent ability points in intelligence, it now exceeded the strength stat.

*The intelligence stat is already close to two hundred.*

As a result, his mana points were over five thousand. Mana had almost no other function but to give him the power to revive his shadow soldiers ad infinitum. But considering the continuously increasing number of shadow soldiers, five thousand might be insufficient.

*All right. Let's get started.*

Every second he spent not fighting felt like a waste.

Jinwoo closed the stat screen. He was currently on the first floor of the Demon's Castle, but he could go directly to the seventy-sixth, having cleared all the floors from here to there. He went straight to the magic teleportation circle.

[Floors one through seventy-six have been opened.]
[Where would you like to teleport?]

Jinwoo didn't hesitate. "Seventy-six."

Lights flashed. He blinked once, and the view changed.

The scene before his eyes was one of a city engulfed in fire. Although he was protected inside the magic circle, it felt like his skin was aflame.

Jinwoo put down the bag he'd brought with him to take out two artifacts. One was a black cloak titled the Robe of Wind by its maker. The other was a nameless ring imbued with water magic. He put them on.

He really felt like a true mage hunter once he pulled the robe's hood over his head.

......*My body is cooling down.*

The robe made Jinwoo feel like he was standing inside a cool cave.

*Will this work against the flames of the Demon's Castle?*

He slowly stepped out of the magic teleportation circle.

Would the robe be worth the price he'd paid? Unlike the last time he was here, the oppressive heat didn't affect him.

*Can I move comfortably with this thing on?*

He tried moving around and found the robe was more comfortable than he'd expected. The Robe of Wind itself felt light as air.

*Nice.*

He was ready, but he wasn't the only one. Having caught the scent of a human, packs of demons began approaching. In the past, he would've taken care of all of them to warm up or hunted down every last one in order to level up.

*Not this time, though......*

Because this had to do with his mother's treatment, he didn't want to spend any extra time. Instead of calling for his daggers, Jinwoo summoned his soldiers.

*Vwoom...*

His trusty shadow soldiers appeared.

*But where's Fang?*

Jinwoo looked around for Fang. Because he was a higher-rank soldier, he'd spawned closer to Jinwoo—right behind him, in fact. He took the Sphere of Avarice out of inventory and put it in Fang's hand.

"You can use this today."

Though he was a mage hunter, Jinwoo couldn't exploit the benefits of the sphere, but he thought it might help Fang's spells.

......

Fang bowed deeply in a show of appreciation.

*Stomp, stomp, stomp!*

Finally, enormous demons came into view.

*Shall we get started?*

Jinwoo gripped Barca's Dagger and Knight Killer tightly and ordered his soldiers to prepare for the battle. Countless demons swarmed toward Jinwoo like bugs, but he also had plenty of soldiers on his side. Jinwoo's expression was much more relaxed than the last time he had been here as he waited for the right moment. He then yelled...

"Move—!"

He'd meant to yell *move out*, but before he could finish his sentence...

*Fwoooooooosh.*

An incredibly large pillar of fire flew over his head and struck the enemy, sweeping over them.

"Wh-what is that?"

*Fwooooooooosh.*

The flames scorched whatever they touched, be it a demon or the ground.

"Kreeeee!"

"Skraaaw!"

Demons evaporated quickly, and Jinwoo heard that familiar electronic alarm.

**[You have leveled up!]**
**[You have leveled up!]**

*No way......*

He looked over his shoulder while trying to keep his heart from beating out of his chest. There was Fang, twice as big as he'd been in his dungeon, with gray smoke billowing out of his mouth.

*Gulp.*

Jinwoo swallowed hard.

*So this is the power of the Sphere of Avarice?*

These demons should have had some resistance to fire magic, since they lived in the Demon's Castle, but Fang had incinerated them all.

*Ha-ha!*

He couldn't help but laugh as he took it all in.

*Looks like I'll be able to clear this place faster than I thought.*

He cheered mentally as he gazed at the charred earth and flaming remains of demons.

* * *

With the buff from the Sphere of Avarice, Fang was a force to be reckoned with.

*Hwoooo.*

When Fang inhaled, the air around him turned cold for a moment, and then…

*Fwoosh.*

…he spat out fire left and right, reducing the enemy to ash.

[You have defeated a high-rank demon.]
[You have acquired 1,700 experience points.]
[You have defeated an archdemon.]
[You have acquired 2,200 experience points.]
.

.

[You have defeated a high-rank demon.]

Notifications about defeated enemies and acquired experience points kept coming and coming. The electronic chimes wouldn't stop.

Jinwoo smiled.

*Absolutely incredible!*

Fang eventually ran out of mana and ceased his attack. With one strike, Fang had been able to destroy most of the demons that had been approaching them, yet some lucky ones managed to escape. His other shadow soldiers took care of any survivors.

*Stomp, stomp, stomp, stomp!*

He finally felt like a genuine Shadow Monarch as he watched over his army of more than a hundred shadow soldiers in action.

[You have defeated a high-rank demon.]
[You have defeated a high-rank demon.]

The good news kept coming. Without lifting a finger, Jinwoo had annihilated the monsters with his shadow soldiers. Fang had contributed the most, of course.

*Way to go, Fang...*

Jinwoo looked up. The former high orc shaman turned shadow mage was as big as a giant, and the Sphere of Avarice in his hand had become proportionally bigger as well. The sphere was supposed to double the user's magic just by holding it. Though Fang had been nerfed when Jinwoo turned him into a shadow soldier, the sphere more than compensated for it.

*I'll let Fang hang on to the sphere for a while.*

Jinwoo had no skills that could use the doubling effect anyway. Jinwoo called up his skill window.

[Number of shadows extracted: 127/820]
[Number of shadows stored: 127/155]

Shadow Extraction, Shadow Storage, and Monarch's Domain... None of these skills was affected by the Sphere of Avarice. The only way to increase the extraction and storage numbers at the moment was to increase the intelligence stat.

Jinwoo closed the window.

*Tmp, tmp, tmp.*

At the end of the battle, soldiers gathered around Jinwoo. The corners of Jinwoo's mouth twitched as he surveyed the mounds of dead demon bodies.

*So many demons, so much loot.*

*Ping, ping, ping!*

This time, notifications about acquired items kept coming nonstop.

*Gotta take what I can.*

Jinwoo gladly accepted all the items and mounted Tank, the ice bear shadow soldier. He'd yet to find the entry permit for the next floor, which meant he had to kill more monsters.

Jinwoo gave the order to move.

"Giddyap!"

As Tank lumbered forward, his shadow soldiers followed.

\* \* \*

*Well, this is inefficient.*

Jinwoo thought it was a waste of time and resources to keep all 120 shadow soldiers moving as a single unit. There was strength in numbers if the soldiers were weak, but these soldiers had leveled up nicely and fared well against the demons. Plus, there were now A-rank dungeon magic beasts on the clock.

His army was next level.

"Kreeeeee!"

"Skree!"

[...defeated a high-rank demon.]
[...defeated a high-rank demon.]

But the sheer size of the army meant that it took longer to mobilize and locate monsters than it did to defeat them. And the problem was that a single floor in the Demon's Castle was as expansive as a big city.

*This will never end.*

Jinwoo decided to divide his army into six teams of twenty soldiers. He then sent them in different directions to hunt down monsters. He gave two orders.

*One, defeat all the enemies you encounter. Two, report to me as soon as you find a permit for the next floor.*

Jinwoo was unable to precisely communicate to his soldiers, but simple hand signals helped. Since soldiers couldn't pick up items, he had to meet them wherever the permit was spotted.

He'd have to abandon some loot, but the permit was his priority.

"Roll out."

With that, the six teams went their separate ways. Soon after...

[You have acquired 1,500 experience points.]
[You have acquired 1,500 experience points.]
[You have acquired 900 experience points.]
[You have acquired 1,100 experience points.]

Experience points came flooding in from all directions.

*Looks like they've gotten to work.*

Jinwoo happily watched his overall experience points steadily increase, but then he discovered something odd.

*The amount of experience points coming in is dropping?*

He hadn't seen any low- or mid-rank demons ever since he'd entered the upper floors. The most common monsters he came across here were high-rank demons and a few archdemons.

High-rank demons gave 1,700 experience points, while archdemons yielded a hefty 2,200 experience points. Yet Jinwoo was now raking in much lower numbers.

*Do I get less experience points the farther away my soldiers are?*

He silently monitored the experience points as they came in and noted that the amount was steadily decreasing for sure. He was nearly certain the distance between him and his soldiers affected the amount of experience points he received.

*Good to know.*

Thanks to the unique setting of the Demon's Castle, Jinwoo was able to glean new information about experience points. He hadn't sent out any soldiers on the lower floors. Down there, he'd preferred getting the combat experience and hadn't wanted to miss a single demon soul to complete his quest. He realized now how that had been a good decision.

Still, he wasn't really disappointed about the decreased experience points. Although each acquisition was lower, the overall balance was up, thanks to the more efficient patrol across these widespread hunting grounds.

The experience points notifications kept coming. Thanks to all those points, his stagnated level started rising as well.

**[You have leveled up!]**
**[You have leveled up!]**

Jinwoo pumped his fist.

*Nice.*

He felt like it was a waste to leave all that loot behind, but he could deal with that.

*This helps me level up and clear the dungeon quickly. I'm killing two birds with one stone.*

Jinwoo was more than content as he gazed at his new level.

\* \* \*

Jinwoo's plan was a slam dunk. He was able to head to the eightieth floor quicker than he'd expected. He summoned his soldiers as soon as he arrived.

*Vwoom...*

One hundred and nineteen soldiers spawned at once. Thanks to the experience points they'd earned from defeating monsters, they'd leveled up quickly as well.

*Oh? Tank went up ten levels already?*

He was surprised by this. Tank reared up on his hind legs and roared at the sky, excited that he'd leveled up to 28 and earned his master's attention for doing so. Jinwoo wasn't the only one benefiting from the efficient hunting.

He smiled. "Okay, let's go!"

He went solo, while his soldiers broke into six groups. He was used to working alone and didn't need help from them. He was also confident he could take on his entire shadow soldier army and win, with the exception of Fang with the buff from the Sphere of Avarice.

But...

*What if Fang was in the mix?*

Well... It certainly would be more fun to include Fang. He was daydreaming about the impossible anyway. About a week ago, Jinwoo had ordered a shadow soldier to attack him, both for fun and to test things out. For the first time ever, a shadow soldier had disobeyed him. Jinwoo didn't know if this was due to loyalty or some other force, but the solider wouldn't budge. For Jinwoo, as the master of these shadow soldiers, this wasn't a particularly disappointing discovery.

Wait...

*Why don't I see any demons?*

He tossed Barca's Dagger up and down as he tried to detect the presence of any monsters.

*There should be some around here......*

Jinwoo scanned his surroundings. He definitely sensed a presence but didn't see any monsters. Hadn't something like this happened before? He'd had a similar experience in the past.

At that moment, the ground shook a few times, and a mound of dirt shot up.

"Kee! Kee!"

"Keeee—"

Three cackling archdemons emerged at once and surrounded Jinwoo. Jinwoo frowned at them. The demons mistook that for fear and jumped at him with their mouths wide open. They were aiming for his head, known to be the most delicious part of a human.

But as their prey leaped and spun around in the air...

*Shhhk!*

The demons' heads fell to the ground before Jinwoo could even land.

**[You have defeated an archdemon.]**
**[You have defeated...]**

"Right!" Jinwoo clapped his hands together. He remembered a similar experience in the last C-rank dungeon he'd raided with Jinho.

*The stonemen hid underground and attacked like this.*

Jinwoo, who'd been getting frustrated trying to recall the incident, brightened. It almost felt like a load had been lifted from his shoulders. He happily grabbed the loot from the demons' corpses and then began walking off but stopped after a couple of steps.

"......" Jinwoo's eyes were fixed on the floor. He glared at the ground beneath his feet as he spoke. "Are you coming out or what?"

It was hard to tell whether it was the ground or the demons trembling.

* * *

It wasn't easy for Jinwoo to exit the eightieth floor.

*There must be some powerful demons out there, huh?*

Yet another team returned to him as shadows. He'd recalled his soldiers, as their repeated destruction and regeneration was exhausting his mana. This had never happened before. From the seventy-sixth floor to the eightieth, using the divide-and-conquer method of hunting had proved most efficient.

*Is it because the monsters are archdemons?*

The majority of monsters on the eightieth floor were archdemons instead of high-rank demons, and their attack of choice was to hide underground. Still, these demons didn't seem to have the power to be this difficult an obstacle for his soldiers.

There was something else going on. All the defeated soldiers were from teams without leaders. The groups led by Fang, Igris, Iron, and Tank were fine, but the two with no leader had been beaten down.

*Are the demons targeting the weaker teams?*

If so, that meant there were monsters out there with enough intelligence to figure out their enemy's vulnerabilities. What if these creatures weren't only strong but smart as well? Whatever they were, they were a pain in the ass.

There were four teams left. Five, including himself.

*If those things can find the weakest link, they're telegraphing their next target.*

With that thought, Jinwoo vanished into thin air.

Jinwoo quickly materialized at Tank's location. He spotted the team of shadow beasts, which was a mix of black bears with black steam rising from their backs and high orcs in full ebony armor. Tank, the leader of the pack, marched ahead of the rest.

*This will be their next target.*

When he was alive, Tank had led the ice bears, and he'd been a magic beast with the power to overwhelm shadow soldiers. Even after he became a shadow, only a handful of the soldiers were capable of defeating him in battle.

But that point was moot. The leaders of the other teams—Iron, Igris, and Fang—were on another level. Sure, Tank was of a higher rank, but he was still only a foot soldier. Igris and Iron were knight rank, and Fang was even an elite knight rank. Tank was no match for them.

So if these enemies had the intelligence to figure out their opponent's weakest link, they would strike here next.

*I'll hang back and observe for a bit.*

Jinwoo masked his presence as well as he could while keeping pace with the shadow beasts from a certain distance. His soldiers didn't notice that he was nearby.

How much time passed? Jinwoo was surprised they'd wait this long. There was no sign of the enemy.

*Was I wrong?*

He was entertaining the thought that maybe there had been too many monsters for his soldiers to battle at once when... His eyes narrowed.

*......Something's happening.*

The enemy was masking their presence until they got closer so Jinwoo didn't notice them until they were nearly on top of their target. Jinwoo closed his eyes and activated his perception. Like a radar, it detected all the enemies nearby.

*There are four of them approaching, twenty of my soldiers, and five demons hiding underground.*

He opened his eyes. He decided to leave the five underfoot for later.

*Stealth.*

*Fwoo...*

Jinwoo turned invisible and made his way toward his soldiers. Soon, he was able to see the enemy with his own eyes.

*They're on horseback.*

*Clip-clop, clip-clop, clip-clop, clip-clop.*

*And they're armed, too?*

They were wearing armor and riding on horses. He was able to see their names as they got closer. Jinwoo had never seen a demon, regardless of rank, wear armor, so he knew they had to be of a different caliber, and true to form, their names reflected that.

*A demon noble and three demon knights.*

Jinwoo had never seen those titles before, but there they were, floating in black letters.

He sensed strong hostility from them.

*I bet they're the thorns in my soldiers' sides.*

They were emitting strong auras of power and animosity. Jinwoo decided to stay invisible and observe awhile longer.

*Let's see how they do.*

He wanted to study the abilities and battle styles of these new demons as much as possible.

*To think there are demons who can defeat my shadow soldiers......*

He was honestly looking forward to the match. Jinwoo stood where he wouldn't impede the battle between his shadow soldier army and the new demons.

*Grrrr?*

Tank spotted the demons, and they promptly dismounted.

*I guess the horses are just for transportation.*

Jinwoo watched the demons with great interest. Spotting the enemy, the shadow soldiers let out enthusiastic rally war cries and charged first. The fight was on.

*Groaaar!*

Tank took the lead. He ran as fast as his four legs could carry him and rose on his hindquarters in front of the demons. Had the enemy been ordinary humans, they would've fainted, but the demons didn't flinch. None of them moved an inch until Tank swung a front leg like a bat with all his might.

*Whoosh!*

Tank's forepaw swiped the air, which was a surprisingly agile attack considering his bulk.

But...the demon noble Tank had tried to target expertly leaped over the shadow bear's leg.

*......!*

Jinwoo wasn't expecting that.

And the surprises kept coming. After spinning in midair, the noble thrust its spear into Tank.

*Shhhuk!*

Imbued with magic power, the attack left a hole the size of a watermelon in Tank's chest. The demon noble's moves were clean and graceful. Jinwoo sensed explosive energy coming from its small frame. His fascination with the new demons grew.

*That's no ordinary monster.*

But it wasn't just the noble. The three knights protecting it were also plainly powerful. The battle was clearly one-sided; the shadow soldiers were no match for demons. Unlike archdemons that were big but easy to hunt, these humanoid demon knights easily trampled all over the shadow beasts.

*This is why the regeneration couldn't keep up.*

Jinwoo was stunned.

"Arrroooo!"

"Arrrgh!"

Shadow beasts were cut down by spears and swords as soon as they regenerated.

Jinwoo felt torn. The shadow soldiers were immortal as long as he had mana. If he ran out, they would simply turn into shadows and retreat to him.

"Aroo!"

Even so, he didn't like seeing his own soldiers getting cut down like this. Was this what it felt like to have a baby brother come home after getting beaten up?

*I've had enough.*

Jinwoo couldn't bear to watch any longer and called back his soldiers. The shadow beasts retreated beneath Jinwoo's feet in an instant to merge with his shadow.

The noble demons exchanged looks and nodded to one another after seeing the shadow beasts give up and run. It looked like they were celebrating their third victory.

Just then…

*Vwoom.*

Jinwoo deactivated his Stealth skill and appeared in their midst.

*Flinch!*

The demons recoiled, but sensing his hostility, they quickly recovered and attacked.

*Whack!*

*Whack!*

Jinwoo knocked the two knights nearest him to the dirt using his bare fists, then flipped a knight that charged at him.

*Wham!*

Cracks on the ground spread out like a spider's web as a message came up.

[You have defeated a demon knight.]
[You have acquired 3,000 experience points.]

The same notification appeared three times. He'd killed three monsters with three moves in less than a second.

*These are just the lackeys anyway. I want the leader.*

Jinwoo's eyes turned to the demon noble. The noble startled when they made eye contact, then pointed a spear at Jinwoo.

*I always wondered if monsters felt fear......*

Now he knew for sure. The tip of the demon's spear trembled a little, which hadn't happened when it had dealt with the shadow soldiers. Being able to assess an opponent's power was also an ability, after all.

*Just because you can feel fear doesn't mean I'm going easy on you.*

Jinwoo threw himself forward right as the demon thrust its spear. Jinwoo avoided the strike by turning his head. It came as a shock to him, however, that the demon was able to continuously attack him with the spear in midair.

The first stab was aimed between his eyes, the next went for his neck, and the last tried to get him in the heart. The noble had impressive moves that flowed as smoothly as water. Yet Jinwoo blocked each attack with Barca's Dagger. During the failed attempt at his heart, he used the dagger to bisect the spear at the handle.

*......!*

The noble froze when it saw its weapon cut in two. With that, the match was set.

*Even three or four A-rank hunters attacking at once would be no match for this guy......*

Jinwoo gave his opponent a high evaluation. It was simply unlucky to have met him.

He grabbed ahold of the enemy's helmet.

"Argh!" The demon was caught by surprise and attempted in vain to free itself, but Jinwoo's grip was too strong.

He transferred energy to his left hand in order to pull the helmet off and go for the neck. As he expected, the helmet came off easily.

*Whud.*

He raised Barca's Dagger high into the air.

"Surrender! I surrender!"

Jinwoo halted his hand.

"A woman?"

The face underneath the helmet was definitely female, not that Jinwoo cared what gender the demon was. But when the monster, raising her arms in surrender, realized her words were reaching him, she dropped to her knees and touched her head to the ground.

*......*

Jinwoo wasn't so coldhearted as to kill her on the spot.

"I'm s-s-sorry. We were in the wrong. P-please spare my life!" Not only had her attitude shifted dramatically, but she was also now begging for her life. A monster, begging for its life...?

"Huh......?"

Jinwoo stared at the slight creature in complete bewilderment.

\* \* \*

Since intelligent magic beasts existed, it came as no surprise that intelligent monsters also existed, but this creature was definitely an anomaly.

......

Jinwoo didn't know what to say or how to respond to the demon. With much difficulty, he eventually spoke. "Are you asking me to spare your life after you attacked my soldiers?"

"I-I've committed an unforgivable crime!" The demon noble slammed her forehead to the ground as she spoke. "But it is my family's duty to protect this place, and we couldn't just stand by while our kind was hunted by those bast— Ah! I mean, by those soldiers. I will forever be indebted to you if you would spare me."

Well, that was fair enough from the demons' perspectives. Technically, Jinwoo and his soldiers had attacked them unprovoked.

So he changed the question. "How can you ask someone who killed your soldiers to spare your life?"

"It is the knights' duty to protect their master. They would have appreciated my safe return."

Jinwoo scratched his temple. Her answer was laughable.

*Is this monster being impudent or overly optimistic?*

The demon noble stole a peek at Jinwoo's expression.

*Eep!*

She sensed things weren't going well for her. She put her head down again and spoke with an urgent tone. "If you spare my life, I will give you whatever you want."

Jinwoo placed his hands on his hips. Even though this demon noble was a powerful monster, killing her now would be like shooting fish in a barrel.

*What should I do?*

He thought about it. It wasn't a question of whether or not to let the monster go but rather a question of what could be more valuable than the experience points or the items he'd get from killing this monster...?

*Oh.*

There was only one thing.

"An entry permit."

"Pardon?"

The demon's head shot up in surprise. She looked much like a human female except for the long, sharp canines that showed when she opened her mouth.

Jinwoo casually asked, "Can you get me one?"

"......" The monster went pale when she made eye contact with Jinwoo, and then she put her forehead back on the ground.

*I guess there's no reason for monsters to know about items.*

Oh well. Jinwoo retrieved Barca's Dagger from his inventory. He had no idea how there was a monster intelligent enough to ask for mercy, but he had no intention of giving up the experience points.

*A demon knight earned me three thousand, so this one is probably worth more, right?*

He might even get that entry permit once he killed this thing. As he was about to reach a decision, though...

"I'll g-give it to you."

"Give me what?"

"Th-th-the permit."

The monster looked up and broke out in a cold sweat as she spotted the dagger in Jinwoo's hand.

"You can get me an entry permit?"

The demon hurriedly nodded. "Our family guards it. If you deliver me safely back to them, I will turn it over to you."

Demons guarded the entry permits? Jinwoo tapped the end of his chin. He had been on the eightieth floor for some time and defeated quite a hefty number of demons, yet there hadn't been a sign of that permit.

*I originally thought the drop rate for items may have decreased on higher floors or that maybe a mini boss would produce one, but...*

Everything made sense if the monsters had been guarding the permits as this one claimed.

Unnerved by Jinwoo's silence, the demon grew more desperate. "I know where all the permits for the higher floors are! If you guarantee my and my family's safety, I can show you."

Jinwoo's mind began to change. Now this was quite tempting. Jinwoo's goal was to get to the highest floor as quickly as possible, so the proposal of being shown the location of all permits was quite attractive. The only issue was...

*Can I trust this demon?*

He reached down and grabbed her by the chin. He sensed her panic but didn't relent. He looked the demon right in the eyes.

*Murderous Intent.*

**[Skill: Murderous Intent has been activated.]**

*Hwoo...*

Jinwoo's eyes sent out a chilling aura. The demon was so frightened, her lips quivered.

"Can I trust you?"

"I s-s-speak the truth."

Jinwoo had made a vow to himself when he first received his powers from the system. He would honor the principle of equivalent exchange. It didn't matter if his opponent was a monster; if she kept her promise, he would keep his as well.

"Fine." Jinwoo deactivated Murderous Intent. "If you hand over the permits, I'll leave in peace."

"R-really?"

He nodded. It was regrettable that he wouldn't be able to earn experience points from the monsters who guarded the entry permits, but spending time searching for the them was an even bigger waste. He'd already squandered more time than he'd expected on the eightieth floor. And besides, if everything was a lie, that would be fine for him, too. He'd be able to go to town on her and her kind.

"Thank you!" The demon noble was visibly relieved.

He wasn't sure if those were her genuine feelings or if she was just naive. Jinwoo raised an eyebrow.

He did have one thing he'd been wanting to ask her. "Before we go, tell me...what exactly are you?"

# 9
## PARTY MEMBER

# 9

## PARTY MEMBER

"I'm Esil, eldest daughter of the Radir Clan. My family is—"

"Never mind that."

Jinwoo cut her off. He didn't care about her family history. He wanted to know why monsters and instance dungeons existed. How should he approach this topic? He didn't even need a complete answer. Any clue would be great.

He had asked the same of magic beasts, but the only thing he'd learned was that they kept hearing something in their heads ordering them to kill humans.

*Do monsters also hear a voice in their heads?*

He decided to ask a simpler question that would allow him to compare them to magic beasts.

"Do you also keep hearing a voice in your head telling you to kill humans?"

"Pardon?" Esil raised her head and blinked.

Since she was still on her knees, Jinwoo had to look down to maintain eye contact with her, and it was making him quite uncomfortable.

*Tsk.*

Jinwoo clicked his tongue and helped her up like he would a child.

He looked her in the eyes again. He could hear Esil's heartbeat accelerating, as if scared by his sudden touch.

He continued questioning her. "I'm asking if someone keeps whispering to you to kill humans."

"Oh..." Esil thought for a moment, then spoke with a little bit of hesitation. "No, but we hear something else."

"What's that?"

"It tells us...to protect our home." She spoke cautiously while trying to get a read on Jinwoo.

*Monsters have a different reason for existence than magic beasts.*

The magic beasts existed to kill humans, and monsters existed to protect the instance dungeons. Their reasons for being were quite different.

*Wait......*

*So does that make me like a magic beast to monsters?* Jinwoo now felt a little guilty that he'd frightened Esil half to death by exposing her to Murderous Intent. But the guilt was minimal.

"When did you start hearing that voice?"

"Ever since we woke up in this place."

*Woke up here?*

Had these monsters lived somewhere else before? Whether this was a real memory or something planted in her mind, there it was. This could be a clue to unraveling the mystery of the system.

Jinwoo pressed further. "Then where were you before you woke up here?"

"In the demon world. Then one day, we woke up here."

"What were you doing in this demon world?"

"We were...preparing for a war."

"A war?"

"Yes."

Was Esil remembering the past? She looked somber now, different from how she'd looked when begging for her life. "We were on the brink of war against a terrifyingly powerful enemy, so we had to unite demons from all over our world, but—"

Esil stopped there. "……"

No, she continued talking. Jinwoo could see her lips were moving. But no sound came out of her mouth. Instead, he heard the system's electronic voice.

[The conversation includes confidential information and has been blocked.]
[The conversation includes confidential information and has been blocked.]
[The conversation includes confidential information and...]

The message repeated until Esil finished answering. Jinwoo's eyes shone. *Ha, I wouldn't have even noticed if the system had stayed quiet.*

Jinwoo would've thought Esil's explanation was just some kind of backstory added by the system, like leveling up, instance dungeons, quests, rewards, penalties, and the job change process, which were similar to elements in a video game. A backstory for monsters wouldn't have been out of place. But the way the system intervened just now convinced Jinwoo of one thing.

*Talking to this monster will lead to more clues.*

The system had exposed a flaw.

"Was it s-s-something I said?" Esil looked worried because of Jinwoo's harsh expression.

*What is the system trying to hide? Who the demons were going to war with? The reason for the war? The outcome of the war?*

Jinwoo asked a more pointed question to find out. "Who was this terrifyingly powerful enemy?"

But then…like a toy whose battery just died, Esil stopped moving. It didn't last long, though.

"Ohhh…" Esil passed out.

Jinwoo caught her and laid her on the ground. She was still breathing, and it didn't look like anything too serious. She grimaced like she was in pain, though, and she appeared to be having trouble breathing.

Jinwoo ripped Esil's armor off with his hands to help her breathe more easily.

*Crunk.*

The armor came apart quickly. He then tore off the cape attached to the armor, rolled it, and placed it under her head as a makeshift pillow. It was a hassle doing this, whether it was for a monster or not, but it wasn't necessarily done out of the kindness of his heart.

*This enemy of the demons......*

The system was ultrasensitive about their identity.

*Maybe there's something there?*

If they had some kind of transcendental power they could use to affect the earth and him somehow...

Jinwoo called up the shop. He tried to wake Esil with a potion, but it didn't help.

*I guess I have no choice but to wait.*

*Whump.*

He took a seat beside Esil and proceeded to calmly organize in his mind all the clues he'd gleaned from her until she woke up.

* * *

"Huh?" Esil bolted upright.

She sensed a presence to one side. Esil flinched seeing Jinwoo sitting there silently.

*It wasn't a dream.*

She slowly came back to reality and scanned the area. The dead bodies of archdemons were strewn everywhere. Her eyes went wide. Demons without intelligence didn't consider demons with intelligence as their own kind. She would've been easy prey for them while she was unconscious. Yet she was still alive.

"Did you protect me?"

Jinwoo got up instead of answering her. He then extended his hand.

Esil took it and carefully rose to her feet, genuinely touched. "Thank you."

"How far to where the permit is?"

"It's close. I will show you the way." She put her wrists together and held them out.

"......?"

"......?"

Both Jinwoo and Esil looked puzzled. Frustrated, she spoke first. "You need to bind my hands, since I'm a hostage."

"Don't need to." He was confident he could stop her from resisting or trying to escape without restraining her. There was no need to waste any more time on something pointless. Jinwoo turned her around and gently pushed her forward.

He detected Esil's heart beating faster, as if she was still afraid of him, but didn't say anything. He looked at the horses the monsters had ridden.

"What about the horses?"

"I'll take them." Esil reddened as she led the way, pulling three horses along by their reins.

Jinwoo quietly followed her.

* * *

Just as Esil had said, they soon arrived at a place that definitely looked as if it might be guarding an entry permit. It was a huge castle.

*A demon's castle within the Demon's Castle…*

The Demon's Castle dungeon was more of a tower than a castle, but the castle before Jinwoo's eyes really looked like something from medieval times. The soldiers guarding the castle gates instantly tensed at the sight of Jinwoo. But…

"A guest." They immediately opened the gates as Esil casually pointed at them with her chin. Soon after, a group of knights emerged from within the castle.

"Lady Esil, we've been waiting for you."

"Where is my father?"

"He's in the throne room."

"Understood."

One of the knights peeked at Jinwoo and asked, "Lady Esil...who is the man behind you?"

"He's an important guest, so be polite."

Taking a cue from Esil's solemn voice, the knights bowed as they cleared the way.

Jinwoo followed Esil into the farthest corner of the castle. After walking down a hallway for a time, they arrived at a huge chamber similar to a boss's lair in a dungeon.

*Is this the throne room?*

Jinwoo looked around. Other than the columns that stretched toward the ceiling, the room was quite empty. It was like the space was made for fighting.

*If I fought my way in here, this is where the boss battle would take place.*

That meant the demon noble sitting on the raised throne at the far end of the room would be the boss of this castle. Esil and Jinwoo stood before him.

The boss spoke first. "Esil."

"Father, this is..."

Before Esil could explain, the boss's eyes met Jinwoo's. His pupils dilated.

"You! Who the hell did you bring here?"

"Father, he's a guest..."

He wouldn't calm down even after Esil's desperate explanation. "A guest? What kind of guest brings an army into the host's house?"

"Pardon?" Esil looked at Jinwoo.

*What army?*

Without taking his eyes off Jinwoo, the boss spoke with a shaky voice. "Esil, can't you see the many soldiers hidden in the dark depths of that man?"

Jinwoo narrowed his eyes. Esil shuddered and took a step back at the change in Jinwoo's mood. He appeared to have been caught off guard.

*He's got keen senses.*

The boss seemed to be able to detect the soldiers hiding in Jinwoo's shadow.

*I'm not sure whether that's a good thing or not.*

Jinwoo had recalled all his shadow soldiers from wherever they were just in case a fight broke out.

"How dare you bring soldiers into my house?"

Knights rushed into the room upon hearing the boss's raised voice.

"Father!" Esil yelled.

The boss had risen and was glowering at Jinwoo.

Jinwoo, who'd been silently watching this all unfold, finally spoke up. "I made a promise."

The boss's eyebrows twitched at how unfazed Jinwoo looked. "What did you promise?"

"The entry permit." Jinwoo took a step forward. "I will leave here in peace if you hand over the entry permit."

The boss swallowed hard.

*Is this the man who's been killing demons and clearing floors at an incredible speed?*

He had been disheartened when he heard that the trusty Vulcan and Metus had been killed.

Despite the Radir Clan's noble status, they were some of the weakest demons, ranking twentieth in strength overall. If this enemy had defeated Vulcan and Metus that easily, the boss was prepared for major losses. But this terrifying foe was offering to leave on his own.

*Can I trust him...?*

The lord of the castle had his doubts. "Is that the only condition?"

Jinwoo had been waiting for this. "That, and..."

Of course not. The boss frowned as his suspicion was validated. A powerful being's demands were never-ending. How much more humiliation would this man heap on the Radir Clan, and how much further would he provoke the knights with his unreasonable demands? The demons' leader was already disgruntled even before hearing out Jinwoo.

The man put his hand on Esil's shoulder.

"I'd like to take her."

"What?" The boss and knights simultaneously burst into protest.

Jinwoo looked around at the demons.

*Huh?*

Esil had said she knew where all the entry permits for the higher floors were. Jinwoo wanted to take her with him because he needed her to show the way…

*Did I say something wrong?*

Jinwoo observed the boss shaking like a leaf, the shocked knights, and the blushing Esil as he blinked in confusion.

\* \* \*

"A guide?" The boss composed himself after hearing Esil's explanation and Jinwoo's request.

He took a seat on his throne again.

*The permit and a guide. Is that really all he wants?*

For as long as they'd been here, they had been told to protect this area. They weren't being overtly forced, but it had become a basic instinct to them, like eating when hungry or closing one's eyes when sleepy. Thus, his heart sank when he heard that black-armored soldiers had invaded and were hunting down demons. He'd thought this was the end.

The boss had sent out a counterattack force after much debate and was surprised at how easily the black soldiers were defeated. However, scouts then reported that there were soldiers on a whole other level from the ones they had successfully eliminated. The scout doubted they could stand against the units led by a fire-breathing beast, a giant knight, and another fierce-looking knight in a helmet with a large mane. That was why the entire Radir Clan had been preparing to go to war.

But there had been no word in the report about the man now standing before the boss. In other words, the enemies' main power came from elsewhere.

*Had I known this monstrous human was the master of the shadow soldiers, I wouldn't have even started to counterattack.*

The boss could see the reality of the situation. The black soldiers he'd thought they'd taken care of weren't gone—they were present in the dark depths of the man. They were lying in wait for their master's orders. The boss got chills from the hostile glares of those countless soldiers.

*It hurts my pride to compromise with a human, but...*

Of course, the entry permit was included on the list of things they were to protect. But wasn't the price to protect the scroll too high? The boss wasn't confident they could defeat the black soldiers even by sacrificing their entire army. On top of that, there was this human.

*......He's concealing his true abilities.*

The boss didn't know what Jinwoo's endgame was, but he could tell he was seeing only the tip of the iceberg above calm waters. It was a truly frightening thing to face off against an enemy without knowing the full extent of what one was dealing with.

The boss spoke with a nervous look on his face. "So...is that really all you want?"

If he could protect everything else by simply giving up the permit, then there was no reason to deny the request. This wouldn't be going against the order to protect the area, since it would actually shield it from further harm.

Jinwoo nodded.

"You won't harm my daughter, will you?"

Jinwoo could feel Esil's eyes on him.

*A monster who worries about his daughter......*

Fascinated at the concept, he shook his head.

The boss thought about it for a beat and then beamed. "We'll do that, then."

The boss felt like a weight had been lifted from his shoulders. If this damn piece of paper could stop the foretold disaster, wasn't that cause for celebration? "No, I would very much appreciate it if you did that."

Jinwoo had been preparing for the worst-case scenario, but the boss's bright smile had him relaxing and laughing along.

*I guess Esil got her personality from her father.*

Was this just the system's programming, or had her explanation actually been true...?

Jinwoo let that thought rest for now and gave a firm answer to his waiting host. "I'll keep my promise."

"Good." The boss snapped his fingers, and a soldier brought a large scroll to Jinwoo.

He opened it.

*It's an actual entry permit.*

Jinwoo smiled as he looked over its contents.

**[ITEM: ENTRY PERMIT]**
**Acquisition Difficulty: ??**
**Category: ??**
**This permit grants access to the eighty-first floor of the Demon's Castle. It can be used only on the magic teleportation circle on the eighteeth floor.**

Jinwoo hadn't thought he could negotiate with monsters to acquire an item. Yet this was the real deal. The only difference between this permit and the ones from lower floors was the mark of Radir stamped in red.

*Am I supposed to get permits from different clans from here on?*

Jinwoo smiled. He liked this much better than having to randomly hunt down monsters in the hopes one would drop what he needed. He rolled it up and put it into his inventory.

"Shall we leave right away, then?" Jinwoo turned around, rushing Esil along, but knights were blocking the exit.

......?

Jinwoo looked suspiciously at Esil, who grinned at him.

What was going on?

The boss approached Jinwoo and stood in front of him.

"The Radir Clan can't let a guest leave just like that."

It might have looked like he was trying to intimidate Jinwoo with his huge, monstrous body, but his face bore the smile of a friendly middle-aged man and wasn't threatening in the least.

The boss wheedled. "Why don't you have a meal with us to celebrate our successful transaction? My daughter will probably need to prepare for the long journey."

Jinwoo looked at Esil. It appeared she was hoping he'd accept. She had kept her promise, so shouldn't Jinwoo do the gentlemanly thing? Besides, he had to eat anyway, and he was starting to get tired of the bread and meat from the shop.

"......Sure."

The boss laughed as Jinwoo acquiesced. "Good!"

Esil's and the knights' expressions also brightened.

Soon, the boss was bellowing at his subordinates. "What are you waiting for? Go and prepare the meal!"

* * *

After all that time spent on the eightieth floor, Jinwoo didn't want to waste any more time than necessary on the other floors. Fortunately, his one concern—whether or not Esil could use the teleportation circle—was quickly and unexpectedly resolved.

[A demon noble would like to join your party.]
[Would you like to accept?]
[If you accept, your companion may use the teleportation deviation circle, and it is possible to share experiences points based on her contribution.]

*Share experience points with my party?*

The word *share* annoyed Jinwoo, but upon closer inspection, the "contribution" part registered in his brain. In other words, he wouldn't have to share experience points if he didn't give his companion a chance to fight.

Jinwoo ironed this out with Esil. "If a fight breaks out, don't get involved. I'll take care of it."

"......Understood." Esil responded bashfully.

......?

So Jinwoo accepted her as a companion and hurried along. Esil carried a pack much bigger than herself and had a hard time keeping up. The pack wasn't heavy, but Jinwoo moved like the wind. He sometimes stopped and waited for her to catch up.

"There it is." Esil, who'd been consulting a map of the eighty-first floor, pointed at the castle coming into view in the distance. Jinwoo had already spotted it and nodded.

"Hold on, please." Esil put down the huge pack and started digging inside. She withdrew a ceramic bottle containing liquor.

Jinwoo asked, "What's that for?"

"This is a drink favored by the Garsh Clan. If you bring this to the negotiations—"

"Negotiations?" Jinwoo grinned and called upon his shadow soldiers.

*Come forth.*

Shadow soldiers sprang out immediately.

*Vwoom.*

*Ah......!*

Esil couldn't believe what she was seeing. There were three black-clad soldiers as powerful as high-rank nobles. The one who had summoned them now held two daggers in his hands. She found it hard to believe that the man in front of her, emitting an energy so sharp that it felt like it could pierce her skin, was the same person she had been speaking to moments earlier.

"A-aren't you going there to negotiate?"

Jinwoo responded with a question. "Is your family close to this Garsh Clan?"

"N-n-no. Nobles have fought over ranks since we resided in the demon world... But they're not an unreasonable clan."

Jinwoo smirked at her response. "That's fine, then."

One exception was enough. Leveling up was just as important as getting the permit.

"Wait here." Jinwoo speedily led his soldiers toward the castle.

"P-p-please hold on!" Startled at his sudden disappearance, Esil belatedly looked toward the castle. "What?!"

The castle of the Garsh Clan was on fire.

*Fwwwoooosh.*

From a distance, it looked like the giant black beast was blowing fire onto the castle gates and walls and effortlessly melting them. The castle's knights rushed out in shock and were slaughtered by shadow soldiers one by one.

"Oh no……" It wasn't clear if it was an exclamation or a groan spilling out of Esil's mouth.

"Aaargh!"

"Gaaaah!"

Castle Garsh was several times more heavily fortified than Castle Radir, but it was helplessly falling apart.

Esil swallowed nervously.

*If Father hadn't surrendered the permit easily……*

The castle she was looking at now could've been Castle Radir. Just thinking about it made her feel faint. She felt fortunate that things had worked out with Jinwoo.

*Craaaaash.*

A tower behind the castle walls toppled with a loud crash.

*How could we hope to stand up to those monsters……?*

Esil wiped the sweat from her chin, relieved that her family had avoided this disaster.

\* \* \*

The executives from the Hunter's Association of Japan and senior officials of the Japanese government were all gathered in one place. The air was heavy inside the meeting room as the president of the association spoke quietly.

"The people of Korea are excited about their tenth S-rank hunter."

The senior government officials smirked. Japan had more than twenty S-rank hunters, but the Koreans were all worked up over hunter number ten. Though it did make sense, considering Korea actually only had eight S ranks currently in their midst. One had immigrated to another country, and another had died in an accident.

But the purpose of today's meeting wasn't to mock Korea. If it was, the mood wouldn't be this serious.

The minister of defense sat frowning in his chair. "So what's that got to do with today's meeting?"

The tone of his voice reflected his unpleasant mood. Jeju Island, in the southern part of Korea, had been invaded by magic beasts after a dungeon raid had failed. These weren't just any regular magic beasts, either. They were ant-like magic beasts known for their ability to stay organized and multiply rapidly.

The Japanese government would've been satisfied if that was the end of it, sneering at the Korean government's problem. But the issue had reached Japanese soil as well. Yesterday, a small village had been erased from the map by an ant suspected of flying in from Jeju Island.

They could no longer ignore the danger. The immediate priority was to calm down the prime minister, as he was worked up about counter-measures. Everybody's job was on the line, so it was time to dispense with the banter. No wonder the minister of defense was so tense.

The president of the association continued. "Mistakes happen when people act too hastily." The president's age and experience were evident from his gray hair and the wrinkles on his face. "But I think this is the right time."

People in the meeting had been distracted, but everyone paid attention to him after this important statement.

The minister of defense now sounded nervous. "Do you…have a good plan in mind?"

"Better to call it *appropriate* rather than *good*."

The senior government officials, including the minister of defense as well as the executives of the association, were all ears now. There was a pregnant pause before the president spoke again.

"If someone claims a piece of land is theirs even though they don't have the power to protect that land, do you acknowledge them as the landowner?"

"......"

There was dead silence. What was the president of the association trying to say? Considering the relationship between Korea and Japan, this wasn't something they could dismiss as the ramblings of an old man. Not to mention, the person who had uttered those words was currently leading the Hunter's Association of Japan.

"So what are you trying to say?" a minister of state asked cautiously.

The president of the association looked around the room confidently.

"We will rid Jeju Island of those magic beasts."

The room exploded in murmurs.

"And..."

The commotion subsided as the president continued.

"We will make Jeju Island ours."

# 10
## IMMINENT THREAT

# 10

## IMMINENT THREAT

Take over Jeju Island?

The executives of the Hunter's Association of Japan remained level-headed, as if this was something they'd discussed previously. But the senior officials of the government were the exact opposite.

"What are you talking about?"

"Do you want to start a war with South Korea?"

"They've been prepared for war for over sixty years."

"This is madness!"

The government officials' voices rose.

They were stuck between a rock and a hard place. They had no idea how many of them would still have a job if they didn't get answers for the prime minister and the media soon. They'd turned to the president of the Hunter's Association for a solution, and what did he suggest? A what of Jeju Island?

This absurd notion infuriated the incredibly busy officials of the government. They would've berated Shigeo Matsumoto, the president of the association, for wasting their time if he hadn't had hunter body-guards beside him.

*It's fascinating how these people never change.*

President Matsumoto smiled despite all the harsh criticism being directed his way. This reaction was part of a calculated plan.

*Tsk, tsk.*

President Matsumoto clicked his tongue and remained quiet for a time before speaking up again.

"I'm not saying we go to war or to take the island by force."

"What?"

"Then what are you planning to do?"

"Could you just spit it out already?"

A smirk spread across President Matsumoto's face. "We have to make South Korea hand the island over to us of their own free will."

President Matsumoto's icy demeanor brought down the fevered temperature of the room. Based on what he'd just said and how he'd said it, he was being completely serious.

......

The deputy prime minister, known to be quite a coolheaded man himself, opened his mouth for the first time today. "President Matsumoto."

He was here as the official representative and right-hand man of the prime minister. As his representative, anything he said at today's meeting was tantamount to the prime minister himself saying it.

"What you just suggested... How do you propose to make it happen?" The second most powerful member of the Japanese cabinet relayed his interest in President Matsumoto's plan.

Were they willing to listen now? President Matsumoto began his explanation in earnest. "Korea doesn't have the power to take care of an S-rank gate. They didn't four years ago when the ants first emerged, and they still don't at this point in time."

The deputy prime minister nodded in agreement.

Jeju Island was a large island and made up 2 percent of South Korea's total landmass. For such a large area to be overrun by magic beasts... Need he say more? The Korean government had given up on Jeju Island after three failed attempts at containing the beasts, or so people believed.

"How do you think they'd react to the suggestion that we send in our Japanese S-rank hunters to deal with the ants?"

The news that some ants could fly had reached Korea as well. It was only a matter of time before the ants themselves reached mainland Korea. The Korean powers that be would be crazy to refuse the help. However...

"Do you think they'd just hand Jeju over to us because we helped them?" The deputy prime minister saw a lot of holes in this scheme.

Sneers came from government officials here and there, but the deputy prime minister wasn't pointing this out to scorn or berate the president. He calmly continued. "Say we help Korea with the ant problem on Jeju Island like you said."

President Matsumoto was confident in the abilities of both the Korean and Japanese hunters to get rid of the ants. Nobody was questioning that.

"What's in it for us?"

Despite the damage done on Japanese soil, the ants on Jeju Island were still solely Korea's problem. Japan couldn't sacrifice their hunters to help Korea.

*That can never happen.*

The deputy prime minister was good at calculating things for his and his country's interest. Equivalent exchange—that was the basic principle of politics. If Japan lent Japanese hunters to help Korea, they'd need to receive compensation.

*Gaining possession of Jeju Island wouldn't even cover it.*

The deputy prime minister's ideas were in line with the president of the association's, which was why he'd shown interest in the first place. But President Matsumoto's ideas were about as feasible as trying to catch a cloud. The deputy prime minister immediately lost interest.

Just then, President Matsumoto laughed. "Who said we're actually going to help Korea?"

The deputy prime minister frowned.

*Is he messing with me?*

He was about to politely ask President Matsumoto to stop wasting time when...

*Wait......*

The deputy prime minister's eyes widened. President Matsumoto had said they would offer help... He'd never said they actually would help.

"Are you...?"

"Exactly." President Matsumoto casually confirmed. He could tell by the deputy prime minister's startled expression that he'd caught on to the true plan.

"You're going to...throw the Korean hunters to the ants?"

President Matsumoto expected as much.

*There's a reason he's lauded as a clever man.*

He looked at the deputy prime minister with a pleased smile. "When Korea's top hunters trust us and accept our help, we'll let them go after the queen ant while we withdraw our hunters."

Korea had already experienced three failures. Who would suspect that a fourth would be the result of a betrayal by Japan? And it wouldn't matter if they caught on, because it would all be over by then.

The deputy prime minister's voice was shaking. "Are...are you going to wipe out all of Korea's highest-rank hunters?"

"Their fate was sealed when the gate opened on Jeju Island and they didn't have the power to close it." President Matsumoto emphasized the inevitability of this situation. "They've been on borrowed time for a while now."

"That means..."

"South Korea will be extremely vulnerable with all their highest hunters gone!"

What if the flying ants made their way to Korea's mainland while there were no S ranks left? Would they still be able to continue ignoring the ants? If it was only one or two ants, their guilds might be able to take care of them, but statistics showed that the ants multiplied rapidly, and that would endanger all of Korea.

*They would probably cry to other countries for help.*

But who would aid them? Both China and Russia had legions of hunters, but they also had great swaths of land to protect. The United States had outright refused to help when the S-rank gate had first opened. North Korea would just send in S-rank hunters to invade Seoul.

*No, they would only have Japan to turn to.*

Japan would also suffer if the numbers of flying ants increased. Korea would have no choice but to beg for Japan's help, and Japan would be able to demand whatever it wanted in return.

*The Koreans might actually hand over Jeju Island without a fight if they found themselves in that situation......*

It would all go according to the president's plan. The deputy prime minister got goose bumps. President Matsumoto was willing to lead all of a nation's best hunters to their deaths for the sake of his gambit, which could then lead to that country's ruin.

*Shigeo Matsumoto is a terrifying man.*

The diabolical plan gave the deputy prime minister the chills.

But that wasn't the end. President Matsumoto continued. "Jeju Island is only the beginning."

Little by little, Korea would have to come crawling to Japan every time they needed the help of S-rank hunters. It would be possible to take over the whole of Korea without firing a single shot.

"...And those are my thoughts on the matter."

The government officials finally exhaled after listening with bated breath to President Matsumoto's lengthy explanation. They'd thought he was somewhat crazy earlier, but now they were hanging on his every word.

President Matsumoto spoke quietly. "What say you, Deputy Prime Minister?"

All eyes turned to him.

"......" He swallowed hard.

Whatever he said would be taken as the word of the prime minister, and the prime minister wouldn't walk back on the decision because he trusted his aide.

He had to think carefully.

......

The deputy prime minister debated the issue over and over in his mind. Finally, he raised his head. "How can the government help you?"

\* \* \*

[You have defeated a demon knight.]
[You have acquired 3,000 experience points.]
[You have defeated a demon knight.]
[You have acquired 3,000 experience points.]
[You have defeated a demon noble.]
[You have acquired 4,500 experience points.]

Jinwoo received nonstop notifications whenever shadow soldiers defeated demons inside castles. He was steadily leveling up in preparation for the battle on the highest floor. After all, bigger rewards meant bigger danger.

*The elixir of life, bonus ability points, the best-quality rune stone, et cetera...*

When he considered the rewards for defeating the Demon Monarch, he decided he couldn't slack off on leveling up for even a second.

[You have leveled up!]

Since most of the demons nearby were taken care of, Jinwoo called up the window to check his stats.

[Level: 87]

He'd been level 80 when he first stepped into the Demon's Castle for round two, and he was now at level 87. Jinwoo couldn't stop smiling as he looked at the increased stats.

*Nice.*

He pumped his first.

* * *

[You have defeated a demon noble.]
[You have defeated a demon noble.]

Shadow soldiers finished off the remaining demons. It was a clean victory. Once the battle was over, the soldiers gathered in front of Jinwoo as usual. True to form, Iron was the fastest among them.

*Thmp.*

Iron stood at attention with his chest puffed out as if he was waiting for Jinwoo's praise. Jinwoo smiled at the huge body occupying his field of vision.

"Get it all done?"

Iron nodded.

"Are you sure?"

Iron nodded again firmly.

Jinwoo raised his perception with a smile on his face. He then spun around and launched Barca's Dagger.

*Dagger Throw!*

The dagger reached the wall in the blink of an eye. And...

"Argh!"

The dagger lodged inside a demon that had been using Stealth and waiting for Jinwoo to become separated from his soldiers.

"Ahhh..." The demon was shocked to see the blade in the left side of its chest. It would've impaled its heart if it were human.

*How did he know?*

This meant the man was familiar with the stealth magic the high-rank noble had used.

*But he's a mere human...*

By the time the demon looked up from its wound, it was surprised to find Jinwoo standing in front of it. There was dread in the demon's eyes.

"How...?"

Jinwoo pulled out Barca's Dagger and used his single close-quarter attack skill.

*Fatal Strike!*

*Shhhk!*

The demon that had barely clung to life with the damage from the dagger was now dead from a max-level Fatal Strike.

[You have defeated a demon noble.]

Jinwoo sent Barca's Dagger back into inventory and stood before Iron again. "Now, how do you explain that?"

......

Embarrassed, Iron scratched the back of his head, or rather, the back of his helmet, and looked at the ground.

Soon, Igris, who had gone deeper inside the castle to flush out hiding demons, returned. But...

*Huh?*

Something about him felt different.

*What's going on?*

He stared at Igris. His suspicions were quickly confirmed. Upon approaching Jinwoo, Igris anxiously dropped to one knee and bowed his head. Nothing unusual there. But then came an unexpected electronic chime.

*A message?*

[Knight-rank Igris has requested permission to rank up.]
[Would you like to promote him?]

*A promotion?*

Jinwoo rushed to check Igris's info after reading the contents of the unusual message.

**[IGRIS LV.MAX]**
**Knight rank**
**This soldier has reached the maximum possible level for his rank.**
**With the monarch's permission, he may rise to the next rank.**

*   *   *

*Igris's level has what...?*

His level had been in the upper 30s but had now changed to "Max." Instead of leveling up, it looked like his soldiers could rise in rank once they reached the designated limit.

*Looks like they rank up around the upper 30 to lower 40 mark?*

Jinwoo made an estimate as to where his soldiers would rank up. Considering his troops' average level was in the lower 20s, this would be a high milestone to reach.

*And they need my permission on top of that.*

No wonder Igris had been giving off an air of desperation when he approached Jinwoo.

......

Igris kept his head bowed. Jinwoo could feel the determination coming from the soldier as he waited patiently for his master's decision. He felt a sudden desire to give Igris a pat on the shoulders for how great he'd been thus far.

*Honestly...*

Jinwoo looked at the system's message again.

### [Would you like to promote him?]

The message was slowly blinking as if to remind him to respond.

Igris had been one of his first soldiers, and he'd definitely fought the hardest. Was there any reason to say no?

Jinwoo answered the system's message without any hesitation. "Yes."

### [Please designate a command word.]

*Do I really need a command word for this kind of thing, too?*

Jinwoo frowned at first but then considered the situation once again.

*When I think about it...*

Jinwoo tended to summon large groups of soldiers at a time. Though Igris was the only one to be promoted this time around, it would be tricky to approve multiple promotions at the same time, especially in the middle of a battle. A command word would be useful.

Jinwoo mulled it over.

"Permission granted."

It was best to keep it simple. As soon as the command word was registered, things began changing. It started beneath Igris's feet.

*Aaahhhhh!*

Countless black hands erupted from the shadow under Igris's feet, accompanied by screams of agony. The ebony appendages grabbed at Igris all over.

*What's going on?*

Jinwoo watched the process with great interest.

At first, it looked like Igris was being dragged into his shadow, but it was actually the opposite. The black hands clutching Igris transformed into black smoke and swirled aggressively around him. Eventually, he finished absorbing all the smoke. It was like Igris had melded with it.

*Fwshhhh…*

As the smoke dissipated, Igris's aura felt completely different.

*Ping!*

A system notification signaled the change.

[Igris has been promoted from knight rank to elite knight rank.]

*Yes!*

Jinwoo tried to rein in his excitement as he checked out Igris's info window.

**[IGRIS LV.1]**
**Elite knight rank**

*His level reset, but his rank is the same as Fang's.*

Fang had only recently joined the shadow soldiers, but he used to be the boss of an A-rank dungeon. For Igris to now be the same rank as that terrible creature meant his abilities were on the same level as Fang's.

*Ba-dump.*

Jinwoo's heart pounded. The assumptions he'd made when he'd first become the Shadow Monarch turned out to be right.

*I'm not the only one who can grow stronger.*

Jinwoo scanned his shadow soldiers one by one.

*Their abilities are improving along with mine.*

Looking at Igris, who had completely changed with this promotion, it hit him that all his soldiers could rank up. Jinwoo was suddenly overcome with the urge to get his entire army promoted.

*My to-do list just keeps growing.*

As he was proudly surveying his troops, Tank approached from afar with a runaway demon's limp body in his mouth.

*Huh?*

Tank was rushing over with an odd look in his eyes, the same look and energy that Igris had just been emitting.

Jinwoo studied Tank in awe. "No way! You too?"

Tank threw the dead body aside and lay down on his stomach with his front paws outstretched toward Jinwoo.

"Aroo."

Yet another message appeared.

*Ping!*

[An elite rank shadow beast has requested permission to rank up.]

[Would you like to promote him?]

*Oh boy.* Jinwoo put his hand on his forehead. When he checked Tank's stats, sure enough, he'd also maxed out his level.

**[SHADOW BEAST LV.MAX]**
Elite rank

**This soldier has reached the maximum possible level for his rank. With the monarch's permission, he may rise to the next rank.**

*Wait......*

Something was off. Igris had started at level 7 and was an unstoppable war machine. Tank seemed to be so much further away from reaching max level, yet the two of them had ranked up at almost the same time. There was no way the difference between the two levels had evened out after just one battle.

*Maybe...each rank requires varying levels to rank up?*

If so, that would make sense. If Tank, an elite rank, could be promoted at a lower level, then he'd reach the threshold level faster. On the other hand, if Igris, a knight rank, needed to reach a higher level to rank up, it would've taken him longer. Therefore, it would be possible for them to coincidentally rank up at the same time.

As he considered this, Jinwoo was hit with another possibility.

*Maybe I'll also rank up one day?*

Perhaps he just hadn't reached the right level yet.

Right, as if.

Jinwoo laughed, then approved Tank's promotion.

"Permission granted."

As soon as he gave permission, Tank went through the same transformation as Igris. Hands came out of his shadow, which quickly turned to black smoke and were absorbed by Tank.

*Fwshhh...*

Just like Igris, Tank had become more powerful.

**[An elite shadow beast has been promoted from elite rank to knight rank.]**

However, there was one difference.

*Ping, ping, ping!*

Notifications popped up one after another.

[You may bestow names upon shadow soldiers of a knight rank or higher.]
[Bestowed names will be kept until a shadow is released.]
[Please choose a name.]

Tank had been a nickname. His official title was still "Shadow Beast" because a rank lower than knight couldn't be given a name. There had been no way to differentiate Tank from the other bears except for the fact that he was twice as big.

Jinwoo could officially name him now. He beamed.

"Tank."

[Would you like to use "Tank"?]

"Yes."

With Jinwoo's approval, the change was input into the shadow beast's info.

**[TANK LV.1]**
**Knight rank**

Tank hoisted himself up on his hind legs once the ranking-up process was complete. When he stood on two feet like this, he was as tall as a house.

Jinwoo was proud of him. "You finally have a real name, Tank."

Tank raised his head and roared triumphantly.

"Good job, everyone."

They could rest easy until the next floor. Jinwoo recalled his soldiers inside his shadow. Iron caught Jinwoo's eye. His shoulders had drooped sadly. Among the old guard, Iron had been the only one who hadn't ranked up.

*Vwoom.*

After all the soldiers had disappeared into his shadow, Jinwoo left the castle. Esil was waiting for Jinwoo with a worried look on her face.

"Um, Jinwoo, sir."

"I told you, you don't have to call me 'sir.'"

"Right."

Jinwoo's stern reaction gave her pause, but Esil eventually spoke again.

"Um, Jinwoo…sir."

Demon tribes appeared to be sensitive to hierarchies.

"What?"

"Do you know how many families have been vanquished now?"

They were on the eighty-ninth floor now, and Esil had come from the eightieth, so that made nine? She seemed to become more concerned the more families he beat.

"Archnoble clans defend the ninetieth floor and beyond. They're on a completely different level than regular high-rank nobles."

Jinwoo spoke without missing a beat. "So?"

"Why not approach them with words? If you negotiate peacefully like you did with our family, they may give you—"

Jinwoo cut her off. "If I were weaker than you, would you have even talked to me?"

Esil snapped her mouth shut. A mere human daring to visit a demon's castle uninvited only to then list off a bunch of demands? It would have been impossible for him to go home alive.

"It is what it is." Jinwoo grinned from ear to ear.

Relationships between humans and magic beasts or monsters only went so far.

*The strong devour the weak.*

Jinwoo believed in this law of nature, and he had no intention of easing up since he desperately needed to both acquire permits as well as level up.

……

Jinwoo looked sideways at Esil. He wondered why she was so quiet and disappointed.

"Isn't it a good thing if there are fewer noble families?"

"Pardon?"

"You said there was a lot of competition among noble families."

"Oh… That's true, but…"

Starting from the next floor up, archnoble families ruled. Should Jinwoo's attacks fail, Esil and her clan would face the wrath of these archnobles. That's what Esil feared most.

Jinwoo turned to her confidently. "I'll make the Radar Clan the number one family."

…*Our family name is actually Radir.*

Esil timidly kept the correction to herself.

Soon they would be venturing to a higher floor. Could this lone man eliminate all the archnoble families as well?

……*Oh, whatever.*

Her job was to guide the way. Esil decided to stop making things complicated.

*Oh……*

There was one more thing she wanted to ask him. "Um, Jinwoo… sir."

"What?"

Jinwoo turned to look at her.

Afraid to look him in the eyes after witnessing him destroy castle after castle, Esil focused her gaze on his feet. "Why did you show our family mercy?"

Certainly, the Radir Clan was no match for this man. Esil was convinced of this, knowing her family's strength and seeing what Jinwoo was capable of. Yet they'd been spared by this otherwise ruthless human. Why?

She had to know.

Jinwoo stepped onto the teleportation deviation circle, then turned his head to look at Esil.

"Because I like you."

Despite being a monster, she'd known when to surrender and when to cut a deal. Most important of all, she'd provided him with a ton of information.

"Wh-what?" Esil was shocked. She blushed from the neck up and simply stood in place, fingers fidgeting awkwardly.

When she didn't move after some time, Jinwoo glanced back at her. "Are you coming?"

He looked at the system message requesting a destination.

"If you don't get on, I'm heading back to the eightieth floor."

"I'm s-sorry." Still red in the face, Esil hastily stepped onto the circle.

......

But she kept her head down for a long time, even after they reached the next floor.

*　*　*

At Incheon International Airport, officials from the Hunter's Association of Japan were in Korea to discuss the ant problem on Jeju Island. They had an appointment with all the important people in Korea related to this matter.

President Matsumoto of the Japanese association and the S-rank hunter considered to be the strongest in Japan, Ryuji Goto, made their way through the terminal.

Sensing chaotic energy, Matsumoto scanned his surroundings.

"What's going on?"

"......There's a powerful presence nearby."

"More powerful than you?"

Ryuji snorted. Shigeo noted his reaction and didn't bother asking him to elaborate.

*There's no such person in Korea.*

Soon, an employee of the Hunter's Association of Korea rushed toward them. "My apologies! I was running a little late. It's so busy here today, I got turned around."

The employee bowed in apology.

President Matsumoto kept his displeasure to himself and smiled politely. "It's fine. But may I ask what's going on here?"

"Oh...nothing, nothing. I hear a hunter from the US is visiting."

"What brings an American hunter to Korea?"

"I was told it was a personal matter. Nothing to worry about." The employee assumed President Matsumoto was worried about a dungeon break, so he attempted to reassure him.

President Matsumoto continued to look concerned.

*A hunter from the US, huh? Does it have anything to do with why we're here?*

Ryuji's gaze hadn't left the commotion. That was probably where the American hunter was. Shigeo checked the time. Even if they left for the meeting now, they were going to be late.

President Matsumoto made a decision. "Let's get going."

\* \* \*

President Go and President Matsumoto sat across from each other. A row of Korean and Japanese officials from both associations and both governments' related departments flanked the two presidents. It was an important matter, so the summit moved along quickly.

"What about a combined strike squad with the highest hunters from both Japan and Korea?"

Officials on the Korean side looked surprised by President Matsumoto's unconventional proposal. They'd assumed this meeting would be about compensating Japan for damages. Instead, Japan wanted to help solve Korea's problem? How fortunate.

Once they got over the surprise, all the Korean participants looked delighted...except one.

President Go's gaze was shrewd as he asked President Matsumoto, "Are you suggesting we form an alliance to deal with the ants?"

"That is correct."

"We know that Japan's best hunters are formidable, but it's too dangerous to attack Jeju Island directly." President Go explained that the ants had multiplied by hundreds since Korea's last failed attempt to subjugate them two years ago.

President Matsumoto had a sly smile on his face. "Of course, it's always dangerous to invade hostile territory without a plan."

One of the Korean politicians who'd been happily surprised by the proposal asked, "Do you have any good ideas?"

"Yes." All eyes were on President Matsumoto, but he took his time before elaborating. "Of course."

He gave an order, and the files he had prepared, with all the numbers having already been crunched, were placed in front of each of the Korean participants. "This contains all our observations on these ants."

The Korean delegates flipped through the files as he continued.

"Ants are as powerful as high-rank hunters, but they have a weakness— their life span."

Ants could live for only a year.

"In other words, once we eliminate the queen ant, all the other ants on Jeju Island will naturally die off within a year."

That was true. The Koreans nodded as they looked over the well-researched files.

Killing the queen ant sounded like a more realistic goal than trying to get rid of several thousand magic beasts originating from an S-rank gate. Yet President Go's eyes were cold.

*What nonsense......*

He knew the truth: Getting rid of the queen ant wouldn't be any easier than trying to kill all the workers.

"Do you realize that the ants will sacrifice their own lives for their queen?"

President Matsumoto laughed and waved off President Go's concern. "Yes, you have to move past their defenses in order to get to the queen ant."

President Go was bewildered by President Matsumoto's casual attitude.

*What is he up to?*

President Matsumoto pursed his lips. "But what if all the ants left the hive for a time?"

The queen ant lived in the deepest part of the cave. Had there ever been an occasion when every single worker ant had left the queen and her eggs unprotected? President Go and the other Koreans looked doubtful until President Matsumoto spoke again.

"They have. Exactly three times."

Three times? It had happened three times? But how did Japan know this?

The answer hit like a bolt out of the blue.

"Each time Korean hunters arrived on Jeju Island, the ants emptied the caves to face them—all three times."

*Ugh.*

President Go's hands clenched into fists on top of his knees. Japan had secretly observed the Korean hunters risking their lives and fighting magic beasts. No one blamed Japan for not helping, but did they have to use Korea's tragedy as a subject for study and then proudly present the facts to the victim? An S-rank hunter had lost his life during the third attack, and countless others had as well. President Go himself had seen their deaths with his own eyes. His fists were trembling with anger.

*Hmm......?*

Ryuji, Japan's mightiest hunter, released some of his magic energy as a response to President Go's shift in attitude. It was a warning—make one wrong move, and he'd retaliate.

Jinchul, who was at the meeting as President Go's bodyguard, rushed to his side. "Mr. President?"

"......I'm fine now." President Go reassured Jinchul, and the other man silently stepped back.

Regardless of Japan's attitude, if their research was accurate, then this was an opportunity to kill the magic beasts.

*I can't let my personal feelings get in the way.*

President Go kept his anger to himself. With the tension subsided, President Matsumoto finally got to his main point.

"Our Japanese hunters will take on that role."

They'd divide the Japanese S-rank hunters into groups and invade Jeju Island from different directions. All the ants would confront the invaders, leaving the hive empty except for the queen.

"Korea's best hunters can then take care of the queen."

Korean S-rank hunters would sneak in via helicopter and get out the same way once they'd eliminated the target.

The room erupted into discussion. Japan's highly detailed and seemingly plausible plan excited all the Korean participants.

"If we do as they say, isn't there a high chance we'll be able to take back Jeju?"

"I see Japan's finally making their move now that they're in danger, too."

"This is our chance."

"Let's use the Japanese hunters to restore control over Jeju Island."

President Go didn't participate in the conversations but instead quietly evaluated President Matsumoto's proposed plan in his mind.

*It might just work.*

There were twenty-one Japanese S ranks, while Korea had only eight. Only six could actually participate because President Go had mobility issues and another had retired.

*Six alone can't distract several thousand ants.*

They'd need the Japanese hunters for that. They could split up into four strike squads of five or so hunters and buy enough time for the Korean hunters. The only problem was whether or not Korea's highest-rank hunters could defeat the queen, an S-rank dungeon boss.

*Would that be possible?*

At that moment, Jinwoo Sung's name popped into President Go's mind. What if Jinwoo, who had killed an A-rank dungeon boss all on his own, worked alongside other S-rank hunters?

*Ba-dump, ba-dump.*

President Go's heart was racing.

*We can't delay this any longer!*

The magic beast ants were evolving rapidly. No one knew how long it'd be before the entire army would gain the power of flight. It could be a decade from now, five years from now, or, heaven forbid, next year… They had to exterminate those damn ants before that happened, even if it meant accepting assistance from another country.

But first things first.

"What does Japan want in return?" President Go didn't miss a beat.

President Matsumoto flashed his most benevolent smile. "We would like half of the essence stones once all the ants are dead in a year."

That was all?

President Go cocked his head. "Is that all you want?"

The officials from the Korean government frowned at his question.

*If that's all they're asking, just agree gracefully. Why make a fuss about it? What is he going to do if they change their mind…?*

*His experience in the private sector has made him too suspicious.*

They glared at President Go with accusatory looks, so he had no choice but to back down. The Korean participants had a brief discussion where no one objected to the plan. Eventually, Japan's proposal passed unanimously.

When the summit was over, a smiling President Matsumoto extended his hand to President Go.

"The future of both countries hinges on this important mission. Let's combine our forces and do our best."

\* \* \*

Back in his hotel room, President Matsumoto stuck a cigarette in his mouth.

Ryuji lit it for him. "Great job today, sir."

"You did all the work, Goto."

"Please don't mention it."

"No need to be humble. Did you see the expression on Go's face?"

President Matsumoto smirked. It'd been for only a brief moment, but President Go had been furious. President Matsumoto had been able to remain smiling when faced with the fury of the most powerful S-rank hunter in South Korea only because Ryuji Goto, the best brawler in Japan and his reliable right-hand man, had been there as well.

President Matsumoto scoffed as he recalled President Go's expression. "It must be hard being the underdog and needing a hand from someone you want nothing to do with."

Ryuji snorted.

As President Matsumoto had predicted, Korea had taken the hand Japan had extended. Everything was going smoothly.

"Korea is only the beginning," President Matsumoto continued. "Hunters are the new superpower and the new authority. I'm going to establish a new empire with the power that has been bestowed upon Japan."

His gaze landed on Ryuji. "And I suppose you will be the next emperor."

As President Matsumoto's second-in-command, Ryuji would later inherit the empire from the emperor. This was why Ryuji put his boss on a pedestal.

President Matsumoto then remembered something. "Oh, right......" He put out the cigarette. "Any information on Korea's new S rank yet?"

"It looks like no one here knows much about that man, either."

"......I see."

They knew all of Korea's greatest hunters like the backs of their own hands with one exception. They had absolutely no information about the newly registered S-rank hunter. This unknown variable could be an issue. With his goal revealed and his plan underway, Matsumoto did not appreciate wild cards.

*One person shouldn't be a concern, but......*

There were five hunters in the entire world who were so powerful, even S ranks were no match for them. They'd been dubbed as "national-rank hunters" because each had the might of an entire country's military force. Another thing they all had in common was that they'd cleared an S-rank dungeon at least once.

A hunter wielding that kind of power could certainly be a thorn in their side.

*But the likelihood of that is very low.*

Considering how the estimated population of the world was seven billion people, the odds of this new hunter being a national-rank hunter was less than a billion to one. Besides, if Korea had a hunter with that kind of power, they wouldn't keep them under wraps. It didn't look like President Matsumoto had anything to worry about.

*Being too cautious will also ruin my plans.*

President Matsumoto picked up his phone. The Japanese association had been on standby, awaiting his orders. "Korea is all in. Summon the S ranks as discussed."

\* \* \*

President Go contacted the Korean hunters as well. The first order of business was to explain the gravity of the situation to them. That was why he was trying to schedule a meeting with them when…

"What?"

The news was an unexpected blow.

"You can't reach Hunter Sung?"

Jinwoo was the only one they couldn't contact.

"We couldn't even locate him because his phone's been off for a few days now."

……

President Go was silent for a moment, then reluctantly gave the order. "Gather all the hunters, even if he's not there, as soon as possible."

"Yes, sir." The employee bowed before rushing off.

President Go was stunned, lost in thought.

*Where could he be?*

President Go had a bad feeling about this.

\* \* \*

As Esil had alluded to earlier, the difficulty level of the raid had gone up drastically. The number of monsters protecting each floor's castle and their levels were incomparably higher than those on the lower floors.

Jinwoo couldn't even put his increasing intelligence stat to good use because his mana was being depleted so quickly. His MP now fluctuated in big gaps every time there was a battle. That meant countless shadow soldiers were dying, regenerating, and repeating the cycle over and over again.

However, Jinwoo hadn't reached the ninetieth floor through sheer luck. He'd spent every single floor up until the ninetieth honing his skills, forging himself into shape with a proverbial hammer, until he finally reached floor ninety. Even as the clans of archnoble demons pushed back, Jinwoo and his shadow soldiers pushed back harder.

### [You have leveled up!]

Jinwoo had secured an entry permit for the ninety-seventh floor when he noticed some kind of steam rising from his body. It was his sweat evaporating due to the heat generated by his overpowered moves, a clear indication of how fierce the battle had been. Jinwoo was pleased with the sweet taste of victory.

As soon as she spotted him, Esil came out of hiding and ran toward Jinwoo. The permit was clutched in his hand, and the castle behind him was on fire.

*First the fifth-ranked Ricardo Clan and now the fourth-ranked Pathos Clan......*

Esil didn't have the energy to be shocked anymore. If every intruder were like him, forget protecting their territory—escaping and surviving the intruders' attacks would be impossible.

"Are other humans as powerful as you?" Esil asked anxiously.

Jinwoo thought about it before casually responding, "Maybe two of them?"

Gunhee Go and Haein Cha—Jinwoo could tell those two were

definitely stronger than most S ranks. He didn't think other S ranks, like Yoonho Baek, Jongin Choi, or Taegyu Lim, were quite as powerful.

Jongin, who was often called the Ultimate Hunter, was mistaken to be stronger than he actually was because he owned the Hunters Guild, the top guild in Korea.

*When comparing their energies, I'd put Haein a few levels higher than Jongin.*

There were different levels of strength even among S ranks. The wide differences in power level among S-rank hunters were probably due to the difficulty of getting a precise reading once a hunter's strength surpassed a certain point.

Jinwoo smiled in spite of himself.

*How will I feel about them once I get out of here?*

Would Jinwoo feel differently about President Go's power the way he'd changed his mind about President Baek's strength between their first and second meeting? Jinwoo became excited just thinking about how much more powerful he'd become.

*But before then......*

He needed to clear the Demon's Castle. There were only four floors left. He was so close to clearing this dungeon.

He turned to Esil. "You can go back now."

Esil's head had drooped after hearing there were two more humans as strong as Jinwoo, but it shot up at Jinwoo's proclamation.

"What?"

"I'll find my own way from here on."

Esil had been a great help in locating the nobles' castles, but he no longer required her services. His raised perception stat was probably a factor, but archnoble demons were so strong that he could easily find their location. He no longer needed her help. Because she didn't have any other role besides that of a guide, having her tag along would just be an extra, unnecessary burden from here on out.

Jinwoo explained all this to her.

"Th-then I'm useless to you now?" Esil's face grew pale.

*Her reactions are funny to the end.*

Jinwoo tried not to laugh as her expression once again exceeded his expectations. He then stood face-to-face with her.

*Oh!*

Esil's eyes went wide at how close he was standing.

*Is th-this the end for me, too?*

*Ba-dump, ba-dump.*

Every heartbeat sounded like thunder. Esil watched Jinwoo slowly raise his hand. As it drew nearer, she closed her eyes tightly in fear. However......

*Huh?*

Jinwoo gently placed his hand on her shoulder. Feeling the warmth of his touch, Esil cracked her eyes open. Jinwoo's face was extremely close to hers. He smiled right then as if he'd been waiting for her to look at him.

"You did a good job. Thank you."

That would do. Jinwoo figured that was a sufficient enough farewell and strode toward the teleportation circle.

*Ping!*

**[Floors one through ninety-six have been opened.]**
**[Where would you like to teleport?]**

When Jinwoo turned back to face Esil, her face was a mix of surprise and disappointment. Fear, worry, surprise, disappointment... Monsters with intelligence had shown a range of emotions. Were they actually creatures from another world or merely illusions created for a purpose by the system?

*I don't know yet......*

But one of these days, if he kept collecting clues, Jinwoo could probably solve the mystery of the system's origins.

Esil hesitated, then called out to Jinwoo. "Um..."

At that exact moment, Jinwoo raised his head and called out to the system.

"Ninety-seventh floor."

\* \* \*

Ninety-seven, ninety-eight, ninety-nine. Jinwoo finally had the key to enter the Demon Monarch's domain.

**[ITEM: ENTRY PERMIT]**
**Acquisition Difficulty: ??**
**Category: ??**
**This permit grants access to the hundredth floor of the Demon's Castle. It can be used only on the magic teleportation circle on the ninety-ninth floor.**

How much suffering had he endured to find this…?

Jinwoo checked his status one last time before stepping onto the hundredth floor, where the Demon Monarch was waiting for him.

**[Level: 93]**

Jinwoo's level was already pushing 100. He could feel the increased stats coursing through his body. He had overflowing strength, and his perception was much keener. He was in peak condition.

*Perfect.*

Jinwoo called up the shop. He replenished his stamina and mana levels and purchased potions as well as extra bandages. He wrapped said bandages around his hands while holding his daggers so he wouldn't lose his grip on them.

It had been a while since he felt this anxious. With the bandaging done, he started warming up.

*Hwoosh.*

*Shf.*

*Not bad.*

Little by little, Jinwoo started upping his speed. His moves were sharp and accurate. Faster and even faster! He moved so quickly, he'd become a blur of afterimages before he abruptly came to a stop.

*Tmp.*

Steam rose from his shoulders. He'd warmed up enough. His preparations were done.

"Whew…" Jinwoo breathed in and out deeply, then stepped onto the teleportation circle.

As always, the circle asked for his destination, and Jinwoo answered firmly.

"Floor one hundred."

His surroundings changed in a blink. Jinwoo scanned the area.

*There's no fire…*

The lower floors had been engulfed in flames. Only the remnants of fire lingered here. He looked up to see something falling from the sky.

*Snow?*

He extended his hand because the color of the snow seemed off. Strangely, the snow didn't melt in his palm. Upon closer inspection, he realized it was ash. Ash was drifting down like snowflakes.

Just then, the usual electronic sound chimed.

*Ping!*

Jinwoo, sensing something, focused on the sky overhead.

*It's coming from above…*

The system soon informed Jinwoo of the enemy's appearance.

**[Balan the Demon Monarch has detected an intruder!]**

A black dot moved in the distant sky. It got closer to the ground and landed quite a ways away from where Jinwoo stood.

It appeared to be a lizard-like animal with wings. Once it landed, the lizard flapped its big wings and cried out.

*Kreeeee!*

Jinwoo then spotted a blue demon's face behind the lizard's head. A male creature sporting regal armor was riding atop the dragon. Four words could be clearly seen above the rider's head.

### [Balan the Demon Monarch]

A remarkable amount of energy radiated from him. Cold sweat ran down Jinwoo's forehead. Balan was truly a boss fit for a final dungeon this grand.

Then something else caught Jinwoo's attention.

*Hmm?*

The lizard Balan was riding also had a name.

### [Kaisellin the Wyvern]

*A wyvern?*

Based on its name and how it looked, it didn't appear to be a type of demon.

*Wait... If it's not a demon, then could I...?*

No matter how many demons he felled, the system hadn't let him extract any of them, so he'd dismissed the idea of ever acquiring a useful shadow from this dungeon. But a monster that could fly?

*......I want it.*

If it was possible to extract its shadow, he'd obtain it no matter what it took. This was the first time Jinwoo was lusting after a possible shadow soldier since Barca, the leader of the Ice Slayers.

Just then, Balan raised his hand toward the sky.

*Ping!*

### [Balan the Demon Monarch has used Skill: Army of Hell.]

*Army of Hell?*

*Ping, ping, ping!*
One warning after another sounded.

[Demon soldiers have been summoned!]
[Demon knights have been summoned!]
[Demon generals have been summoned!]

With each notification, more demons appeared in the army forming around the boss. The final demon count appeared to be over a thousand.
*This is it.*
Jinwoo also revealed the full extent of his magic power.
As Balan lowered his arm to point at Jinwoo, the black swarm of demons rushed forward.
*Thmp, thmp, thmp, thmp!*
Their charge made the ground quake.
Jinwoo sneered as he surveyed the approaching army.
*I have soldiers, too.*
His lips moved. "My shadows."
Instantly, Jinwoo's shadow started spreading out from under him. He activated Monarch's Domain. Once the Demon Monarch's soldiers stepped into the boundary of his shadow, Jinwoo summoned his army.
"Assemble."
His shadow soldiers shot out from the ground.
*......!*
Jinwoo sensed the enemies' panic.
*Ahhhh!*
*Grrrahhh!*
Two hulking knights, Iron and Tank, took advantage of the situation and raced toward the army at full speed.
*Crash!*
"Graaaaah!"
"Kreeee!"
Dozens of demons were bowled over by the two powerhouses. A wave of

over a hundred shadow soldiers followed behind. Among them was Igris, the pièce de résistance! He leaped over Iron's head, landed smoothly on the ground, and proceeded to slaughter demons with a sword in each hand.

"Kreeeeek!"

"Gahhh!"

It was a textbook performance from an elite knight rank.

*But Igris isn't the only elite knight.*

Jinwoo looked to one side. Fang, who had just finished expanding in size, stomped forward as if it was his turn on the battlefield. Jinwoo beamed with pride as he watched him.

*Hwoooo…*

Fang breathed in deeply. His chest puffed up. Jinwoo recalled the shadow soldiers in front of Fang so the shadow mage could go all out on his attack. The soldiers who had melded back into shadows moved in the direction that Jinwoo indicated.

And…

*Fwoooooooooosh!*

The powerful blast of fire from Fang's mouth disintegrated the demons. And it didn't stop there.

*Fwooooooosh!*

Fang moved his head left and right to roast demons alive. Those engulfed by Fang's flames didn't even have time to cry out. Some shadow soldiers were caught in the crossfire of Fang's attack, but they could simply be regenerated later.

*Yes!*

Jinwoo pumped his fist. A little over a hundred of his soldiers had managed to overwhelm over ten times as many enemies. The demon army was being horribly crushed. But right at that moment…

Balan, who had been quiet up until now, made his move. He opened his mouth wide to reveal blue sparks crackling inside.

*Graaaaaaaah!*

The shadow soldiers were bathed in an ominous blue light.

*Krakoooooom!*

*Lightning?*

Jinwoo's eyes widened. The soldiers caught in the blue storm were instantly fried. Those who saw it happen froze as if startled.

*That isn't any ordinary lightning.*

Balan's lightning, which was rather lethal and also had a stun debuff, fell around the entire area. Naturally, the blue storm also targeted Jinwoo.

*Krak!*

Yet, unlike his shadow soldiers, Jinwoo didn't receive any damage. The Robe of Wind he'd been wearing absorbed all fire-type damage.

[The irregular status condition has been removed by Buff: Immunity.]

[The irregular status condition has been removed by Buff: Immunity.]

[The irregular status condition has been removed by Buff: Immunity.]

The stun debuff was neatly canceled out by his immunity buff.

Jinwoo dashed toward Balan. Because Balan's magic affected a wide area, if Jinwoo didn't do something about it, the scales would tip in his enemy's favor.

Balan turned to Jinwoo.

*Graaaaaaaah!*

A scream rang from the monster's mouth, followed by blue sparks that shot out like hail.

*Krak, krak, krak!*

Balan shuddered as Jinwoo remained unscathed by his direct attacks.

......*!*

Jinwoo could sense that the monster was rattled. In the blink of an eye, he used his maxed-out Dash skill to reach Balan and took a giant leap. Balan also drew his sword, and Jinwoo struck it with Barca's Dagger.

*Klang!*

The force of impact made Balan fall off his dragon and pushed Jinwoo back a distance. Jinwoo and Balan both took a tumble but got back up at the same time. They glared at each other for a beat.

Then they both instinctively charged at each other with all they had.

*Graaaaaaaah!*

More sparks flew out of Balan's mouth.

*Krakoom, krakoom!*

Jinwoo was awash in blue light. He continued running, relying on the robe for protection, but something was wrong.

*......Is it getting hotter?*

When he looked over his shoulder, he realized the edge of the robe had caught on fire. He quickly pulled it off and threw it aside.

*I guess that was the robe's limit.*

Though it was only a human-made artifact, it had actually lasted longer than he'd expected.

The rest was purely up to Jinwoo.

Jinwoo swallowed.

*Graaaaaaaaah!*

As if seizing the opportunity, the monster fanned the flames in his mouth, making them even stronger. Jinwoo heightened his senses as much as he could.

*I can do this.*

No, he *had* to do this.

Time slowed down for Jinwoo, and he was able to evade the streaks of blue directed at him.

He wondered why.

*Krak!*

Memories of his time in the Demon's Castle flashed before his eyes as Balan got closer. As they did, he continued dodging the lightning.

*Krak!*

His heart beat quietly.

*Ba-dump, ba-dump, ba-dump.*

Jinwoo avoided all Balan's attacks by a hairbreadth and stood before him.

*Oh.*

Jinwoo finally realized why all those Demon's Castle memories had played in his mind. It was out of gratitude.

*Thank you.*

He was thankful for having been given the strength to fight such an incredible monster. His abilities had been honed further with each floor. It was like he had been training for this very moment. It had made possible what had been previously impossible.

How could he not be appreciative?

*Shhhk!*

Balan swung his sword down, but Jinwoo blocked it with Barca's Dagger in his right hand and stabbed him in the shoulder with Knight Killer in his left.

*Krak!*

The dagger had been made especially for penetrating armor, so it dug deep into Balan's shoulder.

*......!*

Though Balan didn't let out a peep, Jinwoo sensed he was screaming in pain. Jinwoo pulled out Knight Killer. Sparks seemed to fly out from Balan's eyes as he leveled a vicious glare at Jinwoo. The monster's breathing was labored.

He lunged at Jinwoo. Jinwoo's daggers and Balan's sword struck each other countless times, leaving innumerable wounds on both of them.

*Klang! Klang-klang! Ka-klang! Klang!*

Every time they clashed, the collision of their magic power left holes in the ground where they stood.

Jinwoo frowned.

*His shoulder is severely wounded, but......*

The Demon Monarch lived up to his name. Jinwoo was beginning to feel pain in his wrists. Much more of this, and it would only get harder for him.

*I have to knock him off-balance.*

Both Jinwoo and Balan had two hands. However, Jinwoo had yet another hidden away.

*Ruler's Hand!*

Balan fell to one knee as an invisible force struck him down.

*Whud.*

......?

Before Balan realized what had happened, Jinwoo had punched him in the face.

*Wham!*

Balan tumbled for ten or so meters before managing to stop himself, but he was unable to get up. Jinwoo was already on top of him.

Balan opened his mouth wide.

*Gaak!*

But the Demon Monarch couldn't use his lightning. Jinwoo had shoved his right fist into the monster's mouth to block the magic.

......!

Balan's eyes shook.

Instead of using the dagger in his hand, Jinwoo raised his fist high.

*Wham!*

*Wham!*

*Wham!*

*Wham!*

Jinwoo's strength stat was over 200 and allowed him to rapidly chip away at the boss-level monster's health bar. Finally, Jinwoo concentrated all his power in his raised right hand.

*Hwoooom...*

The muscles in his shoulder and arm bulged, and the air around him grew heavy. The magic power concentrated in his right arm pushed out all the sound around them, and for an instant, everything was dead silent.

......

In the short period of stillness that had washed over them, Jinwoo looked down and addressed Balan in a low voice.

"Thank you for everything."

Of course, there was no answer. The Demon Monarch simply glared at Jinwoo with hatred.

*I guess you'll never understand the thoughts behind my words.*

Regardless, Jinwoo genuinely wanted to express the emotion over-flowing within him. He'd said his piece.

With that, he delivered the final fatal blow to the master of the Demon's Castle.

*Whud!*

As he did, some very welcome messages popped up with the familiar electronic chime.

*Ping!*

[You have defeated Balan the Demon Monarch.]
[You have acquired Balan's soul.]
[You have completed Quest: Collect Demon Souls (2).]

[You have leveled up!]
[You have leveled up!]
[You have leveled up!]
[You have leveled up!]

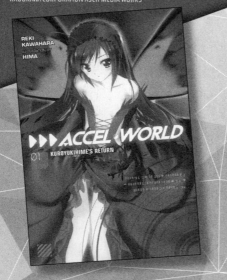